Big City Dreams

T.S. Krupa

Big City Dreams is a work of fiction. Names, characters, places and incidents are the products of the author's imagination or are used fictitiously. Any resemblance to actual events, locales, or persons, living or dead, is entirely coincidental.

Copyright © 2020 by T.S. Krupa

All rights reserved. No part of this publication may be reproduced, transmitted, downloaded, decompiled, reverse engineered, or stored in or introduced into any information storage and retrieval system, in any form or by any means, whether electronic or mechanical, now known or hereafter invented, without the express written permission of the publisher.

Published by Avalon Haddam Press

ISBN-13: 978-1-7362580-0-2

Also by T.S. Krupa

Safe & Sound

On the Edge

The Ten Year Reunion

To my family, I am forever indebted.

CHAPTER 1

The steady rhythmic clicking of the train as it sped over the tracks seemed to help settle my nerves. My fingers idly played with the light gold chain around my neck. A lingering memory reminded me that it used to be much heavier, as I grasped for the familiar ring that used to hang there. I pushed the thought away, tucking the chain under my shirt, and pulled my baseball cap further down as I leaned against the window, watching the scenery speed by.

It could have been hours or minutes later when I finally heard the announcement that we would be arriving at Union Station; it was the final transfer before Penn Station.

New York ... almost there, I thought to myself as butterflies danced in my stomach. I stood and rubbed my hands on my jeans to dry my sweaty palms before grabbing my backpack from under the seat in front of me; my duffel bag dangled over the side of the overhead compartment as I reached up. The train crawled to a stop as I eagerly waited to step off onto the platform.

I suddenly felt self-conscious that my jeans still held a layer of dust from the ranch and my green vest smelled of hay. I froze for a moment and watched as the people around me hustle by in suits, their shoes clattering on the shiny marble floor. A sea of people dressed in monochromatic colors rushed towards their next destinations. A sad smile spread across my lips as I hoisted my duffel a little higher on my shoulder and set out in search of the next platform.

The next train was still mostly empty as I took a seat near another window. While I continued to watch the people below me hustle around the platform, I pulled out a bag of chips and a soda left over from a stop in Chicago. I made up stories about their lives and their destinations. One woman in tall yellow heels caught my attention as she struggled to pull multiple bags behind her with one hand while talking on her cell phone with the other. She was shorter than most of the people around her, but her posture projected a certain attitude. She looked like one of those fancy lawyers you saw on TV; maybe her name was Jessica, but all her friends call her 'Jess.' I imagined her on the phone with a handsome and powerful partner from her high-profile law firm in New York City, and they were planning a getaway. Within a matter of steps, her bags tilted sideways and fell on the ground as she stumbled forward due to the unexpected shift in weight. Like a true professional, she never faltered in her composure. She straightened herself and glanced around only to snap her fingers in the direction of a young man, who came over to pile her luggage back up. She reached into her bag and pulled out a few dollar bills and pointed in another direction to which the young man now headed. I shook my head and let out a small chuckle, it was becoming clear to me that this world was considerably different than back home.

******

I fell asleep shortly after the train left DC. A loud burst of laughter suddenly woke me. The sounds of raised voices and bottles clinking left me momentarily confused. "Where am I?" I thought to myself as I slowly cracked my eyes open and adjusted to the fluorescent lighting. I looked in the direction of the noise and saw a large group of about ten to twelve younger people sitting several rows in front of me engaged in animated conversation. If I had to guess, they were probably in their mid- to late-twenties. Several were holding glasses for a gentleman in a black suit to fill with champagne. The women wore beautiful gowns and had flawless makeup; the gentlemen looked exquisite in three-piece suits and ties. I was drawn to the group as I stared at a woman with long brown hair and bright red lipstick; she had the whitest teeth I had ever seen. She laughed effortlessly at a man's joke and batted his shoulder. He leaned in and whispered something in her ear; she giggled again. My mouth hung open at the intimacy of their moment. I locked eyes with the very attractive bald-headed man, and he smiled at me. I felt my face flush and immediately took to staring out the window again.

  As the buildings and scenery whipped by, I wondered what New York was going to be like. I imagined buildings as tall as the sky, beautiful bright lights, an endless parade of yellow taxi cabs filling the streets, and swarms of people on the sidewalks. Mama had told me stories of going to the city on weekends or during the Christmas season. This one time mama said she and her best friend ditched class just as the weather turned warm and they took the train into the city. They were walking through Central Park and got mistaken for some VIP's at a special event under a big white tent. They decided to play along and were introduced to some wealthy dignitaries. They dined on caviar before they stole a bottle of champagne and snuck out the back of the tent. They spent the rest of the afternoon camped out on the other side of the park with that bottle of champagne, watching people come and go from the tent. They made it home in time for dinner and no one ever knew the difference.

I was deep in thought when I could feel someone hovering over me. I slowly looked up to find the bald-headed man from earlier staring down at me expectantly. He was taller than I originally thought, and exceedingly well dressed. He had a subtle hint of stubble and wore black-rimmed glasses with a full suit and black bow-tie. I wasn't physically drawn to him, but I felt an instant connection; a familiarity that immediately made me relax.

"Can I help you, sir?" I asked, pushing my cap back to see him better.

"Yes. My phone slid under the seats and I believe it's now under your seat." He pointed to the space beneath me.

"Oh, yes sir," I replied, leaning down and feeling around for a phone. My fingers brushed against the side of something rectangular a couple seconds later and I was able to retrieve it.

"Sir? WHO are you calling Sir?" he exclaimed, bringing his hand to his chest in mock indignation.

"I'm sorry, sir, I didn't mean to offend you," I apologized offering him the phone, slightly puzzled by the interaction.

"Again, I am NO sir," he teased. He gingerly took the phone from me and held it between two fingers. I could see the dust and grime on the case.

"Let me help, sir," I said as I took the phone back. I pulled a handkerchief from my back pocket and thoroughly wiped the phone before giving it back to him.

"Aren't you peculiar?" he mused. He stared at me for a moment before taking the seat across from me.

He extended his hand with a flourish and said, "I'm Mac."

I hesitated a moment before taking his hand. "Logan," I replied. He had a firm shake, which Papa always said could tell you a lot about a person.

"Logan, sweetie, you don't seem to be from around here," he said, stating the obvious.

"No sir, it's my first time to the city."

"Uh huh, what brings you to the city?" he asked slowly, clearly taking in my full appearance for the first time.

"Needed a change," I stated without elaborating.

"I see ..." he trailed off and glanced at his friends.

"Sir, I'm really okay if you need to get back to your friends."

After several moments, he said, "I would feel way more comfortable if you stopped calling me sir."

"Sorry, it's a habit."

"Clearly," he said dryly, pulling his glasses down a bit and looking at me again.

"Is something wrong?" I was starting to feel uncomfortable with his silent examination.

"Oh, no. Things are going to work out just fine," he murmured, pushing his glasses back on to the bridge of his nose.

"Where did you say you were staying?" he asked, distracted by something on his phone.

"I didn't say."

"Right ... right." He continued to flip through something on his screen.

"What is your cell phone number?" he asked out of the blue.

"I don't have one, sir." I put my hands into my vest pocket and looked down. I used to have one, but I left it behind. At the time it seemed like a good idea, but now I wasn't so sure. I took a big gulp, looking at Mac.

"Oh. Well that just won't do!" He flashed me a million-dollar smile. He paused and patted down his pockets. He suddenly got up, held up a finger for me to wait a moment, and walked back to his friends. I watched closely as he whispered something to a gentleman, which sparked a spirited conversation. A couple minutes later he came back with a piece of paper and a pen.

"Sorry about that ... the art of the dramatic is strong with this crowd," he quipped, sitting back down. He started writing.

"Where are y'all coming from?" I was unable to hide my curiosity.

He paused and looked up at me. "Sabrina just had to see the new Terrance Kenyon show at the Kennedy Center, as if New York doesn't have enough shows for her already," he said exasperated. I nodded as if I understood.

"Is Sabrina the one with the red lipstick?" I couldn't help but ask.

"No that's Constance, but we call her Connie. The guy next to her is her date, Alistair. The one in the deep blue dress is Sybil and her date is Thaddeus. Augustus is the one with the bad mustache and he's with Marianna in the yellow dress. William and Samuel are twins and they are with Blair and Cam, respectively," he said pointing to each person.

"So, you're dating Sabrina?"

"Oh, heaven's no! Her date was supposed to be Ben, short for Benedict – not Benjamin, but he was called away to Chicago for business. Ben is a saint and he does a pretty good job of taming Sabrina for a straight man, I must say. No, what Sabrina needs in times like this is her opinionated, very well dressed gay best friend. It's a little cliché, but it works for us," he said with a shrug, shifting his focus back to the piece of paper he was writing on. My mind was reeling with information as I tried to draw an imaginary diagram in my mind to understand everyone's connections.

"Okay, when we get to Penn Station, I want you to take this to Gus at The Plaza. He'll be able to get you a room for a night or two." He finished scribbling. "He owes me a favor," he added.

"The Plaza?" I queried, remembering Mama talking about the iconic hotel. I think I may have even seen it on TV once or twice.

"It's a luxury hotel on 5th Avenue and Central Park. You'll have to go about twenty-five blocks, but you can take the metro or a taxi," he said, rising again and handing me the piece of paper.

"Sir, this is very kind of you, but I don't think it's necessary. I couldn't possibly afford it," I stood and handed the piece of paper back to him.

"Nonsense! A girl like you from some country-western, small-town America has no business wandering the streets of New York this late with no destination."

"Oh wait!" he said, pulling the paper from my hand. I was filled with instant regret. Maybe I should have taken the paper. He scribbled something at the bottom and handed it back to me.

"Here's my number, for when you get a phone. Trust me," he stood, "you're going to want to call me." He gave me a quick wink, then turned and headed back to his friends.

"Penn Station," the announcer blared over the speaker, as I stood there holding the paper Mac had placed in my hand. I studied the sheet for another moment and folded it in half. I moved to say something further to Mac only to find he and his friends were gone. I now stood alone on the train.

CHAPTER 2

Standing on the platform of Penn Station, I was in awe as people exited the train around me. I knew this would be a moment I'd remember forever and I desperately wanted to take in all the sights. I stopped to stare at the elaborate ceiling, only to have a man bump into me.

"What the hell lady ... watch where you're going!" he shouted at me.

Welcome to New York, I mumbled to myself, sliding out of the way. I felt an emptiness begin to form in the pit of my stomach, causing me to hold onto my bag tighter as I followed the crowd out of the station and onto the street.

Hot, sticky, humid air blasted me as I exited the revolving doors. It suddenly felt hard to breathe, so I stepped to the side to pull off my vest and long sleeve shirt, leaving me with just a tank top. I tied the long sleeve shirt around my waist and stuffed the vest into my backpack. All the while, people continued to shove past me without bothering to acknowledge my existence. I felt invisible.

I looked at my watch in amazement. It was nearly two in the morning and there were still hundreds of people walking around the city. Everyone seemed to be in a rush; like they knew exactly where they were headed. Everyone but me.

I didn't know what I was doing; I hadn't really planned anything more than getting to New York City. I idly wandered a block or so while looking at the buildings, smelling all the new and sometimes strange smells, and just trying to breathe in the humid air. I should have been exhausted; I had been riding trains in some form or another for the last twenty-four hours. But I felt surrounded by a pulsing energy – it was almost contagious. The city felt alive and I wanted to be part of it. Without realizing it, I turned a city block and found myself standing in front of the largest storefront I had ever seen.

"OMG," I gasped to myself. "It's Macy's." I stopped in my tracks and stared at the department store.

"Watch it!" a voice exclaimed as he raced past me.

"Idiot," I heard another person snicker. I didn't care. I grew up watching the parade with my brothers and sisters every Thanksgiving. Mama would always tell us about the time her high school marching band was selected to participate in the parade. She still claims it was the coldest day she had ever experienced.

"Excuse me, sir?" I stopped the next person that tried to pass me.

"What do you want, lady?" he said, barely coming to a complete stop.

"Which way is Times Square?" I asked in an almost whispered excitement.

"Straight that way," he pointed, giving me an odd look before heading in a different direction.

I was so excited that I struggled to keep walking – I wanted to break into a run just to get there faster. By the time I reached my destination several blocks away, I had beads of sweat running down my back. I walked into Times Square and gaped at the lights and the iconic sights I had watched on TV so many times before. I slowly walked up one side of the square and down the other, trying to memorize this moment and exactly how I felt. I stopped at a cart and bought a bag of roasted peanuts and a bottle of water. I couldn't believe I was actually eating food out of a bag I just bought on the side of the street! It was all so new and exciting; in this moment, I knew I had made the right decision. As I stood off to the side, leaning against a building and eating my peanuts, I watched the people move up and down the sidewalks totally unaffected by where they were. I was in amazement; I wanted to stop them and make them look around.

"Do you know where you are?" I wanted to yell at them. But I didn't. I simply stood and watched. The longer I stood there, the more exhaustion started to roll over me. My legs began to feel like lead, and I couldn't imagine standing any longer. I headed back in the direction I came from, remembering a lovely hotel I had passed earlier. When I turned the corner, I saw a grand building with fancy lettering on a black awning that read 'The Chatwal.' It sounded more like an animal we would find on the ranch than something that belonged in New York City. As I approached the entrance a gentleman in a red suit opened the door, but not before glancing twice at my appearance. Unlike the street, the lobby of the hotel was mostly empty as I made my way to what looked like the counter. I stood for a moment before a well-dressed woman approached the desk.

"May I help you?" she asked, her eyes darting up and down, taking in my appearance.

"Do you have any rooms available?"

"Yes. Our standard nightly rate is $795 per night for a double room with no view," she replied, not making a move toward the computer.

"Excuse me, ma'am. Did you just say $795 a night?"

"$795 plus tax," she said, smiling.

"That's wilder than an acre of snakes! You should be ashamed of yourself," I exclaimed, as I turned and stalked away. The money in my pocket no longer felt like it was going to last as long as I needed it to.

"There's a motel about three blocks away that you might find more suitable for your ... needs," she called after me.

"Which direction?" I stopped momentarily for her to answer. She pointed to the left and I nodded before the same gentleman in the red suit held the door open for me again.

"Thank you, sir," I said and quickly headed in the direction of the motel. I wearily glanced at my watch – it was now nearly four in the morning.

Finding the motel was not as easy as I thought it would be. I walked almost five blocks before I realized I must have missed it and backtracked. I eventually stood in front of a run-down looking building with a flickering red-letter sign only partially lit up. "Vacancy," it read. There was no gentleman to hold the door open for me this time as I pulled on the handle. The door wouldn't open, so I pulled at the door again. Suddenly there was a loud buzzing noise and I could hear the door unlock with a loud click. I pulled one last time and the door easily opened. I stepped inside a small and dingy lobby that smelled of cheap perfume and tobacco. An old woman sat behind the front desk reading a magazine.

"Do you have any rooms available, ma'am?" I approached the counter.

"Hourly or nightly rate?" she droned, without even lifting her eyes to look at me.

"Hourly?" I questioned, not even realizing that was a possibility.

"How many hours?"

"No ... um, ma'am, you misunderstood me. I just need a room for the night," I clarified, flustered. The woman finally lifted her eyes to look at me. As was becoming the norm, she looked me up and down and made a clicking noise with her tongue before she spoke again.

"From out of town, dearie?"

"I just need a room for the night."

"$55 cash," she put down her magazine. I pulled out sixty dollars and handed it to her.

"Sorry, I can't make change," she said, putting my key on the counter and pointing to the stairs.

"Fine."

"No refunds or exchanges. Rooms are as is," she said before sitting back down and picking up the magazine.

"Yes, ma'am." I took a big gulp, grabbed my duffel, and headed up the stairs to room 204.

The hallway was dark, drab, and held a much heavier smell of tobacco smoke than the lobby. There was a guy sitting in the hallway by the stairs who appeared to be sleeping as he clutched a half open beer can. I stepped over him and headed towards my room. To my surprise, the door opened easily. I entered the room quickly, shutting and locking the door behind me. The room was small and covered in green and red wallpaper. I was going to set my backpack down on the floor, but I thought I saw something crawling out of the corner of my eye, so I placed it on the chair instead. I pulled back the comforter on the bed and examined the sheets — they weren't the crisp white linen Mama put on our beds, that was for sure. I pulled the comforter back up to cover the sheets and decided I would just sleep on the top; the room was so hot it wouldn't matter anyway. Sleeping in the horse barn in the hay was cleaner and more comfortable than this five-by-five with stale air. I tried to adjust the room temperature, but the window unit just rattled without any real results. I should have cared more about these arrangements, but I was too tired to care as I laid down and quickly fell asleep.

******

A blaring horn and a woman yelling startled me awake. Confusion set in as I looked around, slowly remembering my surroundings. I glanced at my watch – it was past ten in the morning. As I sat up in bed, I realized my body ached and my skin was sticky. I stood and stretched, twisting and turning in an attempt to ease my stiffness. I pulled the curtain back to reveal a dirty, small square window that had a view of the next building. I stared in wonder. I felt close enough to share breakfast with the man sitting at his table just across the alley. He glanced up from his bowl of cereal to find me staring at him and waved. I awkwardly waved back and closed the curtain. This sure wasn't the wide-open spaces of the ranch. The small amount of sunlight that streamed in the room revealed a large amount of dust floating through the air, making my skin itch. I wandered into the bathroom and turned on the faucet. I jumped. The water held a yellowish hue as it streamed into the sink. I quickly turned it off – even I have limits. I knew I needed to leave this motel as soon as possible. As I gathered my few possessions, the interior wall rattled.

"Baby, please," I heard through the wall as the wall shook again.

I moved closer. "Stop it," I heard a woman plead again, followed by a moan or a scream.

"One more time?" the woman asked as I pressed my ear to the wall. Suddenly there was a loud moan. Grabbing my things, I raced out of the room slamming the door shut behind me.

"Excuse me, ma'am," I hurried to the same lady who had checked me in just hours earlier.

"Yes?" she replied, again, not taking her eyes off of the magazine.

"I think a man might be hurting a woman in the room next to mine."

"203? Nah. They're regulars. Like it a bit rough," she explained without looking at me.

"That's disgusting, I'm leaving," I said to no one in particular.

"Come back soon," the lady mumbled as I headed toward the door. The air felt fresh as I stood in the street and let the sun hit my face, warming me. Across the street from the motel I noticed a diner. It jutted out from the sleek building with a silver façade that made it look like it was right out of the 1950's. Blue and red letters flickered reading Big Easy Diner, which made my stomach growl. Carefully crossing the street, I entered the diner and was greeted by the intoxicating aroma of French toast and eggs – reminding me of home.

"Can I help you?" a large woman asked from behind the counter, flashing me a grin.

"Just one, ma'am."

"Look here, Ma. A true southern belle," the woman hollered towards the kitchen.

"WHAT?" a voice shouted back.

"A southern lady – a southern lady, Ma," she shouted back, forgetting my presence for a moment.

"Before you seat me, may I use the restroom?" I asked, and she pointed to the back. I nodded gratefully and headed to the back. Turning on the faucet to find clean water, I giggled with excitement as I did my best to clean myself up. It felt so good to wash my face and brush my teeth. I dug into my bag to find a clean shirt and jeans, doing my best to change in the confines of the small restroom. I've had worse, I thought, remembering some of the camping trips Papa had taken us on as children, with no modern accommodations. I exited the bathroom to find the lady from the counter standing by a booth.

"Young lady, here," she gestured, setting down a plate and walking away.

"I didn't order yet, ma'am," I said confused, sitting down.

"Don't have to, you get what Mama serves," she replied over her shoulder.

"Definitely sounds like home," I mumbled, thinking of Mama. Not realizing how hungry I was, I shoveled the food into my mouth, taking little time to breathe in between bites. When I was done, I sat there staring at my empty plate and thinking about the day ahead. The lady eventually came by with the bill and a cheese Danish she said was on the house. Looking for change, I dug into my backpack to find my vest. I pulled out several dollar bills and a folded piece of paper fell onto the table. Picking up the paper, I realized it was from the man on the train. I examined it again and thought about my motel experience, causing me to shudder.

"Ma'am, do you know how I get to The Plaza?" I asked before leaving.

"Mmmm, that's one of those fancy hotels. Take a left and then a right on 5th Avenue, about fourteen or fifteen blocks," she said, pointing in that direction.

"Thank you, ma'am," I said, heading in the direction she pointed me. I wasn't sure what today was going to bring, but I knew it had to be better than my unforgettable first night in New York.

CHAPTER 3

The hotel was right where the woman said it would be. As I stood in the lobby, it was as if I had been transported back in time to the 1900's. I tried not to gawk, as that seemed to bring more attention than I was looking for. Another woman in a suit stood at the counter, which suddenly made me as nervous as a fly in a glue pot, giving me flashbacks of yesterday.

"Excuse me," I said, making a conscious effort to drop the greeting I was accustomed to.

"How may I help you?" she gave me a cheerful smile.

"Is Gus here?" I twisted the paper in my jacket.

"He's not due back until later this afternoon. Is he expecting you?"

"Yes," I stated, feeling bad about lying.

"Are you a guest?"

"Not yet."

"I understand. Would you like us to check your baggage until you are able to speak with him?" she asked, looking at my bag.

"Can you do that?" I blurted out.

"It would be our pleasure." Seconds later a gentleman in a suit came around the counter and took my duffel and backpack, the tag on his jacket said Jeffrey.

"What name would you like to put this under?" she asked.

"Logan. Logan Hunter."

"Ms. Hunter, your bags will be here when you need them," the man in the suit confirmed, handing me a small tag with a number on it. I thanked them for their time and headed back out into the city. Fortunately, Central Park was directly across the street. The sun was shining brightly, and it was already starting to get warm. I found an inviting spot near a tree, took off my shoes, and squished my toes in the soft green grass. Lying down, I stared up at the bright blue sky and took a content breath. For a moment, I found if I shut out the city noise, it almost felt like being back home. This was the same sky I looked at while lying in the haystacks at the ranch.

I closed my eyes and felt the steady rise and fall of my chest as my breathing deepened. My thoughts drifted back to three days ago, reliving the anger and confusion I felt when I left home. I could hear Mama's voice in my head, whispering to me before I left.

"Be safe. Do what you feel is right and remember: the world is full of bad people, but there are also just as many good people. Trust your gut and call when you can." We both cried when she hugged me goodbye. She stood on the platform waving and waited until the train pulled out of the station. I wiped the tears from my cheeks until I could no longer see her or the station. That moment seemed like it was years ago. I felt like I had been transported into this new world. I wasn't sure about anything, but I knew I didn't want to go back.

******

At some point, I must have fallen asleep. The sun had shifted and a long shadow from the nearby tree now engulfed me and sent a shiver down my spine, despite the heat. As I rolled over, I saw kids chasing each other around, screaming and giggling. Stretching out, my stomach growled, and I realized that it was getting late. I checked my watch to find it was almost six in the evening; I had slept most of the day away. A feeling of panic set in.

'What if I overslept and missed Gus at the hotel?' I thought to myself. Rushing to put my shoes back on, I left the park and jogged back to the hotel. Pausing for a moment outside the door to gather my composure, I took a deep breath and pulled my shoulders back, prompting me to stand a little taller, and walked into the hotel.

There were more people milling around the lobby than earlier in the day. A couple waited at the counter while being served by a young man. I stood behind them as a tall broad-shouldered man with a full head of black hair and beard emerged from a back office.

"May I help you?" he asked with a slight accent I couldn't place, looking at me.

"Yes sir. I'm looking for Gus," I said, silently kicking myself for using the word 'sir'.

"I'm Gus, how may I help you?" He looked at me a little closer, searching for a sign of recognition.

"Hi, yes. I'm Logan." I reached my hand out to him. Confused, he reached out and firmly shook my hand.

"Hi?"

"Oh, wait. I have this," I said, digging into my pocket and pulling out the wrinkled piece of paper from Mac. I handed it to Gus. He read the note, glanced back at me and back to the note.

"I see ..."

"You do? Because I'm still not sure how this is all supposed to work."

"I can get you into the junior suite for two nights, but that's the best I can do," he said, looking suddenly stressed.

"The junior suite?" I questioned in disbelief. After having slept on a train, in a park, and in the squalor of that no-tell-motel, all I was looking for was a bed with clean sheets.

"Fine. I can give you the Ellington Park Suite, but that's all I can do. The Vanderbilt Suite is already booked," he uttered with a heavy sigh.

"Sir, I can't afford ..."

"No, no. I owe Mac. This is on the house. BUT you tell him that we are even now. He can't keep sending me people in the middle of the day, expecting me to house them all. This is not a boarding house, it's The Plaza for Christ's sake!" he exclaimed.

"Understood, consider the message passed," I whispered.

"I assume you have bags?"

"Yes, I checked them earlier – under Logan Hunter," I said, handing him the valet tag.

"Jeffrey will help you with your bags and escort you to the suite," he motioned to the man from earlier.

"Thank you so much," I said, unable to articulate my gratitude.

"The pleasure is mine," he said, holding out his hand. I looked at his hand. Instead, I walked around the desk and gave him a big hug. I clearly surprised him. After a few seconds he returned my hug and I could feel him relax.

"You are very welcome," he said, more sincerely than before. I finally released him and started to follow Jeffrey before pausing to look back at Gus.

"Oh, Gus, do you have any recommendations for dinner? It's my first dinner in New York I want to make it memorable – affordable, but memorable."

"You're in luck. We have a world-renowned chef here at The Plaza. I'll send something up."

"Sorry, but I don't know if I can afford to eat here," I quietly whispered, leaning towards him.

"Don't you worry about that. You're staying in one of the finest suites in New York, if you ask me. You should dine like royalty – consider it my treat. Welcome to New York," he smiled warmly. I stepped up to embrace him one more time and he chuckled.

"Thank you, sir," was all I had left to say. I followed Jeffrey, who was holding my duffel bag and backpack, toward the elevator. Jeffrey was quiet on the elevator ride up, which did little to settle my nervous excitement, as I played with the ring on my right hand.

"Have you worked here long?"

"No."

"Do you like New York?"

"Yes."

"Not much of a talker?" I mumbled as the doors opened to a short hallway and another door. Jeffrey ushered me forward into the hallway towards a sign labeled 'Ellington Park Suite.' He swiped a key card and pushed the door open for me. I slowly passed through the doorway and gasped, losing all ability to speak. The suite was the biggest hotel room I had ever seen. It was definitely bigger than

Becky's, Emily's, and my rooms combined. The foyer had a beautiful marble entryway that led to a sizable living room with a private terrace. Forgetting about Jeffery, I walked through the living room and pushed the massive French doors open to a grand stone terrace with immaculate plants and greenery, and furniture that belonged in a magazine. At that moment I finally understood the term 'million-dollar-view' as I beheld the picturesque Central Park and New York City skyline.

"Excuse me, Ms. Hunter?" Jeffery approached from behind me.

"Yes?"

"Are you all set?"

"Yes. This is amazing." Jeffrey stood there for a beat or so longer, making the moment awkward. It appeared he was waiting for something, but I didn't understand. He finally cleared his throat, nodded in my direction, and left. Once the door closed, I continued to investigate the suite. There was a huge master bedroom which contained a king-size bed with white crisp linens and a fluffy white comforter. I walked into the bathroom and observed a grand claw-foot tub and a huge shower that may have been even bigger than the kitchen at home; I wasn't sure, but it looked close. On the other side of the suite was a second bedroom, which was smaller in comparison, but still extremely spacious and nice. There were so many emotions raging through my system at that point that I didn't know how to feel. Taking a deep breath, I steadied my nerves before I started to cry. I suddenly caught a whiff of myself and knew what I had to do first. I headed to the bathroom.

CHAPTER 4

After my shower, I dressed in a plush white robe I found hanging in the closet. I had just finished wrapping my hair in a turban with my towel when I heard a knock on the door.

"Hello?" I questioned without opening the door.

"Dinner for Ms. Hunter?" a man replied from the other side of the door.

"Oh, that's me!" I exclaimed, opening the door and forgetting about my appearance. The waiter was about Jeffrey's age, but had more personality as he entered the suite with a huge grin plastered on his face.

"Where would you like to take your dinner, Miss?"

"That's a great question. What are my options?" I asked, surveying the space.

"Traditionally, guests eat at the table in the living room," he said, pointing in that direction.

"Untraditionally?"

"The terrace or on the bed."

"The terrace – definitely the terrace," I said with a clap and followed behind him as he wheeled the cart outside through the French doors. Intrigued, I watched as he carefully set the table with fine china, several glasses, and multiple utensils. He pulled a chair out and indicated for me to sit, I happily complied. He shook a crisp cream colored linen napkin before placing it in my lap. He poured water into the tall glass and reached under the cart to pull out three bottles of wine, which he set on the table.

"Mr. Gus wasn't sure about your beverage preferences, so he sent a white, a red, and a bottle of champagne." I stared at my options, unsure of the correct decision.

"Okay, here's the thing. On the ranch we only have beer, and in town you order a beer, and hanging out with friends in the pasture we only drink beer." I was rambling. I took a breath and continued, "But I desperately want to be one of those people who drinks that stuff," I said, pointing to the bottles. "What's your recommendation? Where do I start?" I asked, looking up at him for advice. He looked startled for a moment and then laughed.

"Our guests don't usually ask for advice. However, I would start with the white wine or the champagne if I were you. Dinner is pasta with lobster and a seafood medley, and a side of summer vegetables tossed in a light olive oil. There's also a garden salad with house dressing on the side. For dessert there's gelato, which I'll put in the fridge until you're ready to eat it."

"Champagne," I finally decided. "I have lots to celebrate." He nodded and put the other options away. He took a step back and with a small flare he popped the cork, sending it flying across the terrace much to my delight.

"What's your name?" I asked while he poured the champagne and uncovered a culinary masterpiece. The food looked too good to eat!

"Thomas." He nodded and stood off to the side for a moment.

"Thomas, the last guy did that too. Am I supposed to say something or give you something? I'm sorry, but I don't really understand," I finally admitted, causing him to laugh out loud again.

"Again, traditionally at the end of a service the guest tips the staff. But there doesn't seem to be anything traditional about you or this visit," he observed, trying to contain his laughter.

"Oh, the tip! That's what Jeffrey was waiting for. How could I forget," I exclaimed, slapping my forehead with the palm of my hand. The towel slid back, and my wet strawberry blonde hair tumbled out. I caught the towel before it fell to the ground and placed it on the chair next to me as I started to get up.

"Ms. Logan, please sit. Enjoy your meal," Thomas said, steadying my chair. "Is there anything else I can do for you this evening?" he asked, retreating to the inside of the suite.

"Wait, are you leaving? Why don't you join me? There is so much food," I queried, causing him to pause.

"I'm still on the clock, but thank you, Ms. Logan Hunter. Thank you for making this a moment I won't soon forget," he said with a wink and left.

I paused to admire the presentation on my plate. I didn't know much about seafood, but it smelled intoxicating and it made my mouth water. Mama usually served beef, potatoes, and greens. Dinner only lasted as long as the food did, and we were never all seated at the same time. The good china and silverware were only used for Christmas and Easter, and Mama didn't own any linen napkins.

I dug my fork into the dish and popped the first bite into my mouth as an explosion of flavor ignited my taste buds. I reached for the champagne and the bubbles fizzled under my nose, causing it to twitch. Cautiously, I took a sip and was delighted by the sensation of the bubbles on my tongue and its sweet taste. I didn't have anything to compare this meal to, but I thought if heaven were to taste like anything, it would taste like this.

"Oh, my God! This is amazing," I exclaimed to myself, as I continued to sip on the champagne and savor my food.

After dinner I wandered through the suite, fully taking in the beauty and the decor. When I passed by the minifridge I remembered the dessert. I pulled out the container of gelato and headed back to the terrace. The sun was setting and the sky was filled with various shades of orange and pink. I lay on one of the lounge chairs, still wrapped in the plush white robe slowly eating the gelato, thinking that each moment seemed better than the last. I sighed in contentment as I pushed everything out of my head.

******

I fell asleep watching TV, still dressed in the bathrobe when I heard a knock at the door. I realized it must be morning as I observed a soft light now streaming through the windows, filling the suite with an early morning glow. The person impatiently knocked again.

"I'm coming! I'm coming," I shouted, getting up and heading to the door. Without looking I pulled the door open to find Thomas with another cart.

"Good morning, Ms. Hunter. Did you sleep well?"

"Pert as a cricket," I chirped to a confused Thomas. "It was the best night's sleep of my life," I clarified, realizing that maybe not everyone understood all of Papa's sayings.

"I have breakfast for you, may I come in?"

"Yes, of course!"

"Would you like to take it on the terrace again?" he asked, heading in that direction without waiting for a reply.

"That would be great, Thomas. Breakfast sounds wonderful, but I'm a little confused because I didn't order any?" I commented, following behind him.

"I did," said a man behind me, causing my pulse to race as I spun around. Standing in front of me in well-tailored brown pants, tan loafers, and a blue short-sleeve button-up shirt with another festive bow tie, was Mac.

"Mac!" I said with more excitement than I intended. I don't know what came over me —perhaps it was the sight of the first familiar face in several days but tears welled up in my eyes as I ran over and gave him a giant hug.

"Gus said he got similar treatment," he chuckled after I released myself.

"How did you find me?" We walked out to the terrace where Thomas had almost finished setting up a massive breakfast.

"Well, I did send you here," he stated, looking at me through his glasses before he continued. "Gus called after you checked in. Said you were the strangest creature I'd ever sent his direction, but apparently, he took a liking to you and wanted to make sure you were being looked after. So here I am ... checking in, if you will," he said, sitting down.

"I can't thank you enough for sending me here, and to Gus. This is the most amazing place. I mean, do you see this view?" I jumped animatedly as I pointed to the park and the skyline.

"I see the view, it's lovely," he replied calmly.

"Is there anything else, Ms. Hunter?" Thomas asked.

"Please, call me Logan. Oh, there is one thing," I remembered, running back into the suite. Rifling through my backpack, I found my wallet and stared at my money. I was unsure of how much to tip in a situation like this. Papa didn't believe in tipping for services that were in someone's job requirement, but he also never frequented any establishments that would have required it. I grabbed a twenty-dollar bill, hoping that I wouldn't insult Thomas and headed back to the terrace. Proudly handing him the money, he smiled and graciously declined the tip.

"Ms. Hunter ..."

"Logan."

"Logan, it has been my pleasure to meet you. No tip is necessary," he nodded his head and left us to our breakfast. I stuffed the twenty-dollar bill in my pocket and took a seat at the table across from Mac. Suddenly, I felt nervous.

"Orange juice?" he asked, pouring himself a glass and I nodded.

"So, Logan Hunter, what is your story? What brings you to the greatest city of all time? Aspiring actress, writer, future banker, dancing ballerina?" he speculated, giving me the same look as from the train with his glasses pulled down low on the bridge of his nose.

"How about 'renegade runaway'" I teased, reaching for a bagel.

"What is this 'renegade runaway' running away from exactly? Nothing illegal?"

"No, nothing illegal. Just a life that my Papa and Austin had planned out for me. It wasn't what I wanted, so I left."

"You actually ran away?"

"If by running away you mean: packing up, telling almost no one, and leaving behind everything, then yes."

"Under the cover of night?"

"No, my Mama drove me to the train station at two in the afternoon while everyone was at work," I admitted sheepishly.

"I see. And why New York?"

"Mama grew up near here and always talks about it. It's her favorite place in the world – even more than the ranch. But I don't think she would ever admit it."

"Where is this ranch?"

"West Texas."

"What did you do in West Texas?"

"I worked for my Papa on the ranch. Mostly taking care of the horses, bailing hay, feeding cattle. I don't know – ranch type things," I explained with a shrug, cramming a piece of bagel into my mouth.

"Small-town Texas girl runs away to the big city to start a new life. Sounds cliché," he joked, picking at some fruit.

"Probably is. Nothing about my life seems very original until this point. I'm looking for that great big adventure, regardless of where I end up. I want an adventure that's completely mine dictated by no one but me. If that ends up being cliché, then so be it. But at least it will be my choice." I paused for a moment feeling fired up. "Did Gus tell you I had champagne and lobster last night?" I said, changing the subject.

"Oh?" he said as a smile twitched on the edge of his lips.

"I LOVED it. Never had anything like it before. 'Too rich for our blood,' Papa always said. Austin said it was 'too fancy for our folk.' 'Our folk' what does that even mean?" I fumed, stuffing another piece of bagel into my mouth.

"Well, then, we have a lot of work to do, don't we? Executing big adventures are kind of my specialty," he winked.

I studied Mac for a moment. "Why are you doing this?" I asked earnestly.

"I see a little bit of myself in you, Tex."

"You're from Texas?" I asked, wide-eyed.

"Oh, goodness no," he commented.

"Oh!"

"North Dakota," he clarified, and I laughed. "So, tell me, Tex, where did you stay your first night in the city? I'm dying to know what stubborn plan you hatched completely on your own. I bet it's dreadful."

CHAPTER 5

Mac left after we finished breakfast, but not before we made plans to meet up that afternoon at an address, he wrote down for me. I took another glorious shower and got dressed. I didn't own anything one might consider 'glamorous' by New York standards, so I cobbled together my best 'ranch chic.' This included a pair of dark blue jeans that I only wore for special occasions and a sleeveless sheer green top I stole from my sister's closet. As for footwear I had my boots, a pair of sneakers, and one pair of flats. I decided on the nude flats, also compliments of my sister's closet.

Knowing I still had two hours before I needed to meet up with Mac, I made an impulsive decision to call home. First, I needed to figure out how to make a long-distance call. I called the front desk where Jeffrey answered and walked me through the process. After two failed attempts, I finally heard a ring on the other end of the line. If my sister Becky or Mama didn't answer I was going to hang up immediately. It was the only real plan I'd devised since arriving.

"Hello?" Becky answered after the third ring.

"Becky, it's Logan," I said by way of a greeting.

"Logan, you are as crazy as a bullbat," she whispered fiercely.

"I wanted to let all y'all know I'm okay," I argued.

"Papa has been in a horn-tossing mood since you left. He won't even speak your name. It's bad."

"How's Austin?"

"Austin? He's fine – still comes over every morning at 6 a.m. to help Papa. He's wearing his class ring again," she whispered again, causing me to pull at the gold chain around my neck where it once hung.

"Did you take some things from my closet?" she questioned, suddenly changing the subject. I looked down at my shirt and flats.

"Nope, not me."

"Dang! Emily must be lying," she grumbled, referring to our little sister.

"Is Mama there?" I asked, knowing my time might be limited.

"Yeah. MAMA!" Becky yelled.

"Who is it?" a deep voice yelled back.

"Um, I dunno," Becky replied.

"You have been babbling to them for ten minutes and you don't know who it is?"

"It's ... Mrs. Kerrington from down the street," Becky finally responded, causing the other voice to retreat. Mrs. Kerrington is our cantankerous neighbor who nobody likes – except Mama. They usually spend hours talking, sharing gardening tips and canning advice. Papa does his best to avoid her whenever possible, especially after the shouting match they got into over an apple tree that fell across fence lines several years ago.

"Grace? I didn't expect to hear from you today. I thought you were headed to Florida to be with your granddaughter?" Mama spoke in her soft, melodic tone.

"Mama, it's me," I whispered, hoping she wouldn't be disappointed.

"Oh, your trip plans changed. That's a shame, tell me about this new trip," she said without missing a beat, causing me to smile.

"Mama, the city is amazing. Just like you said it would be. There are so many people and so much to do. Oh, Mama! I saw Macy's and Times Square," I burst out, speaking as quickly as I could.

"That's wonderful. Are you getting enough to eat?"

"Oh, yes. I had champagne and lobster. I actually ate lobster and it wasn't awful! It was wonderful," I rambled. I heard Mama attempt to stifle a chuckle on the other end of the line; Mrs. Kerrington rarely makes anyone laugh.

"I know you can't talk long. I just wanted you to know that I have a warm bed and roof over my head. I made a new friend and he's helping me get adjusted. I think he's a good person. I'll try to call in a couple of days."

"Grace, I think next weekend would be best. The boys are all going to the cattle auction in Forth Worth and that will give us plenty of time to share those recipes," she interrupted me.

"Okay, I'll call then. I love you, Mama."

"I look forward to it Grace," she said.

"Oh and tell Becky I'm the one who took her clothes – she should go easy on Emily," I added as an afterthought.

"I'll pass that along. Take care," she said and hung up. The short exchange brought a smile to my face. I caught sight of the clock and decided it was time to head out. Before leaving, I pulled my hair up into a low loose bun. I grabbed my backpack and headed out into the city.

******

The address Mac left was at 133 E. 62nd Street. I stopped by the front desk for directions. According to Jeffrey, it was a short ten-minute walk from the hotel. He gave me basic directions which included a detour through Central Park and taking 5th Avenue until I reached Park Avenue. The trip took much longer than planned due to the constant distractions of Central Park. I stopped for two or three street performers and watched each act with excitement, leaving a dollar or two in each open guitar case or bucket. I eventually arrived at the address and found myself standing in front of a beautiful red and light Grey brownstone. I walked up to the front door and rang the bell.

"Good Afternoon, Miss. May I help you?" a gentleman asked as he opened the door.

"Yes, I'm meeting a friend and he gave me this address." I replied, glancing at the sheet Mac gave me.

"Are they expecting you?"

"Yes, sir."

"Let me inquire, please wait a moment," he picked up the phone near the door and punched in a few numbers.

"Yes, I have a Ms. ..."

"Logan Hunter," I finished for him.

"I have a Ms. Logan Hunter at the door," he repeated and nodded.

"Thank you for waiting. They are expecting you," he said and motioned me into the vast home.

"Thank you, sir," I smiled and entered. The entryway was covered in dusty gold wallpaper with cream crown molding and held an abundance of mirrors and art.

"Hello?" my voice echoed into the spacious living room.

"Tex?" Mac called out from somewhere above me.

"Yes?"

"Up here," he announced as I tried to follow his voice. This took me through the living room, into an office-like study, up a curved staircase, and down a hallway into a bedroom that seemed to be the entire size of the first floor.

"Hello?" I called again, entering the room.

"Back here," Mac poked his head out quickly and motioned me towards the back.

"Where am I?" I asked as I entered a smaller interior room which I assumed was a closet, although it certainly didn't look like any closet I'd ever seen.

"Tex, meet Maria. Maria, this is Tex," Mac quickly introduced us and we shook hands.

"Who is Maria?" I asked when she left the room momentarily.

"She works for me," he said as she re-entered the room speaking hurriedly with Mac in broken English. Maria finally mumbled something in Spanish, threw up her hands, and left the room.

"What was that about? She looked madder than a hornet in an old coke can," I remarked after she left. Mac paused, cocked his head to the side, and looked at me with an odd expression.

"Ignore Maria," he proceeded. "Her perpetual state is annoyance."

"Welcome, Tex," he declared, motioning around the room.

"Do you live here?" I asked in amazement. I don't know much about New York real estate, but even I could tell I was standing in a multi-million-dollar home.

"No. I know the family who lives here. I did some work for them and they owe me a couple of favors."

"Is there anyone in New York who doesn't owe you a favor?"

"Not many," he joked, flashing me a grin.

"Why am I here?"

"Ah, yes. Well, I noticed your duffel bag on the train, as well as the current state of your wardrobe, and I couldn't help but think you needed a slight upgrade."

"You think?" I oozed sarcasm.

"Good, glad we're on the same page."

"Now the family's granddaughter is about your size and she happens to be clearing out her closet to make way for the current summer and fall fashions. She told Maria to clean it out in order to make room for the new items and to trash the old stuff. Most of these will only have been worn once or twice, might even be some new stuff. You can take whatever fits."

"Seriously!" I exclaimed, glancing around the lavish closet.

"Yup, now get to work," he pushed me slightly further into the closet.

"This is better than anything in Becky's closet," I remarked.

"Who's Becky?"

"My sister."

"Ah! Okay, I have some work to do. I'll be out here if you have any questions," he backed out of the closet.

"You're not leaving me, alone are you?" I squeaked, my voice climbing an octave.

"Yup. Take your time. The family will be in the Hamptons for the next several days. You don't have to do it all today." I simply nodded and watched him leave the bedroom. I slowly turned around to take in my surroundings. There were tags and labels on each shelf, indicating what should stay and what should go. There was more clothing packed into this one room than my entire family owned. Trying not to get overwhelmed, I focused on the task at hand and started with the first row of shelves closest to the door. This section mostly contained jeans, pants, and sweaters. I carefully separated things into piles, occasionally trying on a pair of pants or a shirt. It must have been several hours later before Mac came back upstairs.

"Hey, Tex? Are you hungry?"

"Starved," I announced. I emerged from the closet in a pair of sparkly gold platform shoes with jeans rolled up to my knees and a bohemian top. I topped off the look with a wide brimmed hat.

"Whoa there, Tex," Mac exclaimed, stopping to stare at my ensemble.

"What, you don't like?" I said with a laugh.

"You need more work than I thought," he exasperated.

"No, no. I was just trying some things on. I know you don't wear it all together," I smiled at him as I sat down to take off the shoes.

"Honestly, how do people walk around in these?"

"Pain is beauty and Jimmy Choo knows beauty," he jested.

"Jimmy who?"

"Jimmy Choo – the designer of those shoes you're wearing."

"Good to know."

"Now, I don't normally eat on the job, but for you I thought we could make an exception. Are you in the mood for Thai or Indian?"

"I've never had either, so let's go with Thai." He shook his head in disbelief and disappeared. It was another hour before he returned.

"Tex?"

"Yes?" I said, this time emerging in a one-shoulder floor length lavender Stella McCartney, which I learned from the label in the dress.

"Wow, Tex! You clean up nice," whistled Mac. He motioned for me to spin and I did so happily.

"Where does one wear a gown like this?"

"The theater. Red carpet function. Movie premiere. Classy dinner. To eat Thai food in the kitchen. Let's go."

"In this?"

"Why not," he grabbed my hand and I giggled, following him down the stairs and through the maze of rooms until we arrived in the kitchen.

"Smells great," I said, sitting down on a bar stool at the island.

"Tastes even better," he quipped, pulling out several to-go containers and plastic utensils. I pulled several containers open and some sauce dripped onto my fingers. Without thinking I started licking them clean until I realized Mac was watching me.

"Sorry," I sheepishly reached for a paper towel.

"You're fine. You remind me a lot of my sister." He observed, pulling out two wine glasses.

"I hope you like Chenin Blanc," he said pulling out a bottle of wine from the fridge.

"I don't know enough not to."

"What do you like?"

"Um ... champagne? I liked the champagne from last night," I decided, and he laughed. He poured the wine and raised his glass high.

"To Tex and her great adventure!"

"To friends," I countered, and we clinked glasses.

"So, Becky — is she your only sister?" he asked, making conversation.

"No. I'm one of five. Peter James Jr. is the oldest; then Brett, me, Becky, and Emily. Peter James Jr. is thirty-two this year. He owns a ranch not far from ours with his wife and their three children. Brett is thirty and married to Alex; they live in town with their baby girl, Lizzie. But they might as well live on the ranch for the amount of time they spend there. Becky is twenty-one, still lives at home, and is finishing up her nursing degree at our local community college. She's dating her high school boyfriend, William Thomas. He's planning to propose as soon as she completes her degree. They'll most likely start a family in town. Emily is sixteen and can't wait to graduate — she wants to work on the ranch after."

"And you?"

"What about me?" He gave me a pointed look. I raised my eyebrows and continued, "I'm a twenty-five-year-old Pisces. I went to Texas Tech University, where I got a business degree with a minor in ranching."

"Seriously? Ranching?"

"Yeah ... seriously ... it's called 'ranch management.' Anyway, I'm the only one in my family who ever left town for any period of time. I originally planned to move to Dallas after school, but then Mama got sick for a little while, so I moved home to help. Once I got home, I just felt stuck. Austin was ready to move on and I wasn't there yet."

"Who's Austin?" he interjected.

"My boyfriend since the seventh grade."

"Seventh grade? Boy, do they start 'em early in Texas," he joked. He finished his wine and immediately refilled both our glasses.

"Yeah, but you have to understand. There's this expectation in my family; you grow up, get married, have children, and become a rancher. We live in my great-granddad's house – fourth generation. The expectation is that one of us is going to take over Papa's ranch. Austin wants the ranch; can you believe that?" I laughed dryly. "He wants the ranch and the whole lifestyle, and that's all okay with him. His idea of traveling is going to town to pick up groceries." I didn't mean to reveal the whole story, but it just came tumbling out.

"Hence the adventure," Mac added between bites of noodles.

"When he proposed I just lost it," I sighed. "I saw our whole life together and I didn't know if it was the life I really wanted. It would have been a perfectly good life," I clarified.

"Austin is kind and hard-working, and he loves me. But I realized I want more. So, the next day I packed up and left."

"Heavy stuff, Tex," he remarked, and I nodded.

"What your sister's name?" I asked after a moment.

"Her name was Abigail," he said just as his phone buzzed.

CHAPTER 6

I excused myself from the kitchen while Mac took the call. I headed back to the closet to finish organizing the area I was working on before he grabbed me to eat. He was quiet when he returned and he carefully observed the piles of clothing and the current state of the closet.

"What is that pile?" he pointed to a pile on the bed.

"Those are the things I'm taking with me. The pile on the floor is stuff for Maria to do with as she chooses."

"This closet is immaculate now," he exhaled with a low whistle.

"Thanks. I only made it through about two-thirds. I can finish it tonight or come back tomorrow, if you prefer?"

"Tomorrow would be fine. We actually have plans tonight!"

"We do? On a Monday?"

"Yes. Now pack up some stuff to take back to the hotel. My friend Grey is going to stop by to assist with your hair and makeup in about an hour."

"Where exactly are we going?"

"Network party or something like that. You're going to need something fancy, so I hope you kept that Stella McCartney dress," he added, and I nodded timidly. I retrieved a few trash bags from the kitchen and bagged up the clothes while Mac called for a taxi. When it arrived, I carried four bags of clothes out to the sidewalk to load into the car. At the last minute Mac received a call and decided to walk.

"I'll meet you at the hotel in about 90 minutes or so," he said, while covering the phone. I gave him a quick salute and shut the door.

I gave the destination to the cab driver and he nodded. Even though it was only a ten-minute walk, the cab crawled at a snail's pace back to The Plaza. When we finally arrived, I unloaded my bags. Fortunately, Thomas was in the lobby and kindly helped me load them onto a cart.

"Did you do some shopping today, Logan?" he asked politely.

"Something like that," I smiled back.

"Do you know where I can get a couple of boxes?" I asked.

"Certainly," he nodded. "I'll bring them up first thing tomorrow morning."

Once I was back in the suite, I poured myself a tall glass of water and gulped it down. I considered taking a nap but decided to rinse off in the shower while I waited for Grey.

I didn't have to wait long because soon there was a knock on the door. I wasn't sure what to expect, but my expectations were definitely not accurate. Standing in front of me was a petite young woman with bright Grey hair. She sported sky-high stiletto heels and a cute one-piece black romper. She wore bright red lipstick and a thick black cat eye – she may be the coolest person I had ever laid eyes on.

"Logan?" she asked.

"Yes, ma'am."

"Oh, aren't you adorable! Mac said you were from out of town. I'm Grey. Now let me in and let's see what needs to be done," she said, pulling a small bag behind her. Within minutes she had me seated in the bathroom and was taking full inventory.

"Eyebrows need a bit of shaping, skin complexion's good, great bone structure. Hair is a little long, let's just do a little trim and add a soft wave – very 1940s you know?" she proclaimed, and I just nodded.

"What are you planning on wearing?" I pointed to the purple dress hanging on the back of the door and the pair of gold Jimmy Choo's I had just inherited.

"Perfect, so glam!" With that she set to work plucking, tweezing, and trimming every hair on my head.

When she finished, she ushered me towards the bedroom, "Go ahead and get dressed. Let's see what we need to do with your makeup."

I carefully got dressed and looked at myself in the bedroom mirror. I gasped – I felt more elegant than I did going to the prom.

When I re-emerged, she exclaimed, "What is that?"

I suddenly panicked, "What is what?"

"That," she said pointing to my shoulders. I looked down and laughed.

"My farmer's tan?"

"Is that what that is? That just won't do," she muttered to herself, and dug into her bag. She emerged with a cream and several other products and went to work rubbing down my shoulders.

"Don't take this the wrong way but you're extremely buff for a girl."

"Thanks, lifting bales of hay all day will do that to you," I explained.

"You just say the cutest things," she giggled to herself.

When there was a lull in the conversation, I asked, "How do you know Mac?"

"He dated my brother several years back and it didn't work out, but we became fast friends."

Interesting,' I thought to myself, as another piece of the puzzle of who Mac was fell into place.

"What do you do for a living?" I continued.

"Makeup artist – mostly for low budget productions. I have several clients who are escorts and strippers. I do their makeup or body art for special occasions." As she continued to talk, I could feel her cool factor going up. While she continued to tinker with my makeup, I asked about the various tattoos on her arm. She was about to tell me about the 'full sleeve,' as she referred to it, when we were interrupted by a knock at the door.

"I'll get it," she said, as she practically floated to the door.

"She's in here." Grey led Mac into the room. He was now dressed in a tuxedo with his customary bow tie.

"You look so handsome," I commented with a smile.

"Well, Tex, don't you look simply amazing this evening," he winked.

"Grey, your work is flawless as always," he kissed her on the cheek.

"The model was easy. Natural beauty like her, where ever did you find her?"

"On the train," I chimed in and she rolled her eyes playfully.

"Are you ready?" he turned to me.

"Just one moment," I moved to stand in front of the mirror. I let out a small gasp – I didn't recognize the girl in front of me. Gone was the long frizzy strawberry-blonde hair. My hair was now sleek and soft, and rolled in soft waves around my shoulders. My eyes were a dark smoky color and my lips a glistening peach. My skin held a soft golden glow. The lavender dress clung to all the right places and the heels gave me a little extra height I wasn't used to.

"Oh, wait, you need jewelry!" Grey exclaimed and Mac nodded in agreement.

"I don't have any."

"Here, take these," Grey said, pulling out a pair of hoop earrings covered in diamonds.

"I can't," I whispered, looking at them.

"Oh, don't worry your pretty little head! They're total knock-offs," she assured me. "I have several pairs." I slid the hoops in my ears and the look was complete.

"Ready Ms. Hunter," Mac asked, extending his arm.

"Ready Mr. ...I don't even know your last name," I realized.

"Houston."

"Ready, Mr. Houston," I chirped with a smile. I took his arm with a flourish and he led me out into the night.

******

When the black car pulled up to the Empire State Building, I couldn't help but squeal in delight. There was a line of three of four expensive-looking sports cars and limos as we pulled up. Photographers snapped pictures of the glamorous people as they arrived on the red carpet.

'I wonder if there's anyone famous here,' I thought to myself, excitedly.

"Mac, what am I going to say to these people? I'm from West Texas. I've only been out of the state for about four days," I whispered as the nerves began to build in the pit of my stomach.

"Don't lead with that," he joked. The car reached the front of the line and someone held the door open for us as we exited. The flashbulbs were blinding as we strolled down the carpet. We paused in front of a tall white screen to have our picture taken before we entered the iconic building.

"Do you attend these things often?"

"Often enough. Sometimes, if done correctly, these are absolutely legendary – other times they're total flops. I happen to know the guy who organized this one, so it should be pretty good. If not, at least they have an open bar." His phone buzzed and he was momentarily distracted, allowing me to fully appreciate our surroundings. All of the sudden, I felt a sting on my shoulder from where Mac flicked me.

"Owww," I said, rubbing the area with my hand. "Was that really necessary?"

"Yes. You are wearing a four-thousand-dollar dress, surrounded by the rich and famous. The least you can do is not slouch or gawk at them," he chastised.

"Four thousand dollars!? This dress is four thousand dollars? That's more than my first car," I exclaimed, examining the dress more closely.

"Quit it," he flicked me again as we entered the elevator.

"Yes, sir," I replied dryly.

"I told you not to call me that," he snapped. We stared at each other as the elevator quickly whisked us up to the top floor. All was forgotten the moment the doors opened.

The iconic skyline was on full display. We stepped off the elevator and I pulled Mac directly to the rail to overlook the city.

"It's amazing," I bubbled with excitement. "Don't you dare flick me again!" I whispered to him as he made a movement.

"She has eyes in the back of her head, ladies and gentlemen," he teased with a wave of his hand as I turned to stare at him.

"Mingle, meet the people, stop gawking, and don't say anything too Texas," he instructed while turning me toward the crowd and giving me a slight push.

"Yes, sir," I exhaled as I headed into the crowd. Unsure of what to do next, I headed straight for the bar.

"What can I pour you?" the young woman behind the counter asked.

"Can I get a Bud Light?" I asked. She raised her eyebrows in surprise.

"Bud Light Lime?" I asked again and the man behind me laughed.

"Just kidding. I'll have whatever you recommend," I quickly added, forcing a fake giggle. The tension from the bartender faded and she smiled as she pulled out a tall glass and poured something white and slightly bubbly into it.

"Thank you, ma ..." I started to say, letting the end of the word quietly trail off. With my tall glass of white-something I wandered over to an empty corner to observe the crowd. People seemed warm and welcoming, hugging and kissing each other on the cheeks.

48

"Sickening, isn't it," a voice next to me commented.

"Are you talking to me?" I asked, looking around for other targets.

"Yes, I thought that was obvious," he said, and I smiled.

"It's a little overwhelming, to be honest," I responded before taking a sip from my glass. I was pleasantly surprised by the sweetness and the presence of bubbles.

"Most of these people don't even know each other, but they do a good job acting," he said with a shrug.

"Really? They could have fooled me."

"I'm Luca, by the way," he said, extending his hand to me.

"Logan."

"What brings you here, Logan?"

"Mac."

"Oh," he uttered, practically shrinking away from me.

"Oh, Mac is just a friend. He didn't want to come here alone tonight," I clarified.

"Oh," he repeated, this time taking a step towards me.

"You live in the city?"

"I'm staying at The Plaza – for now."

"Wow, fancy," he remarked, letting out a low whistle.

"Yeah, I'm actually looking for something different," I replied casually.

"What do you do?" I followed up as an attempt to change the subject.

"I'm currently on Broadway."

"Wow! You're an actor?" I choked on the sip I just took. He slightly shrugged his shoulders as a woman approached him and kissed him on the cheek. He rolled his eyes for only me to see, causing me to stifle a giggle. The woman reached out and touched his shoulder as she tried to whisper to him in his ear. He made a face and took a step back. He was clearly uncomfortable by their interaction.

Thinking quickly, I jumped in, "Luca, darling? I'm ready to see that view you promised me." I held out my hand and pointed my wrist and fingers downward like I'd seen in so many movies. The woman pursed her lips and stood tall, darting her eyes between Luca and me.

"Vivian, if you will excuse me, a promise is a promise," he confirmed with a broad smile, shrugging his shoulders and taking my hand. As we walked away, he placed his other hand on my lower back causing my skin to tingle under his touch as he steered me towards a large oval-shaped machine.

"Thank you so much. That woman is always trying to talk me into something," he said, pulling a quarter from his pocket.

"Glad I could help. I know the signs all too well; I used to help my brothers with their crazy ex-girlfriends," I said with a smile.

"Brothers? Good to know. You know, your acting wasn't half bad," he complimented.

I let out a loud laugh and replied, "I'll take that under advisement." We stood and smiled at each other for a moment before he caught himself and dropped the quarter into the machine.

"Go ahead, take a look," he said, spinning it around for me to look through the peepholes.

"What is it?" I asked, leaning down.

"A promise is a promise," he said, but I wasn't paying attention. I was staring into a sea of lights covering the cityscape. In the distance I could see the lights of a ferry crossing in the harbor.

"If you look this way, you can see Brooklyn," he said moving me ever so slightly. Every couple of minutes he would turn the large set of binoculars and point me toward another view until I heard a click and the picture went completely black.

"Ain't that the berries," I exclaimed, standing up, unable to take the smile off my face.

"Excuse me, what did you say?"

"It's amazing," I clarified, forgetting to censor myself.

"Can I get you another drink?" he asked, looking at my glass.

"That would be great."

"What were you drinking?"

"Umm, to be honest I'm not sure," I commented, examining the glass.

"I'll figure it out," he said, walking away. I took a moment to study him as he walked into the crowd. He was tall and slender, with a full head of thick, wavy hair. He wore a blue suit and a lighter blue shirt with his collar slightly open. He had on light brown leather shoes and he walked with a bit of a swagger.

"Whatcha looking at?" Mac said as he approached me.

"Oh, nothing," I said turning to look at him. He had lost his bow tie and his shirt was now open a button or two.

"Wardrobe change?" I asked, raising my eyebrows.

"My ex showed up wearing the same bow tie; it was embarrassing," he said with a pout.

"Your ex wouldn't happen to be the party planner, would he?"

"Perceptive, Tex. I may have underestimated you," he said looking at me with a whole new appreciation.

"I catch on quickly. I hope you didn't think I was dumber than a watermelon."

"When you say stuff like that I do," he said, causing us both to laugh.

"Your drink," Luca said returning with a fresh glass.

"Thank you," I said, unsure what to say next and was slightly distracted by his smile.

"I'm Luca," he said, turning to Mac and extending his hand.

"Mac," he replied, shaking his hand.

"Will you both excuse me for a moment?" Mac said, distracted by something across the room. We both nodded and just as quickly as Mac had appeared, he disappeared back into the crowd.

CHAPTER 7

Over the course of the evening, we eventually found ourselves sitting in a private corner at a small pub top table. Two or three empty glasses rattled on the table as we engaged in a heated debate over the best Macy's Thanksgiving Day parade float.

"Snoopy is the BEST!" I declared.

"No, Garfield is clearly superior," Luca countered. "Especially when he wears that Pilgrim hat. He looks like a boss."

"But Snoopy is classic!" I laughed, gesturing wildly for emphasis. I accidentally knocked an empty glass over but caught it before it rolled off the table. We started laughing hysterically and I almost fell off my seat.

He caught my arm and said, "Steady there." His unexpected touch sent a shiver down my spine.

"Thanks," I practically whispered as I looked up into his eyes.

"No problem," he replied as he leaned in to move a stray piece of hair from the right side of my face. The touch was so familiar that my heart began to race. He had these amazing, steely green eyes; they were unlike any shade I'd ever encountered before. They were mesmerizing. I began to lean towards him when Vivian approached.

"Luca," she cut in. "Unfortunately, I have to leave. I have another engagement I need to attend," she moved to stand by his side, ignoring me completely.

"At two in the morning?" I questioned louder than I intended. I internally chastised myself, blaming it on the never-ending flow of white sweetness they kept serving.

She fixed me with a deathly stare and placed her arm on his shoulder possessively. "We didn't get to catch up as I had hoped," she pouted.

"Vivian, I just don't think this is a good idea," he said more politely than I felt she deserved. He shrugged his shoulders letting her hand fall to the side.

"Luca, we can't just leave these things so unresolved," she said, taking another step toward him.

"Ma'am, I think he has voiced his intentions with you pretty clearly," I chimed in, standing up. Suddenly I wished I hadn't kicked off my heels earlier, so I could look a little taller.

"Really, Luca, who is this twit? She's seriously starting to annoy me," she droned, flicking her wrist in my direction.

"Geez, even the chickens under the porch know that he's trying to tell you to leave him alone," I blurted without thinking, as my blood started to boil.

"Chickens? Seriously, where did you find her?" she squawked.

"Vivian, please leave Logan out of this," he said, also standing and glancing in my direction. Just as I started to step toward him, I lost my footing and tripped instead. Thinking quickly, he reached out to catch me. Winded slightly, I looked up at him as we were now nose-to-nose. Without thinking I leaned in for a kiss. If he was surprised, it didn't register. We kissed gently at first, but then the kiss became more urgent. It was as if the party disappeared for a moment and we were the only two people on top of the Empire State Building.

It was a moment longer before we both finally pulled away and he helped me regain my footing. Vivian gaped at the two of us. Something in her eyes looked as though she now viewed me as a worthy adversary. She huffed and cast a hard glance at me once more before stalking away.

"You do that for your brother, too?" he teased after a moment.

"I'm not usually that clumsy. Honestly, I thought I was getting ready to fight, but that worked out better. Maybe I should try it more often," I said trying to return his humor.

"Have you ever been in a fight before?"

"Sure. Haven't you?" I asked, confused.

"No, not really ..." he trailed off, looking at me strangely for a beat. "You're really not from around here, are you?"

"Define around here?"

"Planet Earth?"

"Very funny," I giggled.

He leaned towards me and I thought he might move in to kiss me again.

"Tex!" Mac yelled, causing me to spin around.

"Yes?"

"What is going on? I told you to meet people and mingle, not insult Vivian Banks!"

"Oh, come on Mac. She's so spoiled, salt couldn't save her," I said with a slight whine. I heard a chuckle behind me, but I kept looking at Mac as he approached.

"I don't know what you are talking about, but all this," he said waving his hand around, "all of this is for her. She's the hostess and she is about to be named vice president of studio affairs! Rule number one of party crashing is not to offend the host," he flared dramatically.

"Mac, she was just helping me out of a jam," Luca said, coming to stand next to me. Mac looked at us and rolled his eyes.

"Oh, Tex ... what are we going to do with you?" he said, leaning over and pulling me into a hug.

"I'm trying," I said as he smashed me into his chest.

"Well, unfortunately that is our cue to leave," he said, releasing me.

"Okay, I have to grab my shoes," I said, leaning under the table.

"You took your shoes off!?" he asked dismayed.

"My feet hurt," I said defensively.

"You can yell, gawk, stare, and even threaten the hostess, but you do NOT, ever, under any circumstances take your shoes off," he snapped, and I nodded. I quickly put my shoes back on, straightened myself out, and gave Luca a wave.

"Luca, it was so nice to meet you this evening," I said, extending my hand.

"Oh no, I'm going where you're going ..." he began. Unfortunately, he was cut off by a sudden commotion near the door.

"Tex. Now!" Mac exclaimed, grabbing my arm and pulling me toward the door. I turned and strained my neck to see several men in security uniforms swarm Luca. He took one final look at me before turning his attention to the men. Mac had us in the elevator and through the lobby in practically no time. He insisted we walk a block or two before hailing a cab.

"Tex, you wanted adventure and I'm not even sure you need my help," he said after a moment before breaking into a deep laugh, causing me to giggle.

"Sorry, I should have warned you that I have a bit of a temper," I said sheepishly.

"Do not apologize, Tex. You should've seen Vivian's face when she stormed off. She was wildly waving her arms and yelling about the impostor that must have trapped the famous Luca Gaines."

"Who?" I said, momentarily distracted.

"Luca Gaines, the guy you were inseparable from all evening?"

"You said he was famous?"

"You know, two-time Tony, Golden Globe and Oscar winner, currently starring in Broadway's wildly acclaimed original production of "Franklin." Yeah ... I would say he's a little famous."

"I had no idea," I said after a moment, dumbstruck by the idea that Luca was a celebrity.

"Okay, where are we off to next?" he said, pulling out his phone and scrolling through his text messages.

"Next? It's almost three in the morning," I groaned as he hailed a cab. Back home Papa's alarm would be going off in an hour or so for him to start his day.

"The night is still young," he said, instructing the cab driver to take a long and complicated detour to SoHo.

******

The cab finally dropped us off in front of a traditional set of brownstone homes. Mac immediately let himself in and we passed through a foyer into a living room where a dozen or so people lounged.

Several faces I recognized from the train, others were complete strangers.

"Sabrina," Mac practically cooed as she came out of the kitchen with a drink in hand.

"Mac, darling, where have you been all night?"

"We went to the studio party for Vivian Banks."

"Was it a drag?"

"Oh, honey, get me a gin martini and I'll tell you all about it."

"And for you, darling?" she said turning toward me.

"I would love a beer," I practically whined to her stunned expression.

"Ben probably keeps something like that in the fridge," she said motioning for me to follow her towards the kitchen.

"Don't embarrass me," I heard Mac hiss in my direction as I ignored him and trailed after Sabrina. With a fancy-looking IPA in hand, I was happily seated next to Mac on the sofa as he held his martini. Augustus, William, and Samuel were all smoking cigars and offered one to Mac, which he declined. Samuel boldly offered me one as well and I almost accepted had it not been for the look of absolute horror on Mac's face.

"No thank you, sir," I replied instead. Not thirty seconds later Mac launched into a full recounting of our adventure that evening.

"So, there we are and Tex here stands up to Vivian Banks herself. She gets up and tells her to back off and mind her own business or they were gonna throw down. And then she plants a kiss on Luca Gaines," he said, retelling the story to a now captive audience.

"Umm, that's not exactly what I said," I leaned over and whispered to him.

"I had to translate your crazy Texas slang for the crowd," he whispered back.

"Then what did you do?" someone asked.

"We ran," he quipped, and everyone burst into laughter.

"Someone get this girl another drink," Sybil shouted. Moments later and almost out of thin air Sabrina produced a round of shots. Mac looked in my direction to make sure I knew what do with the amber liquid in front of me. I nodded and waved him away.

"To Vivian Banks," I said oozing with sarcasm and tossed the shot back much to the amusement of the room. A few new people joined us in the living room. As Mac found fresh audience members the story became bigger and more exaggerated with each retelling, but the wild laughter remained the same. He was relishing the attention. The drinks kept flowing until it was almost six in the morning and Cam begrudgingly commented she needed to head home for a shower before work. Realization quickly set in for the remaining stragglers and people started to depart. The walls had long since started spinning for me and I didn't know if I was capable of walking, let alone riding, in a taxi.

"Come on Tex, let's get you home. It's been a big night," he said cheerfully and impressively unaffected.

The cab dropped me off in front of The Plaza around seven in the morning. I waved to Mac and stumbled into the lobby, waving to Jeffrey and Thomas on the way up to my room. Once in my room, I immediately kicked off my shoes to reveal a large blister on my left heel. I sighed and slid off the dress, draping it over a chair. I fumbled for a t-shirt before flopping down on the bed and instantly passed out.

******

It was hard to tell how long I had been asleep when I awoke to a sudden, panicked knock on the door. Rising too quickly, the room started to spin and I dashed for the bathroom instead of the front door. After throwing up several times, I splashed some water on my face and pulled on some shorts before I finally made my way to the door.

"Hello?" I asked, pulling the door open to find Gus and another man standing there with tense expressions.

"Logan, I'm so sorry to disrupt you. But we need to look at the second bedroom and bathroom immediately," Gus said, taking a step into the room.

"Be my guest," I said, stepping aside to let them in. As Gus passed, a wave of his cologne hit my stomach, sending me back to the other bathroom. After lying on the bathroom floor for about twenty minutes, I was sure the worst had passed. I quickly showered and dressed before emerging again.

"Gus, you still here?" I asked, wandering back into the suite.

"In here," he called. When I entered the second bathroom, I saw that there were now four people crowded around the sink and bathtub.

"What's going on?" I asked wincing at the loud banging noise.

"There's been a massive leak into the rooms below this one. I don't think it's coming from these pipes but opening up the floor in here is going to give us the best access to the pipes below," said the man who was inspecting the area beneath the sink.

"Oh, right. Gus, may I speak to you for a moment?" I asked pointing to the main room. It was only when we walked out of the second bedroom that I noticed several boxes leaning by the front door. I thought fondly of Thomas, who must have dropped them off. I noticed the clock out of the corner of my eye – it was almost one in the afternoon.

"Yes?" he asked, looking over his shoulder as the men continued to make noise.

"I know check-out was supposed to be around noon, but would it be a problem if I had just a little more time? I will definitely be out by this evening," I said, thinking of the growing list of things I had to do, like find my next place of residence.

"Logan, don't worry about ... actually you can stay a couple extra days. We can't put anyone in this suite as long as the construction is going on."

"Really? That is sweeter than stolen honey," I said with excitement.

"What?" he asked half distracted, half confused.

"Thank you," I corrected before wincing again.

He rejoined the repairmen in the bathroom so I took a bottle of water out to the terrace. Not long after lying down in a lounge chair, I quickly fell back asleep. It was dark when I awoke. I laid there staring at the night sky, reliving the last twenty-four hours. I thought about how I met Luca Gaines and how I never knew just how intimate a kiss could be. I considered how improbable meeting a celebrity like him seemed when I heard a knock on the door. I wondered if all hotel guests got this many visitors or if was just me.

"Thomas?" I asked in confusion. He was dressed in jeans and a t-shirt, not the uniform I had become accustomed to seeing.

"I'm sorry to interrupt your evening, but I wanted to bring you this," he said holding up two brown paper bags.

"Come in, come in," I said, ushering him into the room.

"It's some food the kitchen was about to throw away because they made too much. I overheard Mr. Gus telling the staff that the suite was closed due to construction, but that you would be staying here until it was over. I thought you could use this," he finally said awkwardly.

"Bless your heart ... um, I mean thank you," I said and instantly hugged him. He smiled and I invited him out onto the terrace. I asked him to stay but he declined my invitation.

"Thomas, there is more food than I can eat alone. Stay," I urged.

"My wife has been home with our son all day. I really do need to get home."

"What does she do?"

"She's actually been sick for the last year with breast cancer, but she's in remission," he said, and a wave of relief visibly washed over him. I nodded my head in understanding and made sure he had enough food for his family before he left. The kitchen had provided chicken, steak, mashed potatoes, salad, mixed vegetables, and cheesecake – more than enough to feed myself and Thomas's entire family.

"Thank you, Thomas," I said earnestly as we stood at the door. He dipped his head slightly and headed toward the elevator. Thomas reminded me of a much younger Mr. Winters, who used to help me care for the horses on the ranch over the last couple of years. He was an older gentleman, but sweet as could be; it always made me mad when Papa would holler at him.

I released a sigh of content as I opened the first brown paper bag and began to unpack its contents as the hotel phone rang.

"Hello?"

"Tex! What are you doing?" Mac's voice asked on the other end.

"Eating?"

"No. You need to get dressed, I'm coming to get you."

"Get me for what?"

"Another night, another adventure!"

"Do I have to wear another fancy dress?"

"No, not tonight. Just be yourself tonight, Tex."

"I'll be there with bells on."

"Still don't understand you ... just be ready in an hour," he ordered.

"Yes, sir," I said with a grin and hung up the phone.

CHAPTER 8

Last night was fortunately not quite as epic as the night before, but it was still memorable. Apparently my love for beer inspired Mac and his friends to embark on their very own pub-crawl. They were on a mission to give me the grandest tour of Manhattan. We started on the Upper West Side and systematically made our way through each of the major neighborhoods. It turns out most of the beer was craft or specialty beer, which isn't like Bud Light at all. So even though we went on a beer tour, I still couldn't get my hands on a regular beer in what seemed like the entire city — although I knew it was probably just the fancy establishments they choose to visit. The tour ended up lasting until four in the morning, but this time The Plaza wasn't spinning when Mac dropped me off.

I was now sitting in the living room listening to the morning rain pitter-patter on the windows, while drinking orange juice and eating a yogurt. There were three newspapers spread out on the table in front of me as I looked for rooms for rent in the classified sections. Most of the ads indicated I would need a point of contact, so I started a list of things to buy, adding a cell phone to the top of my list. Between the cash Mama shoved in my hand when I left and the money I had saved up in my bank account, I figured I would only be able to survive for two or three months without a job based on the ridiculous rent prices in the ads. I circled a couple of possibilities and compared their locations on a tourist map of the city I had been given at the front desk. After about two hours I finally had a rough game plan as I packed up, ready to head out into the city. I threw on my baggy, comfy jeans and a sleeveless white shirt with a hip length green jacket. I was deciding on footwear when there was a rhythmic knock on the door.

"Mac!?" I opened the door and gave him a hug.

"Tex," he greeted me, stepping inside the room. He was dressed casually for once – well, casual for him – in jeans and a yellow button-up shirt with the sleeves rolled up and the collar open. He was carrying a Macy's shopping bag and umbrella in one hand and wore a messenger bag across his torso.

"I was just about to head out to run some errands," I said, heading back to look at the shoes I had lined up.

"That's funny because I came over to grab you for some errands, as well. Pick those," he said, without missing a beat and pointing to a pair of short brown ankle boots.

"Really? I was thinking I'd go with the sneakers," I said hopefully, but he shook his head.

"I realized with all the fun we've been having, I forgot to show you around to the regulars," he said, glancing at the 'to do' list in my hand.

"The regulars?"

"I have regular clients who have specific needs; I think we can find you something as far as work goes."

"Oh, my God! You're a pimp?" I asked startled.

"What?! Tex, you're crazy," he said, with a mock-horrified expression. "I provide my clients concierge amenities," he clarified. "Instead of calling three or four different people, they can call me and

I will arrange dog walkers, house cleaners, babysitters, drivers, and so on – all for a fee, of course."

"Oh, of course," I repeated, relieved he wasn't about to pimp me out to his friends.

"Is that why you know so many people?"

"Now you're catching on. Let's go! We have a full day planned," he said, motioning me towards the door as I grabbed my backpack.

"Oh, I almost forgot," he added, looking at my dingy bag. He leaned over and pulled a brown leather backpack out of the Macy's bag.

"For you," he said, presenting it to me. I looked at it carefully, running my fingers over the soft leather and the shiny zippers, finally arriving at the gold lettering that said 'Michael Kors.'

"Thank you," I said, hugging him.

"I knew you needed an upgrade. Plus many of my clients can be a little judgmental."

"It's awesome," I said, quickly transferring my things into the new bag.

"That's not all. I think we can take care of number two on your 'to buy' list," he said, pulling a cell phone from his pocket and handing it to me.

"I can't, Mac. This is too much," I said looking at the phone.

"It's my old phone; I upgraded a couple months ago. You still need to get a service plan, but at least you'll have a phone," he said shrugging it off again.

"If I didn't know any better, I'd think you liked me," I bubbled with excitement, putting the phone into my new bag.

"You're growing on me Tex, that's for sure," he said and we finally headed out into the city.

******

Our first stop was back at the apartment near Park Avenue from two days ago. Maria had called in sick today, which was fine because the house was clean and ready for the clients. However, she never finished organizing the closet that I started. Mac told me he would pay me for my time if I finished the closet in the granddaughter's room, and cleaned out the pantry and linen closets. I gladly agreed. He left me to do what I needed to do while he headed further up Madison Avenue to deal with a sudden 'emergency.' I finished the closet quicker than anticipated and bagged up all the remaining clothes that needed to go to Goodwill. There were two additional bags of items I set aside for myself. Moving on to the linen closet, I noticed it was also marked with tags for things to keep and discard. I was unable to find any sense of organization, so I pulled everything out of the closet and started over. I refolded each item and carefully placed them back into the closet. By the time I was finished, there was yet another bag to send to Goodwill. I decided to save a set of twelve fancy white linen napkins to send home to Mama. I knew she would appreciate them far more than anyone else I could think of. The pantry was the easiest task of the day and within a couple hours I had the whole project completed. I called Thomas at The Plaza and he agreed to come over on his break to collect several bags for me to take back to my room. When he arrived, I showed him which bags needed to be loaded up.

"Oh Thomas, I almost forgot. This bag contains some stuff for you and your wife. I don't really know her sizes, but I'm hoping something will work."

"For me?" he questioned with a confused look on his face. I nodded.

"This box is full of food that is perfectly good, but was going to be thrown away." Mac had mentioned his clients are starting some trendy cleanse when they returned home. "I don't know where I'm living yet so I figured you could use it," I said picking up the extra box and helping him load it into the SUV. Thomas was extremely grateful and thanked me several times before leaving.

Mac arrived right after I finished taking out the trash. "Tex, you're quick!" he said, examining my work. "It's not that I don't trust you," he explained as he peered into the pantry and linen closet.

"I understand. Mama did full inspections of all our chores," I said trailing behind him.

"Your ability to organize a closet is pretty amazing," he said, nodding in approval.

"Years and years of organizing the barn and stacking bales of hay," I remarked with a shrug and he rolled his eyes.

"Okay. We're done here, let's move on," he said before placing a call to a delivery service to pick up the remaining Goodwill bags which we left on the back patio under the awning away from the rain. Then we grabbed a cab and headed to 135 West 52nd Street.

******

"This is amazing," I said looking up at the façade of an all-glass sky-rise.

"It's new," he said, waving to the man at the front desk and heading to the elevator. "I have to warn you, this client is really sensitive about her privacy. Please, Tex, don't gawk or say anything too Texas," he said rubbing his bald head for a moment. We stopped on the twenty-sixth floor and walked down a small hallway before he knocked on a large expansive door.

"Mac, it's so good to see you," a young woman with a darker complexion in a maid's outfit said while answering the door.

"Gladys," he said, leaning over and kissing her on the cheek.

"She is off her rocker today. It's worse than usual," Gladys remarked, only then noticing me. "I don't know if today is good for guests," she suddenly said, wringing her hands into her apron.

"Don't worry, Gladys. Logan is a professional. Let's see what we can do about Ms. MacKenzie."

"Suit yourself, she's in the master," she sighed and closed the door behind us.

Describing the apartment as an apartment is an injustice to the space. It had wall-to-wall windows with panoramic views of the city. Everything was white: the walls, the furniture, the kitchen cabinets, and counters. The occasional 'pop' of color was black or Grey on the furniture or in the wall art.

"GLADYS," a voice suddenly screamed and she went whizzing by us as we continued our way to the master. As we entered the room a shoe went sailing by Mac's head and he didn't even flinch.

"Ms. MacKenzie, Mac and a guest are here," I heard Gladys say.

"Send them away."

"It's too late, darling," Mac suddenly piped up, oozing charm.

"Mac, darling. It's so nice to see you," the woman said, switching gears instantly while emerging from a closet to greet him. They kissed each other on the cheeks and she took a step back to examine him. It was only then that I finally recognized her: the long brunette hair, the porcelain skin, and the trademark beauty mark above her lip. Standing before me was May MacKenzie, Hollywood's current 'it' girl. She wasn't even twenty-five yet and the gossip columns touted her as the 'actress of our generation.' She could sing, dance, act and, impressively, has already won an Oscar, a Golden Globe, and an Emmy. I had to subtly check to make sure my mouth didn't hang open as I stood in May MacKenzie's bedroom. Internally I was freaking out.

"May, this is Logan Hunter," Mac said, turning to introduce me.

"Pleasure, ma'am," I said holding out my hand. May turned to me and raised her eyebrows. She never made a motion to shake my hand, so after several awkward moments I put my hand down.

"Turn," she said motioning that I should turn around. Confused, I consented to her request and made a slow circle while trying to give Mac my best 'what-the-hell?' look.

"Interesting ... Gladys, that's all," she said, dismissing her. As she left the room there was a sudden loud bark from inside the closet.

"Princess!" May said and retreated into the massive closet.

"May MacKenzie?" I whispered to Mac.

"You took it really well," he whispered back, much to my annoyance. May emerged from the closet carrying a small white toy poodle.

"Princess has had such a rough day. Her dog walker was an hour late which threw off her nap and then we missed her groomer's appointment," she said gently stroking Princess, ignoring us completely. Sensing new company, Princess started to wiggle in her arms and made a sudden leap onto the carpet. Princess stalked towards Mac first and started to growl and bark at him, sending Mac several steps backward. Next she headed in my direction, barking and growling. Undeterred by the toy poodle, I took several steps towards her and squatted down to her level, letting her smell my hand. She slowly approached, sniffing my hand cautiously before eventually giving the back of my hand of few licks. I laughed and reached out to nuzzle her head.

"Amazing," May said, looking at me with a perplexed expression on her face.

"What?" I asked in confusion, looking at Mac.

"Princess doesn't like anyone except for May."

"She bites the maids, valet, groomer, dog walker and most of my dates," May added in exasperation.

"Oh, really?" I replied casually. Princess isn't that scary, I thought to myself.

"Mac, this is great. I'm so relieved that you solved this dilemma for me. I knew you would, you always do. She's hired. When can she start?" May said walking back into the closet with Princess trailing behind her.

"Effective immediately," he said looking in my direction. "Of course we'll need to fine tune some of the details," he said stepping toward the closet. Princess let out several more barks, causing him to rock back a step.

"Yes, of course darling."

"Overnight stay? Two walks per day? Groomer visits?"

"Yes darling, of course. Only the best for Princess," she cooed.

"How long this time around?"

"The shoot is in Africa for three months and then New Zealand for another month – four months total."

"Twelve, plus the finder's fee," he replied after a moment.

"Exclusive: one dog, her focus is Princess," she said picking up Princess and petting her again.

"Only exclusive to pets, free to do other jobs?" he clarified.

"Yes, of course darling."

"Excellent. That'll be fifteen, plus the finder's fee."

"Option to add errands or other side jobs as needed?" she negotiated

"Could do a monthly retainer or pay per job."

"Let's wait and see. Gladys will switch to a twice-per-week rotation during that time, so we'll see what your little friend can handle. But if it's anything like it is now, we'll probably go with the monthly option." Mac nodded in understanding.

"Use of amenities?"

"Yes, of course. This place is just temporary. The studio lent it to me until the remodel for my apartment in SoHo is finished anyway. Being so close to mid-town and all these tourists makes my skin itch. But what's mine is Princess's and, therefore, hers to use."

"Great. I'll draw up the paperwork and send it over to Alvin."

"Oh, that's wonderful. I leave a week from today, so she'll need to be available then. Gladys will show her where everything is, plus the schedule."

"She'll keep her phone on at all times and be available 24/7?"

"She will." It was like watching a tennis match with all their back-and-forth comments. I wasn't completely sure of everything they were discussing, but I got the gist of it. I was being hired to watch Princess for four months while she was out of town.

"Wonderful, darling ... Gladys!" she suddenly yelled, causing Princess to growl.

"Yes, Ms. MacKenzie," she said, reappearing at the bedroom door.

"Can you tell Mr. Jenkins and Ms. Newcastle their services are no longer needed after next week?"

"Yes," she said, exiting the room quickly.

"Now that we have that settled, what about the other problem?" she asked cryptically.

"Already taken care of. Dr. Santos will be coming directly to you on Friday for a consultation."

"Mac, you're worth every penny," she beamed. I looked at Mac and gave him a questionable look and he subtly pointed to his nose.

"My pleasure, May," he said, flashing her a big grin that caused her to giggle.

"Now if you two will excuse me, it's time for Princess and me to take a nap," she said, abruptly ending the conversation. We let ourselves out of the swanky apartment and were street side before either of us spoke again.

"Thanks for helping me get the dog-sitting gig. Now I just need a place to stay, and probably another job," I commented.

"Tex, did you not understand the conversation we were having?"

"Yes, I'm going to dog-sit for Princess while she is out of town for four months for fifteen dollars an hour," I said, offended he didn't think I understood.

"Oh, Tex," he shook his head with a chuckle. "Not fifteen dollars an hour. Fifteen thousand dollars."

"She wants me to walk her dog for fifteen thousand dollars?" I said, shaking my head in disbelief.

"She doesn't just want you to walk the dog. She wants you to live with the dog, watch it, walk it, take it to the groomer, play with it, the works ..."

"She wants me to live there?" I asked, thinking back to the lavish sprawl of her apartment.

"Full access to her driver, private pool, gym, etc. Additionally, Gladys will continue to clean the apartment and handle the grocery shopping. So your only focus will be Princess."

"God, she must be crazy as a bullbat ... but heck, yeah!" I said, jumping in excitement.

"Are you hungry?" he asked, ignoring my celebration.

"Starved, darling" I mocked and we laughed. "Mac, how did you know that Princess wasn't going to bite me?"

"I didn't. But I made an educated guess that you had probably wrangled a sheep or cow or something crazier than a toy poodle."

I laughed, only to launch into a story about the time I had to hog-tie a cow because Papa was out of town and it had gotten loose in the street. He just shrugged his shoulders and hailed a cab as I prattled on.

"Food, Tex," he reminded me.

"My treat ... what about Indian food this time?"

"Yes, ma'am," he joked in his best imitation of a Texas accent.

CHAPTER 9

It was only three days before I moved into the 52nd Street apartment. The repairs at The Plaza had gone so well that the leak was fixed and the walls were patched much quicker than originally expected. Additionally, Gus somewhat begrudgingly informed me they had actual paying guests that would need the suite. Fortunately, Mac was able to make arrangements with May so I could move in earlier than expected. Everything was falling into place nicely.

On the day of the move, Thomas and Jeffrey helped me pack my things, which had surprisingly tripled in quantity since I arrived, and carry them down to the cab. Before leaving I gave both Thomas and Jeffery my new cell phone number should they ever need anything. I made sure to leave a good tip for each of them with Gus who promised to give to them after I left. I had just one box left as I studied the suite a final time before officially surrendering it back over to Gus.

"Jeffrey, where is the closest post office?" I asked, stopping at the front desk one final time.

"Several blocks away, what are you looking to mail?" he asked, as I held up the box.

"We can mail that for you," he said, reaching for the box.

"Are you sure? I don't really think that's necessary," I said pulling the box back slightly.

"It would be my pleasure, ma'am," he said with a smile, pulling the box from my hands.

"Ya'll have just been the best to me," I remarked with a grin.

Jeffrey confirmed the address and we embraced before I got into the cab. The package was addressed to Becky and contained her shirt and shoes, as well as several other things I collected from the Park Avenue apartment. I also made sure to include the twelve linen napkins for Mama. I didn't dare put a note or anything that Papa could find, but I guessed they'd figure it out pretty quickly once they saw the contents.

I had so much I wanted to tell Mama, but there were still a couple of days until the boys would be in Fort Worth and it would be safe to call. Instead, I focused my attention to my big move into Ms. MacKenzie's apartment. Gladys had already shown me my rooms yesterday when I went to collect the house key and gave me a copy of the daily routine, which included the following:

Princess's Daily Routine

7:00 a.m.	Breakfast
10:00 a.m.	Walk
12:00 p.m.	Nap
3:00 p.m.	Groomer (Wednesday only)
7:00 p.m.	Walk
8:00 p.m.	Dinner
10:00 p.m.	Walk – Four-day rotation
10:00 p.m./11:00 p.m.	Bed

There were several contingency plans written down, along with the veterinarian, doggie psychologist, and nutritionist – all of which I hoped never to use. The cab was nearing 50th Street when my phone rang.

"Tex."

"Mac."

"I have several new jobs for you," he said, sounding winded.

"Great, what and when?"

"Apparently you did such a good job at the Park Avenue apartment, they want you back to organize their other closets, as well as the office. After you finish there, they told their friends about you and those people want you at their Madison Avenue penthouse next."

"What does work like this pay?" I asked, mostly out of curiosity.

"To be honest, I've never had a professional organizer on my staff before so I just quoted them a grand and they accepted."

"A grand!?"

"Per closet," he clarified.

"You have lost your mind," I said in sticker shock.

"Those closets are more like small bedrooms, anyway."

"I'm gonna need to find some stores to stock up on supplies," I said, running through a list in my head.

"There's a Container Store on Lexington and 58th."

"I'm almost to May's place to drop off my boxes and then I can meet you there," I clarified.

"Great. Take the subway and meet me there in about an hour," he said and disconnected.

"Oh sure, take the subway – like it's that easy," I mumbled to myself as the cab pulled up to 52nd Street. It took me 4 trips but I finally uploaded all my things in my new 'home.' Glancing at the clock it had already been about an hour and I rushed back out the door to meet Mac. I spotted a subway entrance and headed down the stairs to embark on my first New York City subway adventure. I stood staring at the map of subway stations for about ten minutes before an MTA worker approached me to ask if I needed help.

"I see that I'm here and that I need to go there," I said following the yellow line with my finger.

"Yes," the woman said looking at me.

"How do I know how much to get a ticket for?" The woman walked me over the ticket booth and got me a subway card. She patiently answered my additional questions about stops and transfers. She almost had me convinced you couldn't get lost on the subway. Almost ...

I saw the yellow line, or Q train, approach and boarded the train and took a seat. As the train pulled out of the third station, I watched in horror as I realized the stops were wrong. The train was going the wrong direction! I departed as soon as I could and got on the next available train in the opposite direction. Mac was impatiently pacing in front of the store by the time I arrived.

"Where have you been?" he said irritably.

"I took the wrong train," I admitted in defeat. He could clearly see the tension and stress the subway ride had caused me and backed off immediately.

We shopped for an hour for the basic items I thought I'd need for my next several projects. After we finished, Mac suggested we take the subway. I almost balked at the idea, but he assured me that he would ride with me, so I reluctantly agreed. The ride was flawless and soon I was looking up at the large skyscraper I was going to call home for the next four months. I couldn't believe this was about to be my life. Taking a deep breath I walked into the lobby with my bags of supplies and waved to the man at the desk as if I had done it a thousand times. He smiled and waved back.

'I can do this,' I thought to myself.

******

"I cannot do this," I mumbled to myself as I stood on the sidewalk somewhere in the middle of 51st Street staring at Princess. It was Friday and it was my official second day on the job, but my first day completely on my own. May MacKenzie left early yesterday morning to take a private flight to Africa to begin shooting her new movie. Per her new schedule, Gladys was at the apartment all day and helped me adjust to Princess's routine. I felt like I was dealing with Jekyll and Hyde, the dog. Princess had been sweet and well behaved in May's presence, but as soon as she left Princess acted as if she had never learned a single command. Gladys said it was normal and the dog was usually depressed for several days after May left on her trips. Today had been an absolute nightmare; she refused to eat this morning, wouldn't walk when it came time for her walks, barked during her nap, etc. But per her schedule, today was the fourth night in the rotation and Princess was due for her late night extra-long walk.

Determined, or stubborn, I was going to make this work. It was already later than I would have liked, seeing as it was almost ten-thirty at night.

"Now listen here you little white fluffy poodle, I have herded cattle, hog-tied wild pigs, ridden a bull, and trained the most ornery of horses. You will NOT give me any attitude, do you understand?" I shouted as Princess cocked her head to the left and just stared back at me.

"Now I'm yelling at the dog ... this is just great," I muttered to myself after my disappointing pep talk with Princess. Things were going relatively smoothly as we walked. When we found ourselves near 51st Street, Princess suddenly growled at a woman and before I realized what was happening, she had latched on to the lady's purse she had been swinging around.

"No! Princess, LET GO!" I yelled as I started a three-way tug of war with Princess and the lady with the purse. Finally, Princess broke free of the handbag and sat down on the sidewalk. The lady with the purse gave me a couple of choice words in exchange for my apologetic ones before she turned down the street.

"OK, listen up or I'm gonna jerk a knot in your tail," I fiercely whispered, staring at Princess as I pulled on the leash to continue. Instead, she pulled back and starting barking at me. I knelt down to try to scoop her up when she suddenly took off down the street. Catching me completely off guard, the leash slipped through my fingers. Panic rushed over me as I chased after the dog for about a block before I was finally able to step on her leash, stopping her getaway. I am not cut out for this, I wearily thought to myself.

Without realizing it we had arrived smack dab in the middle of 53rd Street, where most of the plays were starting to let out. People of all kinds filled the sidewalks; men and woman in jeans and shorts milled around and a group of couples dressed in fancier attire were whisked away in limos. This wasn't exactly the kind of public location where I wanted to make a scene with a ten-pound toy poodle. I took a deep breath, trying to calm my nerves, and I pulled on the leash again. Princess flattened herself on the ground. She refused to budge. I stared back at the dog in disbelief.

"You have got to be kidding me," I groaned to myself. I lost my senses and began pulling at the leash, dragging Princess slowly along the sidewalk, which even further infuriated me. I was not going to carry this dog back to the apartment.

"PRINCESS! You better start walking or I'm not just going to tie your tail in a knot, but I'm gonna cream yo' corn when we get home." I was now openly talking to the dog as it continued to lie on the ground, mocking me.

"You know, the things you say ... you can tell you're really not from around here," a male voice from behind me teased. The shock of hearing another voice sent me reeling around where I came face to face with a familiar smile.

"Luca?" I whispered as he put his index finger to his lips in a motion to 'shhh' me.

"Does the dog usually talk back? Because I'd love to see that," he said with a mischievous smile. He was leaning against the side of a building, wearing low-slung jeans, a tight black t-shirt, and a baseball cap pulled low.

"No. I must sound like I'm a pickle short of a barrel," I said, finally composing myself.

"I think it was the most amusing thing I've seen all day. Which is saying something, because I saw a video of a monkey dancing the tango earlier." I could feel my cheeks darken and the heat of embarrassment rise in my chest.

"I really should get going," I squeaked. I needed to swallow my pride and head home. Leaning over, I scooped up Princess and turned to leave.

"Hold on a minute, Logan, I didn't mean to insult you. But you must admit it was pretty amusing to watch something like that on my end," he quickly offered up. I thought about it for several seconds and finally nodded in agreement. "You know, I've been hoping to find you somehow after that party the other night. I asked around but no one knew who you were," he said after a moment passed.

"Really?"

"Yes, really. That was one of the most refreshing, unpretentious nights I've had in a very long time," he said pushing off the building and coming to stand in front of me. Princess let out a low growl and I held onto her a little tighter as he approached.

"What are the odds of us running into each other like this in New York?"

"Do you want me to answer that? Math really wasn't my thing."

"No, I wasn't expecting you to," he said with a chuckle.

"Did you have trouble with security?" I asked remembering back to that night. It seemed more a like a dream now than a reality.

"Security? No, they wanted to make sure I wasn't being blackmailed or held against my will. Vivian had convinced them otherwise," he said shaking his head in disbelief.

"Glad you got away."

"Me, too. It was an epic second night in the city," I smiled back.

"Second night!?"

"Yes, sir."

"Luca?" I heard someone yell from inside the building and he turned shaking his head.

He pulled his baseball cap down a little further and leaned in, "Listen I have to go, but can I see you again?"

"That would be better than ... that would be great," I said catching myself. He smiled and I gave him my number.

"Logan, where are you from? I've been dying to know," he said taking a few steps toward the building as someone called again.

"Texas," I finally said with a smile, causing him to laugh.

"I should have known ... you don't mess with Texas," he said, quoting the state tag line.

"Thank you," I said before he walked away.

"For what?"

"For being the first decent thing that has happened to me all day."

CHAPTER 10

Saturday things were a little easier with Princess; she ate and went on her walk without any fuss. During her scheduled nap, I slipped away to my room to call home. I had so much to share in the almost two weeks I had been gone. I felt a nervous pit begin to form in my stomach as I dialed home; the phone rang twice before someone picked up.

"Hello?" I heard the melodic tones of Mama's voice and unexpected tears sprang from my eyes.

"Mama," I said, trying to suppress my emotions.

"Logan, are you okay?" she asked, suddenly concerned.

"Yes, it's fine, I just realized how much I miss you," I said between sniffles.

"Oh, honey, that's normal," she said, soothing me.

"How are Becky and Emily?" I asked, trying to change the subject.

"The girls went to town to see a movie. We received a wonderful package this week full of clothes they could only dream of; so of course they had to put them on and show everyone in town," she joked, eliciting a laugh.

"I'm glad they liked them. Did you get the napkins?"

"Yes, I did. They're lovely. I'm trying to figure out what kind of occasion to use them for."

"You don't need an occasion, Mama. Use them just because," I said with a smile.

"How on earth were you able to get all of that stuff?" she asked gently, but I knew she was worried about how I could afford a package like that. I launched into the story of my recent adventures and my new employment.

"Sounds like you're fitting in just fine," she said when I was done, causing me to laugh again.

"I stick out like a sore thumb," I lamented.

"Logan, it's not like you to whine about things."

"I know, Mama. When I got here the city was so magical and amazing – and it still is, but it's not the ranch either."

"No, I don't suppose it is," she remarked. She took a breath, "Logan, you left because you didn't want this kind of life, and that's okay. But you need to figure out what kind of life you do want. When I met your Papa, I had never set foot on a ranch. But that didn't matter because I realized I wanted to be with him. I wouldn't change that decision or the life I have had. This is the life I wanted." She hesitated a moment and continued, "You told Austin you didn't want the ranch and, therefore, you didn't want him. You know, you didn't really give that poor boy the chance to choose you over the ranch."

"He wasn't going to leave, he's a rancher, Mama," I defended.

"That may be true, but wherever life leads you, you need to make sure you're doing it for the right reasons."

"Like?"

"Running away to New York. Are you running away because you're scared you actually might like this life or are you really a big city girl at heart? You've always had these big dreams, but I sometimes worry they aren't truly yours. I want you to find out who you are, Logan," she said in a way only Mama could say.

"I know, I'm trying," I said, sniffling again.

"I know dear, and I'm so proud of you."

"Is Papa still mad?"

"He's coming around, dear. He's just hurt you didn't feel like you could talk to him about it. He's rough and tough on the outside, but he would have listened. Yes, he likes Austin. But you're his daughter, and if you don't want to get married or take over the ranch, all you need to do is tell him that. You're more like him than me, you know," she said gently.

"I don't know if he would have listened."

"That's never stopped you before," she countered, and we both laughed. Mama proceeded to fill me in on what was going on with the ranch and the neighbors. About two hours later we disconnected.

I felt better after the talk with Mama. My spirits lifted as I left the room and walked toward the kitchen. Passing through the living room, something caught my attention. My heart sank and I felt like I'd been punched in the gut. The room was covered in fluffy white material. Smack dab in the middle of the chaos sat Princess chewing on one of the large black throw pillows that once decorated the sofa.

"You little ..." I growled, stomping into the room. She stopped mid-chew and looked at me as I looked at her. We stared at each other for about sixty seconds until she finally rolled over on her back, exposing her belly.

"Oh, no, you don't! We tried doing things your way, now we're doing them my way," I said scooping her up and taking her upstairs.

She had a crate in the office, but May said it 'traumatized' her too much. I disagreed and commenced her crate-training immediately. Every dog we ever had on the ranch had been crate-trained and I was now determined that Princess would be, as well. I prepared for a battle as I put one of her plush blankets in the crate with a treat. To my surprise she walked in, sniffed the treat and her blanket, and lay down looking me at me with a 'now what?' kind of expression. I cautiously closed the door and laid on my belly, staring at her until my phone vibrated in my pocket.

"Hello?" I answered.

"Logan?"

"Yes."

"It's Luca."

"Oh, hi!" I said, suddenly nervous.

"Listen, I don't know if I should have called this soon, but I wanted to see if you'd like to spend some time together on Monday?"

"This Monday?" I choked down.

"Yeah."

"I could make myself available," I said, thinking through my schedule.

"How about I pick you up at seven?" he said after a moment.

"What if I meet you somewhere at nine?" I countered, thinking of Princess's schedule.

"That works. I'll text you a location."

"Sounds great, looking forward to it," I said, and he agreed. There was a slight awkward pause before we disconnected. Suddenly, seconds later it dawned on me that I had a date with Luca Gaines! I let out a half scream half shriek as I buried my face in the carpet to stifle the noise. I was still lying on the floor with Princess, who had now fallen asleep, cuddled under her blanket in her crate. Princess may need structure, but maybe it was a different kind of structure she needed, I thought to myself as I got up to deal with the mess in the living room.

******

"Hi Grey, it's Logan ... Mac's friend," I said quickly when she answered the phone.

"Who?"

"Strawberry blond hair, good bone structure," I said.

"Oh, yes, how are you darling?" she said as recognition set in.

"Listen, I need a huge favor. I have this date coming up and I've never been a dress-up-and-wear makeup kinda girl. I've always been the ripped jeans, covered in dirt and sweat, hair in a ponytail kinda girl and I was hoping ... well, really I was thinking ... that maybe you would give me a couple of beauty tips?" I finally asked after letting myself ramble on.

"You're in luck! I'm free tonight," she said.

"How about nine? I'll order food."

"Indian?" she offered.

"Apparently not my thing," I countered.

"Sushi?"

"Haven't tried it yet, so sure," I said and she laughed. I gave her my address and she promised to be there around nine. I called down to the concierge desk to get recommendations for Sushi restaurants and they suggested several places that delivered. I called the first on the list and found that I couldn't understand the woman on the phone, so we were unable to communicate enough for me to place an order. The gentleman from the second place I tried spoke much better English and patiently answered all of my questions. Unsure of what Grey liked to eat, I over-ordered in hopes of getting something right.

At promptly nine o'clock the front desk buzzed Grey up. When I answered the door, I was surprised to see she was now sporting a short purple pixie hair cut.

"Do I still call you Grey?" I teased, inviting her in.

"Yes, of course. Grey is my actual name, not a nickname," she clarified, rolling a bag in behind her.

"Logan ... nice apartment," she said, pausing to look around.

"Not mine, I'm just house/dog sitting."

"Girlfriend, you have got to own it! If someone compliments you, just say 'thank you' or something like that." I pointed her toward the living room when the door buzzed again, indicating the sushi had arrived. A minute or so later I pointed the delivery boy toward the living room as well. Grey had settled in on the floor, her sky-high heels kicked to the side. She was dressed in baggy jeans and a bohemian top that revealed a large back tattoo.

"Beer?" I asked, leaning into the living room from the kitchen. I finally had asked Gladys about buying beer in the city a couple days after moving in and suddenly Bud Light just started appearing in the fridge.

"Yes, thank God," she replied with a smile.

"I wasn't sure, not many people around here seem to drink it," I said, sitting down in front of her.

"I agree, especially if you hang out with Mac and his friends. Don't get me wrong, I love the man, but his tastes are a little rich. Sometimes you just need an ice cold beer, ya know?"

"Amen, sister," I said, raising my bottle of Bud Light to the spread of food. She took one look at me and the food, and launched into a mini-lesson on how to eat sushi. I was nervous as I held up the first piece with my chopsticks, but I bravely took a bite and was surprised to find how refreshing it tasted.

"How's Mac?" she asked as we happily ate and drank.

"Good, I guess. I haven't seen him since the day I officially moved in here."

"I see."

"What?" I said, eying her suspiciously.

"Well, it's just with Mac, it's hard to get close to him. He knows everyone and has a million connections, as you know, and everyone owes him a favor; but no one really knows him. He only lets people get so close to the real him."

"Really?" I said, thinking over the statement.

"The real MacAllister Houston is a bit of an enigma, if you ask me," she said, finishing her beer and hopping up to get another.

"Do you know anything about him?" I pressed.

"I know he's from out of town and he doesn't like to talk about it."

"Does he have any family?" I said, thinking back to the sister he mentioned.

"Dunno ..." she trailed off. "See what I'm saying? Total puzzle."

"I see," I said, keeping what little information he had shared to myself. If he was a private person, it was not my business to share his secrets.

"What about you?" I asked, changing the subject.

"What about me? My parents were hippies who settled in Vermont. They named me Grey Raine. I moved to New York when I was eighteen to become a dancer ... ballerina, not pole," she clarified. I just nodded in response, popping another piece of sushi in my mouth. "The dancing thing didn't really work out, I'm much too short according to the industry standard. But I loved New York, so I stayed. In addition to dance, I'm pretty good at painting, which led to painting people – and thus Grey the makeup artist was born," she said with a flare of her arms.

"You are seriously the most interesting person I know," I commented.

"God I hope not, sister," she said with a laugh. Just then I heard a faint bark from upstairs.

"I'll be right back," I said, dashing upstairs. Princess was sitting in her crate, pawing at the side. Her favorite toy alligator had fallen through the cracks and was just out of her reach. I picked it up and pushed it back through the side. She happily danced around in her crate and did a couple of circles before settling back down.

"Good girl," I cooed and headed back downstairs. Grey was clearing the plates and I found there was surprisingly little food left over. I took over the final cleanup while she started to unpack her bag.

"So, this emergency you have ..." she commented.

"It's not so much of an emergency as it is a problem. See, I have this date on Monday and I really like him, but as I explained on the phone I don't know what I'm supposed to wear or how to do my makeup," I gushed and she smiled.

"You called the right person. What do you normally use?"

"Daily?" I asked and she nodded in confirmation. "Daily, I don't normally wear anything other than a little bit of lip gloss and some type of SPF face lotion that's been on sale. Too much sun makes my freckles go crazy," I said, pointing to my cheeks.

"Something that's on sale?" She nearly passed out. "You need more help than I realized. What about special occasions?"

"I'll add mascara and tinted lip gloss," I said with a cringe, expecting her to explode.

"Oh, Logan," she said shaking her head. With that, she pulled out product after product. She showed me how to use foundation, eyeliner, eye shadow, and an array of countless products.

"Now, you don't need all of this stuff. If you start out too strong, people will think you're trying too hard," she commented at one point.

Hours later, she finally packed up her things and got ready to leave. "This was fun tonight, Logan," she commented at the door. "I don't get a chance to just hang out very often. It's a nice change of pace from the bar scene."

"I don't normally get a chance to hang out with other girls that aren't my sisters. Not many girls around the ranch either," I added with a shrug and she smiled.

"You still say the weirdest things," which caused me to laugh and I couldn't disagree.

CHAPTER 11

Sunday afternoon while I was out for a walk with Princess, I decided to take a detour to The Plaza. Gus, Thomas, and Jeffrey were all working and I wanted to stop by for a quick catch-up.

"All y'all don't seem to be working very hard," I commented when I entered the lobby causing them all to look up.

"Logan," Thomas and Gus said at the same time, coming over to great me. Jeffrey waved from his location behind the desk, as he was finishing up with a customer.

"Heard you have some swanky new apartment you are freeloading in," Gus said with a grin.

"Yes sir. Meet my client, Princess," I said, setting her down on the marble floor. She sat instantly and looked at me and back to Gus and Thomas.

"Speak," I ordered and she barked on command. Gus and Thomas clapped with delight.

"Lie down, roll-over," I instructed next and she listened. When she was done I gave her a small treat.

"I never took you for a little dog person," Thomas commented, raising his eyebrows.

"I'm not, really. I'm more of a horse person, but this is starting to work out," I commented and Thomas nodded.

"How's your wife?" I whispered to him when Gus became distracted by a large crowd.

"She got a job as a receptionist at a marketing firm near Wall Street, starts next week," Thomas said proudly. I had just finished congratulating him when my phone rang.

"I'm sorry, I need to take this. It was great seeing you," I commented. I scooped up Princess and headed out to the street, but the call dropped before I was able to answer it.

On my way home from The Plaza my phone rang again. I was about to answer it when Princess started barking and pulling on the leash, distracting me. It rang for a third time when I entered the apartment.

"Hello?" I said, leaning over to give Princess her treat.

"Tex?"

"Mac?"

"What are you doing?"

"Hanging out with Princess, my new best friend," I said, patting her on the head while she just stared at me.

"Do you mind coming over today? I need the company," he said in a hoarse whisper.

"Um, sure. Everything okay?" I said, suddenly on alert.

"It's been a tough day, I just don't want to be alone."

"Okay, I have to put Princess down for a nap and then I'll be right over."

"Thanks, Tex. I'll text you my address in a couple of minutes."

It turns out his address was in the Greenpoint area of Brooklyn, which required me to take the subway. After transferring trains successfully, I arrived at Mac's building about an hour after his phone call. Two bottles of wine clinked in my bag, which made me think of Mama. Mama always taught me that when someone was in need, you should never arrive empty handed. I dialed his apartment number on the keypad from the stoop and he buzzed me in.

I guess I expected Mac to live in some high-rise penthouse apartment with the most modern amenities. What I saw was completely different when I entered his apartment. It was much more traditional and much less organized than I expected.

"Mac?" I called, entering the apartment.

"Tex," he said, coming into the living room. He was dressed in sweatpants and a t-shirt with a two- or three-day layer of stubble growing.

"Going for a new look?" I teased, setting my bag down and taking a good look.

"I should ask you the same," he said, observing my newly straightened hair and the small amount of makeup I experimented with this morning.

"I brought wine," I said, pulling out the bottles from my bag.

"Want a beer?" he asked, shuffling over to the fridge and offering me one.

"Yes," I said, confused as to why Mac would ever have beer in his house.

"Mac, what's going on? Right now I feel a little bit like I'm in The Twilight Zone." He handed me a beer and shuffled back to the sofa, where he sat down with very little fanfare.

"Today is her anniversary," he mumbled to no one in particular.

"Whose anniversary?" I sat down next to him.

"Abigail, my sister. She died ten years ago today," he exhaled, leaning forward so his elbows rested on his knees and his head hung low.

"What happened?"

"It was an accident."

"What was an accident?"

"We were out on my granddad's land in North Dakota and I was driving the ATV. Things were going fine. Then out of nowhere I thought I saw something and I pulled too hard to the left on the handles, flipping the ATV. The problem was that we were right on a small ditch, so we tumbled with the ATV about fifteen feet downward. At first we both thought we were fine. We got up and brushed ourselves off, and that's when the pain started. I felt it in my leg and she just hurt all over. We had a walkie-talkie, but it was thrown during the accident, so it took me awhile to find it. Once help arrived, they rushed us both to the hospital. I knew she was hurt, we both were, but we were joking with each other until we were separated at the hospital ..." he trailed off. "I never saw her again," he said, his voice barely a whisper.

I exhaled, not realizing I had been holding my breath until that point. "Mac, it was an accident," I barely whispered back.

"That's what everyone said. No one blamed me, and that was almost worse, people not blaming me. She was my best friend and she was gone. Mom and Dad were never the same; they got divorced two years later. It didn't feel like home anymore, so I left. I went to Chicago for a while, but I got restless, so I headed even further away. I arrived in New York six years ago and never left."

I just sat with him in silence for a while. I didn't know what to say and I wasn't always good with my words in these types of situations.

He raised his head and said, "It's not easy to just run away; the past always has a way of finding you and haunting you."

"Is that why you let me in and no one else?" I asked, choosing my words carefully.

"Perhaps, it wasn't a lie when I said you reminded me of her. You're so full of life, so much emotion. It was like I was getting a second chance with Abby," he said and I smiled.

"I feel like you're teaching me a life lesson," I commented, leaning back in the chair and looking up at the ceiling.

"I think it's called guilt," he mumbled, also leaning back.

"Is it like this every year?"

"Usually. I try to stay busy and not think about it, but meeting you made it harder to ignore this year."

"When was the last time you talked to your parents?"

"A couple of years ago."

"You regret anything?"

"Several things."

"You still have time to fix it, you know," I said finishing my beer and setting it on the table. "You're always fixing everything for everyone else, but maybe it's time for you to do something for yourself? Maybe then you can be happier with who you are and let more people in," I said, suddenly sounding like my Mama.

"Tex, you're so wise," he said, getting up to retrieve two more beers. There was a long pause as we both reflected on our conversation.

"You know, you made me feel crazy that I was the only person in the city who likes beer," I said after a moment and he laughed.

"That's what you got from all of this?"

"Well, no, but you made me feel crazy."

"I can hear your clucking but I can't find your nest," he said after a moment.

I looked at him stunned for a second and then burst into laughter. "You do understand me!" I proclaimed, giving his shoulder a squeeze.

"I do. I wish I didn't, but I do," he said, the tension finally easing.

Mac proceeded to pull out some photo albums and show me pictures of his sister and family. I eventually convinced him to shower while I ordered a pizza. He was still sad when I left around six, but he seemed better.

"Hey Tex, I think I might go out of town for a couple of days. You gonna be okay without me?" he asked, standing at the door before I left.

"I'm gonna be fine. What's the worst that could happen? Fashion mishap? You just need to accept that it's going to happen," I joked and he waved me off. I gave him a huge hug before leaving.

"McAllister Houston, New York will not be the same without you," I commented. I gave him a little wave before I left, causing him to smile for the first time that evening.

******

The following day I successfully walked Princess and got her settled in her crate, where she was now taking all her naps. I was on my way to the Park Avenue apartment to organize their closets when my phone rang.

"Hello?" I answered.

"Logan?"

"Yes."

"It's Jeffrey from The Plaza. There's a gentleman here asking for you."

"For me?" I questioned, confused.

"He asked for you specifically. He talks an awful lot like you," he said, causing me to stop dead in my tracks on the sidewalk. My blood went cold and it was suddenly hard to breath.

"Is he wearing a cowboy hat and boots?" I prayed the answer was 'no.'

"Yes," he said vaguely.

"I'll be right there," I said, cursing silently as I turned around and headed the other direction. I ran through a thousand different scenarios in my head as I jogged towards the hotel. It just didn't seem possible that he would find me in New York. It seemed less likely he would leave Texas to do so, but with each thought my anger grew. As I rounded the corner, Thomas was standing outside with an odd look on his face.

"He's inside," he said and I nodded, but the look on my face must have told him not to say anything further. I burst into the hotel lobby and saw him standing by the counter, talking with Jeffrey. He was wearing his Sunday best: cowboy boots, a white cowboy hat, pressed jeans, a short-sleeve green button-up, and a belt with a large belt buckle.

"Austin." I seethed, coming to a stop in the middle of the lobby. He turned and flashed me that familiar large lopsided grin, but the smile faded moments later when he saw my face.

"Logan ..."

"You must have one oar out of the water," I snapped, crossing my arms over my chest.

"You're being as friendly as a bramble bush, is that any kind of welcome?" he said, practically sauntering towards me.

"You're as welcome as a wet shoe."

"Logan, you clean up real nice," he said, and for once his twang was noticeable to me as he drew out the last two words.

"What are you doing here?" I whispered fiercely as he got closer.

"Logan, you made your point. Let's go home."

"You must be madder than a wet hen," I said, not moving from my spot as he reached out to put his hand on my arm. The entire lobby was now silently watching us. I think I saw Thomas taking odds out of the corner of my eye, which almost caused me to break my facade.

"Austin, you shouldn't be here," I said as he brushed my arm.

"Can we talk somewhere privately?"

"You look more nervous than a long-tailed cat in a room full of rocking chairs," I commented. "Take this thing off," I said, pulling his hat off and running my hands through his hair so that it wasn't so flat. I finally nodded at his request before turning toward the door, giving a slight wave to Thomas and Jeffrey. Austin stepped back and grabbed a bag before tipping his hat in the direction of the front desk, causing me to roll my eyes.

"I think bramble bush is a bad thing," someone commented, trying to understand our conversation. We walked toward the park, mostly in silence.

"It's hot as Hades here, Logan," he said, taking his bandanna out of his back pocket, wiping his brow and the back of his neck.

"You get used to it," I replied overly casual. I sat down on a bench and took a deep breath, trying to keep my anger at bay. "Austin, how did you find me?"

"You sent a package home. I heard Emily and Becky talking about it one night after dinner. The next morning I bribed Emily to give me the address. It took me a couple days to build up the courage, but I bought a plane ticket; figured it was the only way to talk some sense into you."

"You flew?" I asked, momentarily replacing anger with amazement.

"I knew this was important, and I figured if you could do it, so could I. But don't think I'm going to make it a habit. Most unnatural thing I have ever done," he commented and a knot formed in the pit of my stomach.

"I took the train," I admitted sheepishly, staring into the park.

"Oh Logan," he simply said, shaking his head.

"Austin, nothing has changed. Do you still want to be a rancher?"

"You betcha I do," he said earnestly.

"Do you still want to live in West Texas, get married, and have a million children?"

"I've been thinking about this," he said proudly. "We could get a place and start our own ranch for a couple years, and then when your Papa is ready to retire, we can take it over. We don't have to rush into anything. Yes, I want to get married and, yes, I want to start a family. Three or four children would be fine, a million is a bit excessive," he said, trying to crack a joke.

"Your dream is still the same," I sighed, sadly tugging at the gold chain around my neck. It was a habit I found myself doing more and more lately.

"Logan, I asked you to marry me. I want to be with you. Don't you want to be with me?"

"It's not about wanting to be with you, Austin. It's about me not wanting that life. I don't want to be a rancher and I don't want to be barefoot and pregnant at twenty-four," I admitted, finally saying the words out loud. "We've been together since middle school. You were my first kiss, my first love. But I don't want the same life you want, Austin; you deserve to be with someone who does."

"Fine, then no ranch. Do you want me to move to New York? I'll do it."

"You're crazy as a bullbat. You won't be happy here!"

"Why? You and I grew up the same and you're happy here. I could be happy here."

I stared at him in amazement. "Okay, sure. Let's try this," I said, suddenly rising from my spot.

"What, right now?"

"You want to see what the city is like? Let's take her for a ride," I said with a mischievous grin.

CHAPTER 12

For having so much to say to each other moments earlier we were now both eerily quiet. It was noticeable people giving Austin odd stares for his pressed jeans and cowboy boots as they clicked on the pavement, not to mention his large silver belt buckle that glistened in the sun and the cowboy hat that now dangled from his bag. When he wasn't looking I tried to take in his appearance, his blond hair was cut short on the sides and left a little longer on top. His brown eyes were squinting into the sun which made his nose wrinkle. It was a strange feeling, I knew every feature on his face and was present to almost every scar. I had witnessed first hand as he grew into his large chin and broad shoulders. The scar above his left eye was from a very angry mama cow as he tried to help birth a calf whereas the scar under his chin was from his brother's elbow during what was supposed to be a friendly game of football. He walked with his shoulders back as the muscles under his shirt flexed when he shifted the duffel bag he was carrying from one hand to the next.

"We are almost there," I faintly said as we turned to the corner and he just nodded. My mind was racing over the current situation. It was almost four weeks ago that Austin had asked me to marry him and three weeks six days since I packed up and ran away to New York City and three weeks four days since meeting Mac and having my life turn all cattywampus. The ranch and Austin seemed like another lifetime since I arrived in the city.

With Austin's appearance I felt more confused than ever. My feelings for him seemed to be tied to my past and I wasn't sure if there was room for him in my future. Suddenly, the phone in the back pocket of my jeans vibrated interrupting my thoughts. Having too much to deal with I ignored whoever was calling. Letting out a long sigh, I steered Austin up another block and across the street to my current 'home.'

"Hey Jack, can I talk to you for a moment?" I asked the doorman as we entered the lobby.

"Ms. Hunter, how can I help you?" he commented formally walking towards us.

"Jack, this is my friend Austin," I finally said after pausing to debate the best adjective to describe the current situation.

"Pleasure to meet you, Sir," Austin said reaching out a hand to greet Jack.

"He's going to be staying with me for...." I paused to look at Austin realizing we hadn't yet discussed his plans.

"It's undecided at this moment, Sir," he finished my sentence.

"Are you horn-tossing mad?" I fiercely whispered through my gritted teeth forgetting Jack's existence at the moment. "What does 'undecided at this moment' even mean?" I questioned with the realization on just how quickly Austin was able to bow me up.

"It means, I stay until you agree to come back to Texas with me," he replied smiling politely at me.

"Like hell."

"Logan there is no need to show-out in front of this gentleman," he paused and pointed to Jack who was now watching us with a perplexed look on his face. Austin always took the upper hand especially in public.

"Fine. My apologies, Jack," I commented through my still gritted teeth. "My friend Austin will be staying with me in Ms. MacKenzie's suite for an undisclosed amount of time but I'm sure it won't be longer than a few days. I just wanted to make introductions as I know you are always cautious with security," I managed to explain as my temper simmered beneath the surface.

"Yes, of course, Ms. Hunter. I hope you enjoy your stay, Sir," he said shaking Austin's hand again before going to help a couple that had wandered in from the street looking for directions.

"This way," I hissed at Austin heading to the elevator and hitting the button and passcode for the twenty-sixth floor.

"Twenty-six?" Austin said after a moment as the elevator whisked us away.

"Yes, it will be fine," I commented suddenly remembering his fear of heights.

"You can't even tell you're that high up," I added as an afterthought as he gave me a very skeptical glance. When we arrived on our floor, I led him down the small hallway before I opened the door to May's apartment. I was anticipating the reaction and Austin did not disappoint.

"Well butter my butt and call me a biscuit! You little cotton-picker live here?!" he yelled turning around in circles several times before finally turning to look at me. No matter my anger I couldn't help but laugh at his current expression; it was probably similar to mine the first time Mac had brought me to the 52nd Street apartment. The apartment was ridiculously lavish; it was designed to look fabulous and only fitting for the rich and famous. The best feature was the wall-to-wall panoramic views of the city. My favorite views had become the ones at sunset but the night view — it was then the city felt alive.

"My client lives here, I'm just staying here while she is out of town so I can watch her dog," I said trying to be casual leading him further into the apartment.

"Your client?" he asked following me staring at everything as his mouth hung open in disbelief.

"Sorry I probably shouldn't say..."

"May MacKenzie?!" he shouted dropping his duffel causing me to panic. The way he said it made me think she was standing in the room with us. Austin may have been a rancher but even he had heard of May MacKenzie and shared the male population sentiment about how attractive she was.

"How could you possibly know that?" I asked once I made sure she was not in the room.

"Every wall is adorned with her face," he said slowly walking from one picture to the other.

"I guess," I huffed. In reality, since I had been there, I hadn't really paid attention to all her self-portraits.

"Will I get to meet her?" he asked suddenly peeking at me from behind one of the many abstract sculptures on the first floor.

"Doubtful. She is clear across the globe in Africa or New Zealand or something like that for the next several months," I explained before leading him to one of the guest bedrooms on the main floor.

"You can stay in this room."

"Where do you sleep?"

"I sleep in the upstairs guest room so that I'm closer to Princess."

"Princess?" he let out a howl of laughter.

"Austin, you better watch your manners, or I'll call your mama," I said and I meant it. He set his stuff down still chuckling to himself as I gave him a tour of the rest of the apartment.

"Hey there," I said as we entered May's bedroom and I made a beeline for Princess. I noticed that Austin didn't follow me but hung by the door. I unlatched the crate and Princess happily danced out and was wagging her tail.

"Is this her bedroom?" he said in almost awe.

"Ugh, really? It's her apartment so logic would tell us that she also has a bedroom. That question was as dumb as prairie dirt, Austin," I commented. In the meantime, Princess locked in on Austin and started barking.

"Whoa, that little thing has a temper, doesn't she?" Austin commented taking a step back.

"She's not that bad," I said reaching down and scratching behind her ear causing her to stop her barking and lean into the scratches. She surveyed Austin one more time, huffed and followed me out of the room. So began the parade of myself, Princess, and Austin back down to the kitchen. Princess got a treat and settled down on one of her many fancy pillows, always keeping a wary eye on Austin. Austin settled down at the counter and watched me as I busied myself making something to eat.

"I assume you're hungry?" I asked after I was done making two sandwiches.

"I could sit for that," he commented back.

"Drink?"

"Sweet tea."

"It's all unsweet," I replied thinking to my own disappointment the first time I ordered tea at some fancy restaurant Mac had taken me too.

"That's as dumb as a watermelon," he commented mostly to himself as he settled in and ate his food. Instead of tea I grabbed two beers that were left in the fridge and set one down in front of him. He was about to comment on the beer and I shot him a glance that caused him to pipe down and eat his food. The phone in my back pocket vibrated again and yet again, I continued to ignore the call.

"Austin, why are you here?" I asked after several quiet moments, trying to be as calm as possible.

"I told you, I'm here to bring you home," he said taking a bite out of his sandwich and wiping his hands on his jeans.

"What if I don't want to go home?"

"You've lost your hold on vertical," he said seriously.

"I've lost my what?" Calm quickly flew out the window as he stared at me.

"You understood crazy as a bullbat earlier?" he said, clearly trying to make his point.

"Austin, I understood the phrase, I'm irritated you were using it. But the point is I'm not ready to be married, to live on a ranch, to be all those things you want," I said ignoring his jabs at my sanity.

"You got this crazy adventure out of your system, come home," he voice hitched a little on the last word.

"Austin..." I was interrupted by a curt knock on the door. The knock caused Princess to jump up and start barking uncontrollably which only caused Austin to curse under his breath and start yelling at Princess. The phone in my pocket started to vibrate and my whole world seemed to be closing in on me ever so slightly. After taking a pause, my temper won.

"ENOUGH," I shouted, glancing at the clock. It was late afternoon and I wasn't expecting anyone let alone did I know anyone that would look for me here. Both Princess and Austin quieted down at my outburst as I made my way towards to the front door. "Quiet out of both of you," I hissed, shaking my finger before opening the door.

CHAPTER 13

Exasperated I flung the door to the apartment open only to find a young women standing in front of me. She was slender but fit and wore the latest sleek black bob. Her navy pantsuit was perfectly tailored and paired with a cream silk blouse. She wore tall Grey stilettos and tapped one impatiently against the marble floor. Over her shoulder she carried a large bag that was bulging with various items. Either she didn't notice the door was open or didn't care as she starred at the screen of her iPhone causing her face to wrinkle and her lips to form a thin pressed line.

"Can I help you?" I asked more rudely than I meant to. At the sound of my voice her head snapped up and she gave me a curt smile.

"Logan? Logan Hunter?" she asked looking back down at her phone not waiting for my reply.

"Yes ma'am. Can I help you?" I asked again.

"I'm Caroline Keneally, Ms. MacKenzie's personal assistant. I've been trying to reach you all day," she said not lifting her head but walking directly into the apartment.

"I'm sorry, no one ever mentioned a personal assistant," I said as my cheeks turned red in frustration.

"I'm not surprised," she said finally looking up and taking in the scene of several different sets of eyes watching her closely.

"How can I help you and Ms. MacKenzie?" I asked for the third time as I felt my patience thin.

"She has made some changes to her travel schedule and needs some items shipped to her immediately," she explained in a crisp tone looking back to her phone.

"Of course, I'd be glad to take care of that," I said offering to help in hopes of her leaving soon. My offer seemed to surprise Caroline as she picked up her head and nodded as if someone asked her a question. After another moment she slipped her phone into her gigantic bag and took several more steps into the apartment.

The silent pact that had been brokered between myself, Princess, and Austin suddenly shattered as Princess erupted into a fit of barking causing Austin to curse one more time. Caroline suddenly got wide-eyed, dropping her bag, and threw herself behind the closest thing she could grab which happened to be Austin.

"Can you control that vicious thing?" she shrilled causing me to chuckle.

"Princess, that is enough out of you," I commented scooping Princess up and scratching behind her ear again, causing her barks to simmer down to a couple grunts.

"Logan, you're so lucky, you always draw the best bull," Austin commented.

"Lucky? Luck has nothing to do with it," I shot back, giving him an icy stare as I strode past him and Caroline back into the kitchen.

"Excuse me, what did you just say?" Caroline said finally regaining her composure and straightening her blouse.

"Just that Logan has always had the best luck with animals; this one time a couple years ago, we were having trouble with an Arabian on the ranch..."

"Arabian?" Caroline asked interrupting clearly confused.

"It's a horse, and she was tough as nickel steel, too. But Logan..."

"To...Tou...Tough as nickel steel?" she stuttered, finally taking in Austin's full appearance.

"The horse was mean and stubborn," I called from the other room, shaking my head at the painful conversation that was attempting to be had between the two of them.

"Yes ma'am. She was stubborn but Logan here, Logan didn't shy away. She got right on that horse even though the horse had thrown three previous riders. Logan had that horse tamed that afternoon, made her papa really proud," he finished beaming with pride.

"Papa?" Again a confused Caroline questioned Austin.

"My father," I translated again.

"Oh, I see, she tamed a horse, fascinating," Caroline commented.

"It was so much more than that; then there was the time she..." Austin said about to launch into another story.

"Caroline, is there anything I can do to make this easier on you?" I interrupted and she looked grateful as she came into the kitchen causing Princess to start barking again.

"I didn't know you had guests," she stated deciding to stand on the other side of the kitchen.

"Austin is a friend from back home and made a very unexpected visit to the city," I commented hoping this wasn't breaking an unspoken rule.

"I see...and where is home?"

"Texas, ma'am," Austin said sauntering into the kitchen and settling down at the counter.

"Explains a lot," she mumbled, getting distracted by the sudden ringing coming from her bag.

"Caroline," she answered quickly.

"Yes...Yes...No, I understand...right away," she answered a series of rapid questions that the caller seemed to be firing at her.

"Princess, she's fine...looks happy..." she paused again looking at me still holding Princess and Austin at the counter.

"I don't know if she wants to talk to you?" she replied looking at me. I had figured out the caller was May and sudden panic rumbled in my gut of the thought of talking to May directly on the phone. I steadied myself and reached my hand out for the phone. Caroline shook her head and mouthed 'Princess' to me causing me to laugh.

"She wants to talk to the dog?" Austin commented in the background causing both Caroline and me to glare which instantly had him quiet. I glanced back at Caroline and I could read the slight panic in her eyes as May continued to talk on the other line.

"Yes, I understand. I'll see if Logan can get her...Logan, the dog sitter," she paused again as May interrupted her.

"Logan, May would like to speak with Princess," she finally said with exasperation as she put her phone on speaker and held the phone out. There were several moments of sheer panic as we all stood there staring at the phone.

"Well..." May could be heard saying through the phone.

"Austin, come here," I whispered, thinking quickly. Austin look confused as I waved wildly at him to come closer. Cautiously he got up and slowly walked toward me. As he did Princess erupted in loud barks, to the delight of May.

"Aww, who's mommy's little girl? Do you miss mommy? Mommy misses you too," May cooed in response. Austin rolled his eyes at me and Caroline stood there holding the phone out with a blank expression for several minutes until Princess quieted down.

"Caroline? Caroline? CAROLINE?" May finally yelled trying to get her attention as she snapped back to reality.

"Yes, May?"

"Have those items overnighted to me. That is all," she disconnected abruptly.

"That was May MacKenzie?" Austin said after several moments of silence.

"Indeed," Caroline said, shoving her phone back into her bag.

"I think it was better not knowing all this stuff about her. Sounds like she has too many cobwebs in her attic, if you know what I mean," commented Austin as he moved to the sofa in the living room.

"I have no idea what you mean or what you are saying," Caroline replied.

"Caroline, can I help you with anything or can you handle this? It's almost time for Princess's walk," I said with exasperation over the turn of events my day had taken.

"I'm all set. Shouldn't take me longer than an hour or two to get everything done. Then I can leave you two alone," she said casting a side glance in Austin's direction.

"No. Nope. No need to be alone," I stammered as I made my way to the door. I had never been so happy to take Princess for a walk as I was in that moment.

******

Walking Princess gave me a moment to clear my head and try to reorganize my day. During the course of two blocks, I was able to move two of my organizing jobs to later in the week and Princess's grooming visit to first thing in the morning. I left two voice-mails for Mac and was about to leave a third before deciding I sounded too needy and disconnected. I was feeling good about things as we entered the building when my phone buzzed. Thinking it was Mac, I immediately answered.

"Logan is tonight still good?" Luca's smooth voice, caught me off guard.

"Well bless my heart, Luca."

"It's so good to know you haven't changed," he commented back. I could hear his smile and picture his steely green eyes. Although, we had just met I felt this connection to him even though we clearly lived in different worlds. He was running with big dogs and I was watching the dogs.

"I just meant..."

"It's okay Logan, I actually know what that one means and it's not necessarily very nice. Is something wrong?"

"I've been burning daylight," I whined unintentionally.

"For a moment there you sounded real Texas."

"The twang always comes out when I'm tired or mad," or both I thought to myself.

"I've seen you mad, I pity that poor soul," Luca commented causing me to laugh.

"I've had an unexpected guest show up that I need to babysit."

"Do you want to bring them along?"

"NO. Definitely not."

"Okay. I'm not letting you go that easily."

"I think I'll be free in a couple days?"

"I don't know if I can be, I have a quick trip to L.A. coming up. Are you sure you can't get away this evening?"

"Maybe I can sneak out later this evening," I mused as I contemplated various scenarios in my head about how that would go.

"I'll take anything you got."

"But it can't be for too long," I said talking myself into an evening with Luca.

"Sold, I know just the place. Can I pick you up?"

"No," I shouted startling Princess who paused to look up at me. "I think it would be best if I met you somewhere."

"Okay, what about if we meet outside the subway at the Roosevelt Island stop around 10?"

"How about 11?" I countered.

"That will work, is that a yes then?"

"As long as I got a biscuit you can have half," I said instantly shaking my head. I just couldn't say no to him but even to me that sounded country.

117

"I think that means yes?"

"Yes," I said continuing to shake my head to no one in particular.

"Bye, Logan, see you tonight."

"Bye, Luca," I said swooning as I walked back into the 52nd Street apartments.

CHAPTER 14

Princess is always more agreeable after a walk. When we got back to the apartment, despite the strangers that were occupying her living space, she happily took a treat and settled in again on one of her fancy pillows. I found Austin and Caroline upstairs in May's bedroom. Correction, Austin was loitering in the doorway as Caroline was deep inside May's closet.

"Seriously, you had never been on a plane before?" Caroline questioned in disbelief.

"No ma'am. Most unnatural thing I have ever done," twanged Austin.

"He should have kept his two bow legs on the ground in Texas," I commented walking past Austin and into May's room.

"Caroline are you sure I can't help you with anything?"

"Actually, I was looking for May's Louis Vuitton travel bag?"

"Why does she need Louis's bag?" Austin questioned.

"Louis is the brand," I responded to Austin as if I hadn't just learned that myself a week or so ago.

"It's the traditional monogram," she responded as if he hadn't spoken.

"I think I saw it in the study," I said turning around and heading downstairs.

"How do you know it's a brand?" Austin questioned following me like a puppy.

"I'm not dumb as dirt, Austin. I have picked up on things mighty quickly," I snapped at him.

"I didn't say you were dumb as dirt. Just the Logan that I know didn't care about stuff like that."

"Who said I cared about stuff like that? I just happened to know about the stupid bag."

"Your hair is done all different, real nice but different. Your clothes are..."

"Are what?" I snapped turning to face him with my hand on my hip.

"Aren't really you but your temper is the same," he finished.

"Uh-huh, got anything else to say Austin?" I said shifting my stance and pulling up my sleeves.

"Calm down Logan, you could always pick a fight with an empty house," he commented taking a step back. Just then the door bell rang and just like earlier in the day the house erupted in chaos.

"Who's that?" Caroline called from upstairs.

"Are you expecting visitors?" Austin questioned.

"I don't know," I yelled but directed to both Austin and Caroline throwing my hands up in exasperation.

"Then why don't you get the door?" Caroline called back.

"Working on it," I said through gritted teeth.

"I wasn't expecting you, I wasn't expecting Caroline, and I'm certainly not expecting anyone else," I hissed at Austin. Princess all the while was barking and running from where we were walking to the front door and back. Before I could reach the door, the bell rang one more time.

"Are you going to get the door?" Caroline called out again causing my blood to boil with irritation.

"Yes ma'am."

"Why you being so sweet to her?" Austin questioned as we approached the door.

"Are you horn tossing mad? I have to be sweet to her, she can report to my boss," I said flinging the door open.

"I thought I told you not to talk like that?" Mac commented striding into the apartment amongst the chaos.

"Mac, I thought you were going to be gone a couple days?"

"Plans changed."

"Now is not a good time, "I said through gritted teeth closing the door and scooping up Princess in one motion.

"You know him?" Austin asked while his neck started to turn red with frustration.

"And whom might you be?" Mac said suddenly realizing we were not alone.

"Mac, this is..."

"Logan did you ever get that door?" Caroline said coming up on our group.

"AND who are you?" Mac asked, waving his finger at Caroline.

"Who are you?" she shot back.

"Logan, I thought you were working today at the Perry house?" Mac turned to look at me.

"Logan, who is this guy?" Austin questioned, his face fully red.

"Logan, what is with all the house guests?" Caroline questioned peering around Mac and looking at me. Even Princess let out a small grunt as if to voice her dissatisfaction with the situation.

"Ya'll never miss a good chance to shut up," I said raising my voice.

"Excuse me?" Mac questioned.

"She's real mad," Austin commented.

"What?" Caroline asked confused.

"Mac, this is Austin...."

"The Austin?" he said raising his eyebrows.

"The Austin."

"Wait, I thought he was your friend?" Caroline interrupted causing me sigh.

"Would y'all just shut up and let me explain?"

"Why didn't you say so?" Mac replied getting defensive.

"I did."

"She did." Austin echoed.

"Right," Mac said, rolling his eyes at me as Austin and Caroline now looked at me.

"Okay. Let me try this again...this is Austin," I said pointing at Austin causing him to give a half hearted wave. "We were childhood sweethearts and he wanted to get married and I did not. So about a month ago, I gave him his ring back and ran away. The first person I met in the city was Mac," I said now pointing at Mac. "He got me a place to stay my first week or so in town, he has introduced me to some of his friends, showed me the city and gotten me several jobs. One of those jobs is dog sitting for actresses/singer and overall talent May MacKenzie's dog, Princess," I said rubbing her behind the ear to which she happily barked and everyone chuckled. "Everything was going smoothly until Austin here," I continued, pointing to him again. "Austin here just showed up in the city today with the idea that he was taking me back to Texas. While we were discussing his sudden appearance and cockamamie idea, Caroline here knocked on the door." I said now pointing at her.

"I tried calling first," Caroline huffed.

"Right. Caroline here is May's personal assistant. Sent here by May to pick up Lord knows what and send it Lord knows where," I was talking so fast I paused to take a long breath.

"You're Caroline?" Mac responded surveying Caroline for the first time.

"You're Mac?" Caroline questioned suddenly equally intrigued.

"I believe we have actually spoken on the phone, the time May needed the thing from down south but needed it overnight," Mac replied cryptically.

"Oh right, you're May's fixer," she commented back.

"Fixer? Are you a contractor?" Austin pipped in.

"Do these hands look like they fix anything?" Mac quickly replied. "Boy, no, I just find solutions to people's unique dilemmas."

"You should put that on your business card," Caroline snapped back.

"Anyway…to recap, Austin isn't staying, Caroline is leaving, and Mac should come back tomorrow." When I finished all three erupted into more questions than I was able to answer. Instead, I turned on my heels and headed into the living room while my entourage followed. The sound of them talking turned into a steady hum that I was able to tune out as I settled Princess on her pillow with another treat, yet again. After which, I went into the kitchen and pulled four glasses out of the cabinet.

"Would anyone like a drink?" I was met with a resounding 'yes' by the group.

"Let me," Mac said disappearing into the study. I fiddled with the glasses as Austin and Caroline took seats on opposites sides of the living room sofa, suddenly very silent.

"Do you need ice?" I questioned when he returned with a tall bottle filled with amber liquid.

"That is blasphemous. The Macallan M is only served neat."

"What does being neat have anything to do with anything?" Austin asked from the other room.

"Neat as in no ice or water," I explained carrying the four glasses into the living room.

"Very good Tex." Mac said as he poured four glasses and carefully handed them out to everyone. Austin sat forward on the sofa raised his glass of amber liquid to his nose before he carefully sipped it.

"This is real good," he said drawing out the syllables the last two words.

"Should be at $5,000 a bottle," Caroline commented, causally sipping from her glass as she sat back on the sofa and closed her eyes for a moment.

"FIVE-THOUSAND-DOLLARS? You've got to have your tail up," Austin exclaimed causing Caroline's eyes to pop open but Austin didn't notice; he was dumbfounded — looking at his glass in awe.

"Excuse me, did you just accuse me of having a tail? Who are you? Who in the world says that?" Caroline quipped to no one in particular.

"The Macallan is worth every drop," Mac commented, ignoring Caroline and sipping from his glass as he casually paced the room.

"Won't May miss this ridiculously expensive bottle of amber gold?" I asked unsure of what exactly the Macallan was as I settled into a square white armchair that was surprisingly more comfortable than it appeared.

"May isn't a scotch drinker — she only has it for show. But given that she has three other bottles of Macallan in her bar area, I doubt she will miss this one."

"She has fifteen thousand dollars worth of scotch?" Austin said in disbelief mostly to himself.

"Amongst other things," Mac commented with a smirk. I still didn't grasp his relationship with May and how much he actually knew about the actress and for how long. He had been frustratingly mum on the topic whenever I asked.

"May actually has really cheap taste in alcohol. In public she is always holding wine or something expensive but it usually gets poured out when no one is looking. She prefers her wine from a box or a bottle of Mike's Hard Lemonade," Caroline commented almost as if to fill the silence that had befallen the room.

"No way," I giggled while Mac had a horrified expression on his face. It was the first time all day that I finally was able to laugh and relax for a brief moment as the room went silent again.

For a while we sat in silence sipping the Macallan M lost in our thoughts and Mac continued to wander randomly throughout the space. I was thinking back to when I was on the ranch, wishing for something exciting to happen to break up the day-to-day chores. Now I had more excitement than I knew what to do with. I guess Mama was right, you had to be careful with your wishes and way more specific.

"As fun as this little soiree has been, I have to finish getting things together for May," Caroline finally said just after seven.

"Oh, I was going to get you that bag and it's almost time for Princess's walk, again," I said jumping up causing Princess to bark in my direction.

"Indeed," she said already on her feet.

"Tex, you know how to throw a party," Mac commented causing me to stick my tongue out in his general direction.

"Real mature, Logan," Austin commented from his stretched-out position on the sofa as he fought to stay awake.

"Speak of the devil and she doth appear," Mac said suddenly holding up his phone, showing the crowd that May was calling.

"Why would she be calling you?" Caroline huffed, now looking at her own phone.

"Good evening, May," Mac answered, gesturing us to be quiet.

"Yes, of course...I told you I had that all arranged for you in the states...but of course May...no May...I can do that May...yes have a good day May," he commented before disconnecting.

"So that is what I sound like talking to May," Caroline mused to herself.

"You are about to get a phone call," Mac postured pointing at Caroline's phone. Sure enough seconds later, her screen lit up indicating May was calling.

"Good evening May," she answered copying Mac. "No, I don't know why people keep telling you that...yes May...of course...I will have to check that account...I can call Frank immediately...yes I understand, I can also call Anne about those pictures...No I left already, sorry you won't get to speak with Princess again...yes May," she finally said before disconnecting.

"What's all the fuss about?" I asked returning with the bag. Caroline paused to look at Mac, Austin, and myself. Austin for his part let out a soft snore from where he now lay on the sofa.

"Tex is in deep with May," Mac commented winking at me.

"I suppose she is at this point. Do you know she has gone through a dozen dog sitters for that dog? No one has lasted past a week. I suppose some sort of congratulations should be in order for you," she said looking at Princess who had just as quickly fallen back asleep.

"No need to be mean as a mama wasp," I shot back quickly.

"Ladies," Mac commented trying to get Caroline back on track.

"I'm sorry. Working with May can be taxing at times," she said rubbing her temple. "May has broken up with her recent boy-toy and is having the procedure," Mac pointed to his nose, "taken care of while on location rather than waiting to do it in New York as she originally planned. Frank is one of her accountants and she wanted some money moved so she can do some retail therapy to help with her break up; and Anne is our contact with one of the entertainment outlets and May wanted several photos of her on the beach enjoying herself 'leaked' to the press post breakup," Caroline explained as she turned and headed upstairs.

"Being famous is exhausting."

"It can be," Mac commented pouring himself a second glass of scotch.

CHAPTER 15

After Caroline left but before Mac left, and much to his chagrin, he helped me carry Austin to bed in the guest room. I tried my best to carefully remove his boots but it took some tugging and pulling before I was successful. I slid his belt and belt buckle from around his waist just as he sighed and rolled over mumbling something about alfalfa hay, slipping back into the hallway before I started giggling.

"I thought for sure you would want him shacked up in your room," Mac said from behind me giving me a fright.

"Are you kidding me, him being here only complicates things."

"Yes, I suppose it doesn't make it easy. Luca Gaines is going to be heartbroken," he said mockingly throwing his hand over his forehead.

"Wait, I didn't tell you about Luca yet? How do you know?" I questioned puzzled by the depth of his statement all the while getting Princess ready for her walk.

"I was joking about Luca but wait is there is something going on?" Now he looked perplexed.

"I saw him again after the rooftop incident and we exchanged numbers. I'm actually going to meet him tonight," I said glancing at my watch.

"Tex, you little vixen. You never cease to surprise me, which is really hard to do."

"Are you coming or staying?" I asked holding the door open for him as Princess and I exited for our walk.

"Oh darling, I'm coming with you. I need all the details." With that I closed the door and we headed out for our walk. Mac walked with me for several blocks, peppering me with so many questions. Many of them I had no answer to as the story wasn't as juicy as he had hoped. Near the turnaround point was a subway entrance where Mac bid Princess and me adieu and headed to Sabrina's townhouse for the evening. I raced home with Princess to get ready for my evening rendezvous with Luca.

****

I allotted for an extra fifteen minutes in case I took the wrong subway. However, this time I was in luck and arrived at the Roosevelt Island stop early. While I was getting ready, Luca had texted to meet him street level by a park bench that was across the street from the subway entrance. I found the bench easily and sat down noticing how quite the area was — a few people hustled down the streets seemingly on a mission to get wherever they were headed. I fidgeted with the hem of my blouse as I waited. My mind drifted back to Austin and more specifically almost getting caught by Austin as I left May's apartment. I had just finished doing my hair so that loose beach-like waves hung perfectly in place and was going to start my makeup just the way Grey showed me how when he wandered into the bathroom.

"Austin, I thought you were sleeping!" I sheepishly said.

"I was hungry so I got up?" As he said this, realization dawned on me that we had skipped dinner that evening.

"There are snacks in the pantry and fridge, please help yourself."

"Are you hungry?"

"No," I lied as my stomach grumbled in that very moment.

"Okay...pantry and fridge," he said as he wandered back off. I waited a couple minutes and followed only to find him asleep on the living room floor.

"Oh Austin," I whispered covering him up with a blanket from the sofa. Thirty minutes later I left the apartment and both he and Princess were sleeping like babies.

****

"You're cute as a speckled pup under a wagon," I heard as someone touched my shoulder causing me to jump.

"What did you just say?" I finally asked after catching my breath for a moment looking at Luca.

"Did I not deliver that right? I should try again," he said earnestly.

"You must be missing a couple buttons off your shirt," I cracked back.

"But I don't have any buttons on my shirt?" he said looking down at his black long sleeved but form-fitting shirt.

"I didn't mean actual buttons," I laughed bursting into a fit of giggles.

"I was trying to make you feel at home. I looked at sayings all day and in two seconds you stymied me with your sass," he said shaking his head.

"You actually looked up the crazy things I say?"

"I think I already played my hand but yes."

"That is just the sweetest thing," I said jumping up and wrapping him in a hug. In a moment the light-hearted banter was gone and a sudden heaviness filled the air between us, making it hard for me to breath. It took an extra moment or two before either one of us spoke again.

"What else did you practice?" I asked.

"I think that is a secret...but so is our current destination so we better get moving," he said ushering me down a side street.

"Come on, you have to tell me," I whined and pulled on his arm. "I promise I won't laugh."

"Yes you will."

"You're right. I promise not to laugh hard," I finally said causing him to let out a deep loud chuckle.

"Logan you are just so refreshing to be around."

"How so?"

"Take this morning in rehearsals. We are slightly redoing this scene and I'm struggling with the rewrite. I know I'm struggling, the director knows I'm struggling, and my scene partner certainly knows I'm struggling. My director yells 'cut' and I think he's about to tell me how awful that was. Instead, he goes on to tell me how much 'improvement' he saw in that scene and I was doing great, but we should take a break. During the break he asks to see me and I think, oh now he's going to let me have it. No, instead he wants to talk about my last movie and the actress I worked with on set. He then asks me if I think she would do the new screen play he just finished writing. I just stared at him dumbfounded and frustrated. After that I go into my dressing room and there are some benefactors there with patrons wanting pictures, autographs, asking me about my next project, for free tickets to my final show and I'm pretty sure one of them made off with a copy of my script as I couldn't find it anywhere after they left. It had all my notes on the rewrite," he let out an exasperated sigh, "I haven't had one genuine conversation today."

"You just eat sorrow by the spoonful," I said mostly sarcastically and without thinking.

"I did just say a lot didn't I?" he questioned himself, lost in thought for a moment. We continued to walk down a curved road in silence passing cyclists, and joggers by the dozen. It continued to baffle me how many people were out so late at night and not just out for a casual stroll but being active as if it were completely normal. I didn't have to be home to know that every single person in my household was already asleep. Papa's alarm would be going off in a few short hours; after he got up he would brew a pot of coffee for himself and mama. Mama would drift downstairs barefoot in her lavender fuzzy robe as the aroma of coffee filled the house. The two of them would sit at the kitchen table and talk quietly until Brett, William Thomas, and Austin (normally) would arrive. Then the four of them would head out to the barn and mama would go about getting the rest of the household up and running.

"What are you thinking about?" Luca interrupted my thoughts.

"Home," I said simply and he nodded in some kind of understanding.

"We are almost there," he said after some time.

"Where is there?"

"How about instead of me answering that I'll tell you another saying I looked up."

"Deal."

"Let's see...oh yes there was one...you can ride any horse in my string. But I felt dirty just reading it and now that I have said it out loud I feel creepy."

"I haven't heard that one in forever and I think you chose wisely."

"We are here!" He said pressing his ear to the side of a closed box office window.

"What are you listening to?" I said suddenly feeling the need to whisper.

"Hold on," he whispered back. After a couple seconds he stood up and knocked three times rapidly on the ticket window. There was a short pause and someone knocked back twice to which Luca responded with one more knock.

"What in the Sam Hill is going on?"

"The park curator owes me a favor," he said as we walked around the box office and he causally jumped the turnstile.

"Lord almighty, does everyone in this city owe someone a favor?" I said with more exasperation than I intended as I followed suit jumping over the turnstile suddenly very happy I wore jeans instead of the skirt I was eying.

"People are always looking to get ahead. Favors are easy to come by in this city. But in this case it's not as complicated as that. The park curator and I went to high school together, we go way back." We had ventured into this quiet serene park that was unlike anything I had seen in the city so far.

"So what is this place?"

"This is the FDR Four Freedoms Park. FDR gave this incredible speech in 1941 to rally America and its allies during World War II. The freedoms that he spoke about eventually became the Declaration of Human Rights," his eyes lit up like a kid at Christmas.

"You sure do know a lot about this stuff."

"I'm a nerd when it comes to history. I love to know about where we came from, helps me know where we are going."

"Have you always come here?"

"No, it was just built a couple years ago. But when I was preparing for the opening of 'Franklin' I would try and come as often as I could. I can't come in the middle of the day without causing a scene. Sometimes I would have luck coming right when the park opens or closes. At first I thought I felt more connected to the character, that moment in time. Over time I realized that it was helping me clear my head and think about being in a place with such great meaning and significance. It helps put all this 'fluff' that occupies my days in perspective."

"Fluff?"

"The public persona of Luca Gaines. The fame, the lifestyle, the paparazzi, the whole industry. It's all fluff in my life." We both fell silent as we walked around the small park. It was a weird sensation being in this somewhat secluded park, desolate of people but surrounded by skyscrapers and the hustle and bustle of the city off in the distance.

"I saved the best view for last," he said pointing to the sky.

"Isn't that all sweetness and light! You can see the stars!"

"It's better from down here," he said lying down on the thick plush grass. I didn't hesitate following his lead. I kicked off my sandals and mushed my toes into the grass as I felt my whole body relax and mold into the soft earth.

"I never thought I would miss the quiet," I mused after awhile running my hand over the grass staring at the sky.

"Growing up in the city is all I have ever known," he commented next to me as his hand seemingly and accidentally grazed mine.

"During the summer the house would get as hot as a two dollar pistol and you can hear Papa snoring all the way from the den. I would sneak out my room, usually by climbing out of the window and down the large oak tree near the house. I could bribe my way past John and Wayne..."

"John Wayne?"

"John and Wayne, our two dogs...and I know, my Papa named them. If I remembered treats they would take them and forget to bark at me. From there I could climb up into the hay loft and crack one of the barn doors ever so slightly. The north wind would blow through and you could see millions of stars spread through the night sky; it was sweeter than stolen honey," I said with a final sigh.

"Sounds like a lot of effort."

"It was easy as pie. I would go there to think or get away from my family, too."

"You take people up there?"

"To the hay loft? Never. Austin tried to come with me a couple times, probably trying to get frisky but I always told him to get lost. It was actually the last place I went before I decided to come to New York."

"I'm really glad you did," he said grabbing my hand and giving it a squeeze. I rolled over onto my side and looked at his silhouette as he laid in the grass still gazing at the sky. I could have stayed there in the moment all night and we almost did. Luca talked about his family and his French bulldog named Alfred; named after the butler in Batman. I told him about the ranch and my horses Jessica Fletcher and Nancy Drew; named after my favorite female detectives. I laughed uncontrollably when he told me about one of his early auditions where he oversold his ability to speak Italian in order to get a chance at an audition and ended up telling the casting agent about a 'pretty bird who turns left at the sight of cake and right at McDonald's' instead of giving simple directions to the nearest McDonald's. It was only much later that he ever learned about his mistake from that casting agent directly. I told him about the time I tried to rope a hog and my pants split open in the back and I was too proud to act embarrassed so I just kept going and later walked off with the back end of my pants hanging down around my knees as if nothing was wrong. Some boy, to this day I don't know his name, made a crude comment and I popped him right there giving him a real shiner. My mama and papa were mortified, probably more about the pant thing than the popping-the-boy-off thing but they grounded me for two whole months.

"I asked for an hour of your time and now I have stolen almost five hours," Luca commented.

"Hush your mouth!" I exclaimed sitting up with a start. "It's almost four in the morning?"

"I thought you knew."

"I had no idea. I have to go; Princess will be up soon and expecting her walk."

"Not a problem, we can get a cab," he said stretching and slow to stand.

"That would be amazing," I said turning to the entrance as he reached down and grasped my hand. With no words spoken he pulled me back towards him and for a brief moment his gaze met mine as he brushed his lips against mine causing a catch in my breathing.

"Be afraid of nothing," he mumbled under this breath.

"Are you quoting Joan Crawford?" I asked as he raised his eyebrows at me.

"I'm impressed," he said before leaning in and kissing me.

"Don't be, she was a Texan; learned about her in my Modern Texas class which was the follow up to Texas History in high school." I said at the next available moment.

"You had Texas History in high school?"

"Sure...didn't you have New York history?"

"No, I had American history."

"Well you're missing out. Sorry your state is lame," I said with a shrug and he laughed.

"Logan, you are just too much," and with that he kissed me again.

"I just had to see if it was real," he finally said when we pulled away.

"What's real?"

"That feeling I get around you, it's like the air suddenly has a weight to it and it's hard to breathe," he said once again holding my hand but interlocking our fingers as we walked towards the entrance.

'Oh that' ... I swooned to myself.

CHAPTER 16

Three days later Austin was still in New York and was driving me insane because he was stir crazy. We had made no progress on the status of our relationship nor the exact date of his return to Texas. On top of watching Princess, Mac continued to line up other miscellaneous jobs for me that kept me busy and tired at the end of the day. I made the mistake of taking Austin with me the first day to one of my jobs. He spent the whole time looking everything up on his phone and then telling me how much everything was worth of the things he could find, and what he could do with that kind of money on the farm. I was about ready to duct tape his mouth by the end of the first hour. After that he stayed in May's apartment when I had a job lined up. He tried to join me for walks with Princess but she spent so much time barking at him and not walking, it became too difficult and I left him home.

"Do you know there is nothing to watch on TV? Ms. MacKenzie has about 1,000 different channels and I can't find a darn thing on any of them," Austin uncharacteristically whined when I got home that evening.

"I'm sorry, did you watch one of d'em movie channels?"

"Ain't nothing on but love stories and end of the world stuff."

"What about ESPN?" Sports was usually a safe go to.

"That was good the first day, but now it's all the same stories told different ways. What do people do all day?"

"You mean people who aren't up at 4 and working by 5 until the sun sets on the ranch?"

"Yes. Remember Misty Douglas?"

"You mean Misty Burgess? She married Jeff last fall."

"That's it, I couldn't remember who she married."

"We went to the wedding," I said hoping this conversation had a point.

"Well she quit her job a couple weeks ago to stay at home with their new baby. I don't know how she does it?" he said truly exasperated.

"I think she is busier than you think she is with a baby and all," I said turning my back on him so he didn't see my horrified expression.

"Maybe, but I still don't see how people sit around. I think I'm losing muscle mass. Today I went to move the sofa a bit because the sun was in my eyes and I almost couldn't do it. I mean I can lift bales of hay all day long on a normal day and today I can't move a sofa!"

"Wait, you moved the sofa?"

"Don't get all cattywampus, I put it back," he said defensively.

"What do you want to do for dinner?" I asked trying to change the subject. "I can pick something up on my walk with Princess."

"Take-out again? I know your mama taught you how to cook. What about some of your famous honey soaked corn bread or BBQ?"

"We really don't have the fixins for that," but Austin was right I thought to myself. I was a bit embarrassed by my sudden inability to cook anything beyond a bowl of cheerios in the morning. "Let me take Princess on her walk and then we will go out and walk around the city and get some food. Then maybe tomorrow Gladys can pick up everything I need to make a good old home cooked meal," it was the least I could do having ignored him for the better part of three days.

"So tonight would be like a date?" he questioned.

"Like a date."

******

My walk with Princess was uneventful and when we returned I told Austin I had to change and I would be ready to go. After getting Princess all tucked away in her crate, I glanced at myself in one of May's full-length mirrors. My hair had grown out, longer than I had kept it in years. Whatever product Grey gave me was keeping it shiny and straight unlike the fuzzy, knotted mess it was back home. I wore a bit more makeup that I had, again thanks to Grey. The jeans I wore hung a little looser than I could remember and the green tunic I changed into was trendier than anything I had previously owned. Overall, I still felt like myself but the person looking back at me in the mirror looked different and I didn't see that as an entirely bad thing.

"Austin, I was thinking we could walk down towards Times Square, Rockefeller Center, the Empire State building, and then see about dinner somewhere near Greenwich Village," I said entering the kitchen, only to find him and Caroline deep in conversation; and for a moment if I'm being honest a twang of jealousy rippled through my gut.

"Caroline, I didn't hear you arrive," I said completely caught off guard.

"Sorry, I tried calling and you didn't answer, again... so I let myself in," Caroline said holding up a key. I glanced at my phone and sure enough I had a missed call from Caroline and then another one from Mac.

"I'm so sorry. I turned the volume down earlier and I forgot to turn it back on."

"It's a bad habit for her," Austin commented taking the words right out of my mouth. For once I just nodded in agreement.

"Can I help you with anything?" I asked after a couple awkward moments.

"No, I just stopped by to get a couple more things for May. Are you guys going out?"

"Logan is going to finally show me the city," Austin commented, picking up his cowboy hat from the counter.

"No, no, no," I said upon seeing the hat. "New York has a different dress code, you need to change," I said also noticing his belt buckle and boots.

"I didn't bring anything else."

"Oh, I can help with that. May always keeps several male outfits in the guest closet and you look about the right size," Caroline piped up.

"Should I ask why?"

"It started after her brother came to visit and they were photographed by paparazzi and he was wearing something off brand according to her. After that she or I stock the closet for seasonal/hottest trends of the season. It's always on a constant rotation," she said heading for the guest room.

"I ain't wearing none of those skinny jeans," Austin commented with a somewhat horrified look on his face.

"How do you know about skinny jeans," I asked as we followed Caroline into the guest room.

"Barbara B was talking about 'em."

"The day-time talk show host?"

"Yeah, that's her, they made a real good roasted ham on the show as well. The trick is to apparently soak the ham in a salt brine and then clean the ham and cook it with honey."

"Do you hear yourself?"

"What's wrong with a little learning? I thought you wanted a more cultured experience?"

"I wanted to live a new experience not watch one."

"Are you two done?" Caroline said looking at both of us and holding several pieces of clothing in her hands.

"Sorry ma'am," Austin replied.

"I have these great non-skinny jeans and this plaid shirt with a Grey vest," she said practically forcing the clothes into Austin's hands.

"Plaid shirt? I have several of these at home, nothing fancy about that," he said almost relieved.

"I doubt you would wear a $350 Burberry shirt on your quaint farm in Texas," she commented.

"$350? I doubt my whole wardrobe costs $350," he said with alarm.

"Don't be dramatic, your boots cost more than $350," I snapped back.

"My church boots were $400 but these boots I brought were on sale at the General Store for $250," he said with pride in his voice. Austin loved a good bargain, sale prices, or anything you can get with a coupon.

"Cowboy boots are expensive? I had no idea," Caroline said with genuine surprise.

"It's actually a ranch with about 100 head of cattle amongst other things," I turned to Caroline to address her previous statement.

"That sounds like a lot."

"It is ma'am. I'm hoping some day it will be mine and Logan's to run," he said heading into the bathroom.

"Yours, not mine," I corrected leaning on the door frame.

"What is your shoe size?" She called from inside the closet.

"Size 10," I responded without thinking.

"That's helpful, thank you," She replied. A couple minutes later she emerged carrying a box.

"What do you think?" Austin said sauntering out of out the bathroom.

"Wow, Austin, you look great. Try these on," Caroline said handing him a pair of ankle high brown suede boots.

"But I already have boots."

"These are a little different," I said with a chuckle. When he was done he stood up and spun around a couple times.

"They are just clothes, I don't see the fuss," he said as Caroline and I applauded at his transformation.

"Now you are ready for a night out on the town. The city is so much fun at night. Where are you two going to eat?"

"We hadn't made it that far," I replied.

"Oh, my favorite place is this little restaurant a block or so from Chinatown. It's on one of the side streets so not many people know about it. It serves great Italian food, lots of wine but it's so cozy and comfortable," she beamed.

"Do you want to go with us?" The question just popped out of my mouth before I thought it through. Austin raised his eyebrows at me and I shrugged apologetically toward him.

"I couldn't impose, you two enjoy the evening."

"Caroline, please come with us. How else could I repay you for getting me all dressed up tonight," Austin laid it on real thick.

"Really, you don't mind? I haven't had an evening off in weeks. This will be great...let me just go grab a couple things from May's closet and I'll be good to go," she practically squealed and ran off. She of course wouldn't have to change because she already looked perfect. Her short bob was slicked back away from her face. She wore a black silk jumper that was long pants and long sleeve but left most of her back exposed. It all perfectly matched the large black bag she was carrying today. I envied how put together she always seemed.

"Sorry Austin," I whispered as we headed toward the front door.

"Don't worry about it. Do I really look okay?" he said after a moment, pulling at his shirt.

"You clean up real nice," I replied causing him to laugh.

"I'm ready to go," Caroline practically sang as she joined us by the door.

"Great, do you mind if we walk around a bit. Take Austin through Times Square?"

"No, not at all, you lead the way," she added. It was about an hour later than planned but the three of us headed out for a night on the town.

******

About three blocks into our walk, my phone rang. Seeing that it was Mac, I quickly hit ignore and texted him instead. It was easier to tell him what we were doing and how I was really feeling about it without everyone hearing. By the fourth block, Caroline had taken charge of our casual walk and had assumed the position of tour guide. She directed all her facts and stories at Austin and would gently touch his forearm when she was trying to get his attention. The feelings in my gut stirred slightly but I was unsure of what to make of it. Mac eventually texted back, wondering what we were up to. I replied that we were currently in line at the Starbucks at the corner of 49th and 7th after Caroline insisted on stopping for a Grande Caramel Macchiato with a shot of espresso and almond milk.

"But why not say large if you mean large and according to the sign it's the middle size so shouldn't it be a medium?" Austin asked utterly confused.

"Because it sounds nicer in Italian," she finally said out of frustration but Austin looked unconvinced.

"Did you just pay almost six dollars for a coffee?" he again questioned. "Your phone must be off the hook. I only pay fifty cents for a cup at Kelly's on the corner every morning, don't I Logan?"

"Yup, every morning."

"What about a phone?"

"Let me translate, honey ... he thinks you're crazy for spending that much money on a cup of coffee," I chipped in after being ignored.

"It's not about the coffee it's about the experience. Here try it," she said offering her cup to Austin as if I hadn't spoken. He cautiously took the cup from her and slowly took a sip. His face puckered and his nose crinkled as if he had just eaten a lemon.

"I'd just as soon bite a bug than drink that again," he hollered and Caroline hastily grabbed her Starbucks cup back and stomped a couple feet ahead of us before stopping and calling back to us.

"Are you guys coming or not?" Austin and I looked at each other and shrugged as we headed off after Caroline.

What are you doing exactly? Mac texted again.

Trying to show Austin the city but also find something to eat, I replied as Caroline was once again pulling and tugging Austin in different directions.

Fabulous — are there any limitations or expectations within those goals?

No? I responded rather confused by his statement.

Then do you mind if I hijack this excursion?

No.

Excellent. Can you and your posse be outside the Empire State Building in fifteen?

Yes, but why?

You'll see when you get here Tex. Now hurry!

"Y'all, Mac wants us to meet him at the Empire State Building," I said looking up and seeing that neither Austin or Caroline were paying me any mind.

"Hey," thoroughly annoyed I put two fingers to my mouth and whistled. Not only did Austin and Caroline stop but so did the whole city block. Most people just stopped and stared but several mumbled under their breath before they continued on their way.

"Was that necessary?" Caroline commented.

"Now why do you have your tail up?" I shot back, feeling my face grow red.

"Ladies," Austin interjected taking a step between us. Caroline and I just stared at each other for another ten or fifteen seconds before I spoke again.

"Mac would like us to meet him at the Empire State Building."

"Why?"

"I'm not sure, inferred that it might be worth our time." Caroline scoffed at this idea and Austin looked skeptical.

"Logan why do you spend so much time with this guy? You barely know him," Austin huffed.

"Mac has...Mac...did..." I found myself stumbling over my words. What did Mac mean to me? I know that without him my New York adventure would look very different.

"Mac can show us a good time tonight."

"Are you sweet on him?" Austin asked.

"Oh Austin, you're more his type than Logan," Caroline commented trying to contain her laugher. Slow realization dawned on Austin as he processed what Caroline just said.

"I still don't like it when he calls you Tex," he finally said with no further comment.

"That's fine but we have ten minutes now to get there, y'all; I promise this will be something adventurous."

"I'm just tagging along in your evening, so whatever," Caroline said as if she hadn't intruded on our plans and been monopolizing Austin's attention this entire time.

"Whatever you think is best Logan," Austin agreed.

"Well then, let's hurry," I said rushing them along to the Empire State Building.

CHAPTER 17

When we got to the Empire State building there were hundreds of tourists milling around. Not seeing Mac, I texted him asking for his location.

Look up, he texted back. My head snapped up and I was looking at a double decker tour bus. There on the second level Mac stood waving with a wide Cheshire cat grin stretched across his face.

"Mac!" I exclaimed with a laugh causing Austin and Caroline to follow my gaze.

"No way," Caroline said in almost a whisper to herself.

"I don't understand," Austin said looking confused.

"I'll be right down," Mac called and disappeared into the bus reappearing before us.

"How in the world?" I commented when he stepped out onto the sidewalk with us.

"Do you remember Sabrina?" he asked, and I nodded. It's hard not to forget the moment when I met Mac and his eccentric friends.

"Well, Ben..."

"Short for Benedict not Benjamin?" I questioned and he nodded in approval.

"That's often a common mistake," Caroline chimed in as she stood closely next to Mac now very interested in what was going on.

"Well, Ben, short for Benedict not Benjamin, just got his huge promotion with work and wanted to do something to make it up to Sabrina for the long horrendous hours he's been working. She suggested renting a double-decker tour bus and turning it into a party bus as we cruise around the city. What she doesn't know is the additional surprise stops along the way he has planned sparing no expense. So here we are," he said with a flourish of his hands.

"How do you know about the surprise stops?" Caroline questioned.

"Who do you think planned them?" he commented as excitement danced in his eyes.

"Mac, darling?" I could hear a women's voice from within.

"Yes, Sabrina?" he slightly tapped on the window of the bus startling the women inside.

"Mac, get back on the bus, we are headed out on the most epic adventure anyone is ever having tonight." She paused to look at the three of us standing around.

"Logan, darling I almost didn't recognize you. You are looking so New York...it's been a while since the Vivian Banks fiasco. Come aboard, grab some champagne or whatever you fancy. There is a full bar and bartender on the first level in the back," she flipped her hand in the general direction. She leaned over and whispered something to Mac and he nodded whispering back.

"You heard the woman, all aboard." I fell in line behind Mac while simultaneously pulling Austin aboard. Caroline needed no convincing, she looked smitten by Sabrina and made an instant beeline for the bar.

"Connie, Alistair, Sybil, Thaddeus, William, Samuel, Blair, Cam, Marianna and Augustus — who has since shaved that awful mustache. The entire gang is here," Mac quickly made introductions. Moments later, the driver announced we were headed out and some minor safety precautions that no one was listening to. Caroline had returned from the bar with a glass of some type of pink drink with a lime wedge. Austin mumbled something about needing a drink and headed in the direction of the bar next.

"The poor boy is going to be disappointed as I know they probably aren't serving beer let alone his favorite, Pabst Blue Ribbon," I said shaking my head.

"That's disgusting," Caroline commented and Mac nodded in agreement. Someone called his name and he wandered off to join an animated conversation.

"So-o-o, did she say something about you and Vivian Banks?" Caroline questioned her eyes getting wide.

"Yes, that woman has too many cobwebs in the attic."

"Do you know that Vivian Banks is May's Godmother? Not blood related or anything, kind of a self-appointed thing. Vivian took May under her wing when she first was coming onto the movie scene. Once she hit it big, Vivian took all the credit for discovering her and making her a success. May never really minded being attached to the image of Vivian."

"Shut your mouth," I said with a horrified look on my face.

"What's going on? You look white as a ghost," Austin said approaching with a glass of something in his hand.

"What are you drinking?" Caroline asked while my mind reeled from this information.

"You know darn tootin' well they weren't going to have anything we drink on the ranch. My daddy always said that when you're drinking on someone else's dime or at a classy-folk event, that rum and coke is always a smart choice." His voice jarred me back into the present conversation.

"I didn't know that about your dad?" I commented.

"You don't know everything about me Logan, think as you may," he said directly sipping on his drink.

"What happened with you and Vivian?" Caroline pressed for more details.

"I'll tell you what happened," Mac said coming over and interrupting. I tried to make some hand gestures indicating for him to stop talking but he didn't. What he did was retell the whole story to Caroline and Austin. The only saving detail he left out was the kiss between Luca and me.

"Now I need a drink," I said at the end.

"Logan always gets into these horn-tossing situations. In school she got herself a bit of a reputation for being a fighter. Girls were always scared of her and the boys wouldn't mess with her," I heard him say as I walked away. When I returned, Connie was telling a story about her latest trip to London where she met with a Prince at the palace. Some connection her mother had through a second cousin or something. About fifteen minutes later, Ben stood up and announced we were making our first surprise stop. This stop was inspired by Sabrina's guilty pleasure of a movie, *Sweet Home Alabama*. There was a collected groan from the crowd as he said this causing Sabrina to playfully bat him in the arm

"I saw that one," Austin piped up next to me, elbowing me in the ribs.

"Yes I know, I was there," I whispered back.

"I wonder what part," he started to say but didn't have to speak further. We found ourselves in front of Tiffany's. The bus stopped and a doorman held open the front door to the store for us and welcomed us inside.

"No way," Caroline gaped next to me.

"Welcome Mr. Kennedy," a man in a very tailored suit said stepping onto the bus.

"Of those Kennedy's?" Caroline asked Mac and he nodded his head.

"Second or third cousin," he whispered back and Caroline was clearly impressed. Sabrina let out a squeal and they exited the bus first. We were all encouraged to follow. As we entered, there were a couple waiters walking around the floor with trays of hors d'oeuvres. Austin was suddenly very quiet but kept close to my side. We walked together looking at the fancy jewelry in the cases. There were several sales associates on the floor ready to show us anything we desired. Sabrina was looking at a large pair of diamond earrings when suddenly Benedict Kennedy got down on one knee and proposed. I didn't hear what he said but it was as if the whole room had the air sucked out of it as we all stood by watching and waiting for her reaction. Sabrina's top lip quivered ever so slightly and a tear slid down her cheek breaking her normally polished facade. She nodded in agreement and crumpled into his waiting arms. The room erupted in cheers and laughter; suddenly champagne appeared on numerous trays as everyone celebrated.

"I realize I never really gave you a proper proposal," Austin quietly said as he stood next to me. I wanted to chuckle at his statement, but I didn't want to pick a fight with him in that moment either; he was right that he never gave me a proper proposal. I would caution even using the word proposal. It was the night after a friend of ours had gotten engaged to this woman he met while traveling to Colorado for vacation with his family. They had been dating six months and mostly long distance as she was from Nebraska but our friend just knew she was the one. I now internally blame him for everything that has happened. Austin found the whole thing to be 'unnatural' and he kept saying how they 'barely knew each other' and 'where are they going to live,' and 'you think you know a guy.' I had honestly started to drown him out when he was talking about it because it had been non-stop. So we were sitting on the sofa in his mama's den and a movie was playing on TV that I was trying to catch the end of and I missed the first part of the conversation he was having with me but I heard the second part, "…and I just think that you and I have the perfect situation. We have grown up together, we know what we both want and there are no surprises with that. I think it's a good idea that we go ahead and get married. It makes a lot of sense, with me working on your papa's ranch and you working the horses; we can help him run it until he's ready to retire and then you and I will have the ranch and we can raise our children the way we were raised. I didn't ask your papa yet but I will in the morning, I don't think he will have any objections. I didn't have time to get a fancy ring or anything. I know you probably wouldn't wear it but it's the proper thing to do. Until then you already have my senior class ring from high school which most people consider to be our engagement ring anyway, so what do you think Logan?" When he finished, he just looked at me with this endearing look and all I did was nod. After that his mama came back into the den and we watched the end of the movie; no one said another thing about us being engaged. I probably looked calm, but I had no words to describe just how scared I was in that moment. I felt as if my freedom had been taken away and I was going to suddenly be imprisoned in a life I didn't want. It wasn't completely Austin's fault. I had talked about traveling or leaving the ranch and in my head I had this whole plan but Austin didn't really know anything about it. I thought I had another year or so before he was going to even think about marriage and by then I would have laid out my whole plan to him. I guess neither of our plans went as we would have hoped. I suddenly realized that Austin was waiting for a reply to the statement he made.

"What's proper for them isn't what is proper for everyone else. But look at that passion, the emotion," I said as Sabrina tried to collect herself, but tears continued to streak down her cheeks but a smile as wide as the Hudson spread on her face and if I had to bet it wasn't going anywhere anytime soon. Benedict shared in her emotion as he wiped a tear from the corner of his eye but held onto Sabrina's hand as they were whisked away to select the perfect ring.

"Logan, I meant it when I asked you to marry me. I will ask you again if that is what you need," he said again quietly.

"Don't you dare get down on one knee," I hissed.

"I didn't mean here," he shot back.

"Everything okay over here?" Caroline said wandering over.

"Yes, why?"

"Just looks a little tense but that seems to be your normal," she said sipping from her glass.

"Caroline," Mac sang her name.

"Yes?"

"I know May has a line of credit here, what do you say we take it for a spin?"

"I don't know...maybe..."

"A nice break up present to help her mend her broken heart?" Caroline nodded in delight and the two of them practically scampered off to one of the showcases where an all too eager salesman was waiting for them.

"Logan, are you ever going to want to marry me?" Austin asked after they left.

"I don't think so," I said quietly looking him straight in the eyes as not to send any mixed messages. He hung his head slightly and I put my hand on his arm and guided him out of the store and back onto the now empty tour bus. We were silent for a couple minutes before I spoke again.

"Austin, you're my best friend. You have been since forever but what I feel for you is protective and fierce friendship," I said suddenly putting a name to the feeling swirling in my gut earlier. "I think if you're honest with yourself, you don't love me like that either. We don't have that passion..."

"It's not just about passion."

"No, it's not but what we have is safe and there is more to love than being safe. Sometimes it's passionate, it's messy, it's emotional, and sometimes it's a fairytale. It's more dimensional than what we have." His head was bowed, and he nodded.

"I know in my heart I love you Logan Hunter but you're right. We are safe and have been together forever. When I asked you to marry me it was what I thought was the next step. I could see us being just fine together if you said yes and moved back to Texas but I also know in my heart we both deserve more than fine." I nodded as tears erupted from the corners of my eyes.

"I still want that ranch Logan Hunter," he said reaching over and wiping the tears away from my cheek.

"It's all yours," I said with a laugh and leaned my head on his shoulder as he put his arm around me in an embrace.

CHAPTER 18

As we waited for the group to come back to the bus, I flagged down a hot dog vendor that was passing by and Austin and I dined on hot dogs and rum and cokes sitting on the top row of the bus looking out on Fifth Avenue. Austin talked about his plans to expand the ranch and grow Papa's business which surprised me. I had heard him talking about stuff here and there, but I never once stopped to listen, really listen to his plans or his future dreams. I had always been so focused on myself and my big adventure; it never occurred to me that Austin might have plans for his own adventure.

"I'm sorry it took so long but here's to our futures," I said lifting my glass to clink his.

"This city isn't that bad...looks like it agrees with you Logan...if you like this sort of thing," he commented back with a boyish grin. The heaviness of the earlier conversation had lifted and things between Austin and me felt familiar.

"Thank you."

"Am I interrupting?" Mac said popping his head up from the stairs of the bus.

"Mac! Join us?" I said with a cheer. Austin even got up and shifted making room for Mac.

"I don't want to intrude on the 'don't mess with Texas' lovebirds," he said sauntering over. He wrinkled his nose over the sight of the hot dogs but kept any comments to himself.

"No love birds. Tex and I have decided it would be best if we were just friends," Austin (always honest to a fault) commented but with a with a cheesy grin, proud that he snuck my nickname into casual conversation.

"Whoa, that's heavy stuff for a party bus."

"Oh, we are ready to party on the party bus," I assured Mac holding up my drink.

"Good to hear as the newly engaged couple are about ready to continue this adventure."

"There's more?" Austin asked surprised.

"With this group there is always more," I commented, and Mac nodded in admiration.

"Where is Caroline?" Austin asked peering around Mac and down to the street level.

"Why do tell Austin, are you sweet on Caroline?"

"What? No! I mean she's nice...oh hell...I dunno," he finally said dropping his suddenly red face into his hands and shaking his head as I howled with laughter and Mac chuckled.

"Caroline is fine, she is just finishing up a couple of purchases. There is a specific pair of pear-shaped sapphire drop earrings that are just to die for, couldn't be left in the case without an owner any longer." Moments later Caroline emerged onto the second level of the bus.

"Why the long face?" I asked moving over to one side and Mac quickly slid over next to me leaving a convenient open spot next to Austin.

"I've spent May's money before and much more than I just spent but sometimes I just wish I could keep something for myself. Those earrings, are going to haunt my daydreams," she said making the saddest face and without thinking leaned over and rested her head on Austin's shoulder. I could see him stiffen quickly as I raised one eyebrow at him and he gave me the most innocent look back, causing me to chuckle.

"Caroline it sounds like you need a drink."

"Yes please," she whined. I hopped up and got her a drink. Luckily the bartender remembered what she was drinking and was able to whip it up quickly for me. She perked right up like a dandelion when I handed her the pink beverage.

"What did I miss here?"

"Tex 1 and Tex 2 decided to just be friends. Discuss," Mac said with a mischievous grin.

"Oh really?" she said closely eyeing Austin and me.

"We are fine," I said and he just shrugged his shoulders. Caroline pressed for more details as loud laughter and cheers could be heard from the street.

"I think our group is finally ready to continue," Mac said disappearing to the lower deck.

"Did you see her ring?" Caroline asked after a lull. We both shook our heads and Caroline let out a low whistle, "let's just say some small countries couldn't afford to buy the massive ring she is now sporting."

****

Without knowing where exactly the bus driver was taking us, it seemed as he was going out of his way to delay our trip. Instead of continuing down 5th Avenue he twisted and turned around each city block until we ended up in the Times Square area.

"See Austin, you do get to see the sights after all," I commented as we sat in the seats with the warm evening air hitting our faces.

"It's a nice city but I miss the ranch," he commented and with that I knew Austin's time in the city was drawing to a close. It made me sad, but I knew this is what was going to be best for us.

"I feel like we are taking the most ridiculous route around the city," Caroline commented slightly slurring her words from the seat next me.

"Patience sweet Caroline. There is always a bigger picture at play with this crew," I commented as we drove through Times Square and continued down Broadway. As I looked around, the streets and landmarks were growing familiar and I recognized it as one of the routes I walk Princess on.

"What are we doing over here?" I wondered out loud and Mac winked in my direction.

"Just wait for it," he whispered. The bus came to a stop in front of a large marquee that read '*Franklin*' causing my heart to skip two beats.

"No."

"Oh yes," Mac said as his eyes had a devilish twinkle in them. There were some squeals and shouts from the group below that matched commotion going on, on the street in front of the theater.

"What in the world?" Austin questioned being the first to lean over the ledge to look.

"It can't be," Caroline said joining him as they now gawked over the edge of the bus.

"Tex, wanna take a look?" Mac said elbowing me in my ribs.

"Your taking too much pleasure in this," I commented finally standing up to look. I would not let the sudden hot sensation I had in my gut make me out to be scared or embarrassed compounded by the fact I was just too stubborn for that. Yet I couldn't force myself to open my eyes to see what I already knew was true below. The sudden harmony of song drifted up from the street level, one voice catching my attention. Finally, I opened my eyes and I scanned the group of singers until I recognized the familiar features of his face. As I watched him with an almost curious detachment, I had never seen him perform before and he carried himself differently now as he sang. He seemed to stand up taller, shoulders back with an almost aristocratic confidence I had not seen before. I swear his eyes almost sparkled with passion he had for what he was doing. The song suddenly changed melodies and the other actors shifted slightly in perfect unison to the right making room for Luca to step front and center and perform what was to be a grand solo. His voice was melodic and almost mesmerizing as he now took center stage of this entire odd scenario that was playing out. I couldn't move even if I wanted to. I was trapped in this magical spell he was weaving. In a matter of minutes his voice softened and the group came back together to finish the song. When they were done, the entire party bus and what seemed to be a city block applauded. I watched him watching us, scanning the street crowd and party bus. The warm sensation in my gut did somersaults when his eyes connected with mine causing me to break out in a smile while clear surprise registered on his face and he soon returned my cheesy grin with one of his own.

"Tiffany's and Luca Gaines? I don't know your friends, Mac, but they certainly know how to throw a party," Caroline finally said in complete approval breaking the spell Luca had cast. The actors now shifted down below, started a new song that seemed more up tempo, causing the crowd to erupt in approval. The small group of actors made their way through the crowd that had gathered and onto our party bus. The words to the song were now muffled as they boarded the bus but the sound grew louder. Mac, not wanting to miss out on the action, quickly descended the stairs while singing along. Caroling blinked for a couple seconds before she snapped out of some daze she was in.

"Come on, Austin," she said grabbing his hand and pulling him toward the stairs.

"Logan, are you coming?" he called over his shoulder as Caroline disappeared below.

"Sure," I said my legs shaky as I followed. When I finally descended to the first floor of the bus it was now crowded. Unable to find a spot, I sat on the stairs of the bus and watched. Everyone on the bus knew the song well as a large sing-along had developed and it was hard to tell who the actors and audience were. As the song ended everyone held the last note for what seemed like forever before the group erupted into thunderous applause.

"Where are Ben and Sabrina?" I heard the voice of a women I didn't recognize ask when a quiet moment presented itself.

"Here, here," Ben said standing up holding Sabrina's hand.

"We heard you were fans of the show and were celebrating some big news — so we thought we could help with that," the women said as the group launched into another song. The actors were now more spread out and the sound bounced off the close walls of the bus as if surround sound had been plugged in.

"I bet Ben paid a pretty penny to get the cast of *Franklin* to sing and tour with us," Marianna, who was standing in front of me, said to Cybil who just raised her eyebrows and pursed her lips but nodded in agreement. As the song progressed, I tried to snake my way to the bar trying to avoid all the extra bodies that were now on board. As the song ended, another round of applause erupted. The strong hum of conversation soon engulfed the bus.

"I need something stronger than before," I told the bartender.

"We need to stop meeting like this," the unmistakable voice of Luca Gaines said next to me. Without giving me a chance to respond he leaned in close and kissed my cheek. "When they told me we had to do an encore performance for some rich benefactors of the theater, I was dreading this evening. Then to my surprise I see you in a sea of strangers and, instantly, I couldn't get on this bus fast enough." His entire attention was now solely focused on me.

"Luca, I...." never at a loss for words, I suddenly found myself without explanation. What I saw in Luca's eyes was excitement and adventure; what I felt in my stomach now was drama and chaos. The bartender set a drink down by my hand causing me to turn away from him for a moment.

"Luca, how are you?" I heard Mac say as he approached us.

"Mac, is it?" Luca said turning to shake Mac's outstretched hand.

"You remembered," Mac said clearly charmed.

"Mac will you introduce me to your friend?" Marianna suddenly appeared at his side. Her eyes were as big as saucers as she took in Luca's appearance.

"He's more Tex's friend than mine," Mac said, turning to look at me with a wink. My eyes got big and my jaw dropped a little as a string of things you don't say around your mama rang in my head.

"Hi, I'm Luca," Luca said saving me from the awkward conversation as he extended his hand to Marianna.

"Could I get a picture?" she asked her voice shaking slightly.

"Not a problem," he said flashing a grin. I was pushed to the side and as I watched, I felt a slight understanding about Luca's previous statement about personal and professional sides of Luca Gaines. I saw him smile but it was fake, it never reached the corners of eyes like it had in the park; his eyes didn't light up as he made polite conversation. He looked like Luca Gaines but he seemed more of a shell of himself. As Marianna walked away, Caroline approached and I expected much of the same reaction from her.

"Luca?" He took a moment to survey her and his eyes widened a little.

"Caroline? Is May here too?" he suddenly looked around in almost horror.

"No she's on location...abroad," she added for extra measure as he physically relaxed by her statement.

"What are you doing here?" he asked.

"Are you talking to me or her?" I asked suddenly confused.

"What an eclectic group of people, how did you all end up here," he finally said surveying the crowd for the first time.

"I'm here because of Logan," Caroline replied.

"I'm here because of Mac," I said pointing to my right.

"I'm here because of the drama," Mac smarted.

"Well that clears that up," Luca commented.

"Tex would say clear as mud...or something like that...but the newly engaged couple is approaching and are eagerly waiting to monopolize your time." Mac whispered the last part as Ben and Sabrina approached.

"I heard congratulations are in order," Luca said without missing a beat as they got closer. It amazed me at his ability to just slip in and out of this character he played. It made me question every interaction we had and which of the two Luca Gaines I had been with. Ben and Sabrina pulled him away to another crowd at the center of the bus. I heard the words 'encore' and 'Sabrina's favorite is' and 'we loved you in.' As I made my way back up to the second floor of the bus I heard him break into song. I felt conflicted, I finally felt that my chapter with Austin had a beginning, middle and was coming to an end. It made me sad, but I felt as if a weight had been lifted at the same time. Seeing Luca on the bus had caught me off guard and made me feel unbalanced for some reason.

Caroline approached me first. I had been sitting on the top deck in the back watching the city as the driver seemed to drive around with no rhyme or reason. The entire crowd on the lower deck was singing in song once again. I had some random thoughts run through my mind but for the most part I was just numbly starring at the sky.

"Logan are you okay?" she said slightly slurring her words.

"Hi Caroline, yes I'm fine," I commented as she tripped and fell into the seat next to me.

"You aren't a big Luca Gaines fan?" she questioned. If only she knew it was quite the opposite actually.

"How do you know him?" I asked instead of answering her.

"He and May dated a while back. He always seemed so normal. I never knew what he saw in her and it ended badly. Plus, Vivian Banks, you remember May's Godmother? She has always been sweet on him and tries to reconcile them. Calls them the next 'modern Hollywood couple'."

"How badly did it end?"

"Oh, you know — May cheated on him with the lead actor in her current project and tabloids got hold of it. Plastered it all over the papers. They tried to make it work but you could tell Luca wasn't into it at that point. They had this huge fight at a restaurant and May stormed out and then burned any and all things related to Luca later that day. May paid someone to take pictures and a video and then leaked it to the press. It was epic. To this day — May will not tolerate anything that has to do with Luca, the mere mention of his name or association with him will send her into a blind rage. The ONLY person that can get away with talking about Luca to her is Vivian."

"Caroline, I think I got my ox in a ditch," I said with a sigh as Austin stumbled over to us.

"There two you are," he mixed his words as he sat down next to Caroline, swinging his arm behind her on the chair. It bothered me that I noticed and that she didn't seem to mind.

"Austin have you had one too many drinks?" I questioned looking closely as his glazed eyes.

"This city is just too rich for my blood...these two people downstairs were talking about eating caviar," except his pronunciation was more like 'cave-rrr.' "Do you know what that is? I didn't know and when I asked they told me it was fish eggs."

"No, really..." Caroline started but Austin continued as if she hadn't spoken.

"Do you know it costs like $500 for this much," he said holding his middle finger to his thumb creating a small circle.

"Yeah, May makes me order that stuff when she's trying to impress guests...fun fact she doesn't actually eat it."

"I just cannot related to this city, the people have more than they can say grace over...you know what I mean," he said looking at me with a frown.

"Yeah, Austin, I know."

"But not me? Right Austin," Caroline said leaning into his shoulder and fixing her large brown eyes on him.

"Nahhh, y'all are good," he said waving his free hand in the air. I blew out a puff of air forcefully causing the hair that had fallen down in my face to move to the side trying to curb my frustration. It could have been seconds later or minutes later when I heard my name and all three of us turned to look at Luca and Mac approaching us on the upper deck.

"I was wondering where you disappeared too," Luca said with a sweet smile.

"Tex, this man sings like a dream. You two should always talk in song as far as I'm concerned," Mac uncharacteristically gushed as Luca sat down and put his arm around me. Almost instantly, Caroline's eyes got big as she eyed the obvious connection between us. Austin sat straight up, abruptly pulling his arm out from under Caroline causing her to fall back.

"Logan, who is this guy?" Austin barked at me.

"Hey! Watch it!" Caroline fussed at Austin trying to sit up.

"Hi, I'm Luca. I don't think we have met yet. I'm Logan's...friend...boyfriend," Luca said extending his hand to Austin. Austin's face grew red and he didn't hesitate to meet Luca's open hand with a closed fist to his left cheek. The impact caused Luca to stumble back into Mac, who easily caught him and set him upright. Once his got his balance, Luca didn't hesitate and lunged at Austin. The two fell onto the center isle of the bus while I tried to pull Austin, who was currently on top, off of Luca. Caroline just sat in her spot and was doing a mixture of yelling and crying in their general direction.

"What idiots," Mac said stepping in and easily lifting Austin off of Luca and setting him down in a seat several rows away from where we were. I was able to help Luca up and set him into a chair.

"Logan, who the hell was that?" he said holding his hand to his cheek. I could already see an angry red mark forming on his perfect face.

"Austin is my ex-fiancé," I said through gritted teeth as I stared down Austin who was glaring right back at me from where Mac was holding him.

"May isn't going to like this," Caroline muttered from her spot, still not moving.

'No, I don't guess she is,' I thought to myself.

CHAPTER 19

The night went from long to longer. Amazingly no one else on the bus heard or saw the brawl between Austin and Luca nor did they hear my long string of cuss words directed at Austin, Caroline's crying pleas, and Mac's deep laugh. After checking on Luca one last time, I climbed over the seats towards Austin.

"What the hell is wrong with you?" I asked standing over him with my hands on my hips.

"Me? You talk about breaking up and us outgrowing each other but you failed to mention that you were already shacking up with some richie rich kid in skinny jeans," Austin slurred raising his pointer finger at me.

"Austin put that finger down before I do it for you," I said taking a step toward him causing him to lower his hand.

"Should we do something," Caroline said somewhere behind me.

"Nah, Tex can hold her own," Mac commented.

"I was more worried about Austin," she huffed back.

"Nothing I said to you was a lie, it was the reason I left Texas in the first place," I said trying to stay calm, but my blood raged with anger over the situation. I wasn't just mad at Austin, I was mad at Luca, Caroline, Mac, and myself. There wasn't a soul in the immediate circle that I felt had any grace in the current situation.

"Logan, that guy called himself your boyfriend. He put his arm around you," Austin said with a hiccup.

"You put your arm around Caroline," for the first time in the conversation he adverted his eyes from mine. Hearing someone talk behind me, I spun around now pointing my own finger.

"You have done nothing but antagonize me all evening. I thought we were friends but now I feel like a puppet in your big game," I said to Mac who instantly stopped smiling. "You knew Austin was in town and you knew that Luca was going to be here, and you invited us on this adventure anyway. It was downright mean what you did tonight." He started to protest.

"Don't," I said shaking my finger in his direction instantly causing him to quiet down. I moved to my next target.

"Caroline, you clearly like Austin, don't be mean with his heart; he's loyal and kind but stubborn — a bit hot headed. I just don't want to see it." She looked at me with big eyes causing tears to spring from the corners of my eyes. My tone softened a bit when I turned to Luca.

"Luca Gaines, what did you think you were doing tonight? You must be crazy as a bullbat thinking that a couple interactions win you an automatic spot in my heart and calling yourself my boyfriend?" I just shook my head, "You didn't deserve to walk into this mess tonight and for that I am sorry." He just blinked at me a couple times and I didn't give him a chance to reply.

"It seems as we were each pawns in each other's dealings tonight," it was something my mama would say when one of us was particularly mean or petty growing up. I turned and headed down to the lower deck. I was about to ask the driver to stop when he came to a stop on his own.

"Finally, I need to pee so badly," someone said quickly moving past me. It seemed as if it was a general concern as people got up and were stepping off the bus. I just let myself be taken off the bus with the crowd. I didn't know where we were, but I needed to get away from that bus and the people on it as soon as possible.

"The Core Club would have been better," William mumbled.

"You know Benedict always prefers the Yale Club," Samuel mumbled back as they quickly rushed past me.

"Are you coming?" Marianna stopped and waved at me as the group entered a single door with a blue awning of the Greyish stone building.

"Y'all go ahead," I said with a wave. I crossed the street and chuckled when I realized I was at Grand Central Station. I could just as easily get on the train and go somewhere else, anywhere else; running away from another mess that I had gotten myself into. But tonight, on this night, I just kept walking. The phone in my pocket buzzed, binged and vibrated several times until I finally just turned it off. As I wandered, I realized that I knew my surroundings better than I anticipated and soon I stood in front of a big sign that said Big Easy Diner. I sighed and pushed the doors of the diner open, the fresh aroma of bacon and eggs greeted me causing my stomach to rumble.

"Sit where you like," the women behind the counter called to me. I waved and eased myself onto a stool near her at the counter.

"What will it be?" she asked after a couple of minutes.

"Coffee and whatever you suggest," I said never opening the laminated menu she had slid down to me.

"Darrell, black with the works," she called over her shoulder.

"Yup, Yup," a voice from the kitchen responded.

"You didn't ask my opinion, but you look the worse for wear," the women said carrying a mug over to me.

"Thanks, I've had better," I mumbled adding sugar and cream.

"Wanna talk about it?" she offered. I glanced around the diner; there were two police officers in a far booth and a couple of women in scrubs that looked like they were ending a long shift as they quietly chatted to each other.

"Slow night?"

"Night? This is our morning shift, Dearie. It's nearly five in the morning." I was only slightly surprised by this information. I had to get home soon to walk and feed Princess ... if I had a job or a place to live anymore. For all I knew, Caroline had already told May my connection with Luca and my stuff was sitting on the curb. I let out a loud sigh and just shook my head. I wasn't ready to talk, I didn't know where to start and who to start with. The lady left me alone only bothering me once more when she delivered a large plate of eggs, bacon, toast, and hash browns.

****

It was about an hour later when I got back to the apartment. I didn't see any of my things on the curb, so I took that as a good sign as I waved to the doorman and rode the elevator up. The apartment was dark and quiet as I entered. Cutting through the kitchen only to trip on what I assumed were shoes, causing a curse to escape my lips as I bent over and felt around until I located the objects. I could tell from the weight and size they were Austin's boots. It seemed like another lifetime that Caroline and I were picking out his outfit, yet we had only returned from the evening. As I approached his room, I could hear soft snores fill the air through the cracked door. Entering his room completely uninvited, I froze in place seeing Austin lying on his back still in his clothes, mouth open, as occasional snores escaped his vibrating lips with Caroline curled up next to him asleep in the crook of his arm. My stomach suddenly protested all the food I had eaten. I couldn't hate them for that moment, but I wasn't enjoying it either. Carefully, I put the boots down and went out to the living room and got a blanket. Returning to the room, I draped the blanket over Austin and Caroline. Caroline stretched and opened an eye, watching me as I moved about the room.

"Sorry Logan...glad you're okay," she mumbled before closing her eyes and rolling over. Was I okay? I backed out of the room and headed upstairs. Princess sat eagerly in her crate, greeting me with half barks and her tail wagging.

"I hope your night was less eventful," I cooed at her opening the latch of the crate allowing her to bound out. She followed me down to the kitchen and sat by her water bowl as I prepared her breakfast. On the menu this morning was scrambled eggs, spinach, and salmon in extra virgin olive oil. Tonight's dinner was a version of beef stew that Gladys was going to make during the day. Shaking my head by the fact that Princess often ate better than I did, I leaned down setting her food down. Knowing that I wasn't going to last much longer without sleep, I deviated from her schedule and we set out on a walk as soon as she was done eating.

My phone binged after the first block. Looking at the message, it was from Luca.

We need to talk. The message read.

Sure do.

Now?

I'm walking Princess.

I'll meet you. With that I send him directions to where Princess and I were walking. It didn't take long for him to find us. I saw him as he approached us coming from the opposite direction.

"Hey," he said pausing to stand by me.

"Hey," I said looking up at him. Princess noticing he had stopped to talk started growling.

"Keep walking," I directed toward Princess but Luca thinking I was speaking to him fell in line next to me.

"How is your cheek?" I asked after several moments. Glancing over I could see the spot on his cheek was a blackish purple already and swollen compared to the other side of his face.

"Hurts like a bitch. My director is not going to be happy."

"Sorry." We stopped walking, lingering and looking at each other uneasily and then continuing down the sidewalk.

"When we first met you asked me a question. I can now officially say I have in fact been in a fight."

"Over-hyped, isn't it?"

"The subject was worthy in this case." His response surprised me causing me to stop walking and look at him.

"Luca..."

"Logan, it's been a long night. Some parts were better than others. I just really needed to clear things up with you. I don't like unfinished business." I nodded and we restarted our walk.

"I'm embarrassed by the drama, I don't like drama," I commented mostly to myself.

"Drama is my life," he said winking and then immediately flinching.

"Luca, I'm truly sorry about Austin's behavior. It was out of line."

"You don't need to apologize for him. I know we have only known each other for a short time but you are worth the fight. I can't fault him for that. But you were right as well."

"I was?"

"I was cavalier and careless, just introducing myself as your boyfriend. I forgot myself and my place tonight."

"Meaning?"

"If I'm being honest, most people would have let me act like I was simply because I am who I am."

"So what you're saying is that most people would have jumped at the chance to have Luca Gaines introduce himself as their boyfriend?"

"Something like that."

"I'm not most people."

"I am keenly aware of that."

"What happens next?"

"I don't know. I have several shows, press, and other obligations as my run draws to a close. I don't want to stop seeing you, that is if you still want to see me?"

"I don't want to stop seeing you either but I have a house guest I need to ship back to Texas."

"Are you and Mr. Left Hook officially over?"

"We have been over for a while but, yes, we are officially over."

"Tonight, certainly complicates things."

"Sure does." We were silent as we walked another block.

"I'm a couple blocks in that direction," I pointed my hand to the left.

"I should go. I need to nap before tonight's performance. I'll call you in a couple days." I nodded and he paused for a moment before leaning down and kissing me on the forehead.

"Bye, Logan."

"Bye, Luca." Princess and I watched him go. It was just a simple good-bye with even a promise of more to come but in that moment, it felt like a permanent good-bye. Perhaps it was the alcohol or lack of sleep or even the stress of everything but whatever it was, tears streamed down my face as I walked the final blocks home. Princess, keenly aware I was upset, twisted herself around my legs, whining and pawing at my legs until I picked her up. Once I did, she licked my face and my tears causing me to cry even harder. The last part of the way home was a complete blur.

Upon returning to the apartment I kicked off my shoes and threw my jeans to the floor; unhooking my bra and dropping it to the floor in one quick movement, I picked up a shirt from the floor and it smelled clean enough as I pulled it on and slid under the covers. In a rare move, I lifted the covers and Princess, who had been following me around, jumped up onto the bed and curled with me as if she had done it a thousand times. Stretching my limbs trying to ease the aches and tension from my muscles, I turned to my left side, drifting off into a dreamless sleep.

******

"Logan?" I heard my name called but it sounded like it was far off in the distance, like an annoying insect that keeps buzzing by your ear.

"Logan." The voice said more sternly this time. The small lump of fur next to me started growling as she wiggled her way out from under the covers.

"Where did she come from?" a female voice chimed in causing Princess to bark several times before huffing and curling up next to my arm on top of the covers.

"LOGAN," I heard again finally causing me to open my eyes slightly. The room was filled with bright light and I could see two figures standing in the doorway.

"Whatdoyouwant?" I mumbled trying to push myself up only to find that I had no strength to lift myself.

"I think we need to talk," Austin's voice was now audible for me to discern.

"Whydoyouwanttotalkabout...sleeping..." I mumbled rolling over on my side and away from the talking heads.

"This isn't working," the woman commented.

"She's just stubborn as a mule...but I ain't ever seen her like this. I have an idea," he said retreating from the room.

It seemed like moments later a sugary sweet aroma wafted into my room. The scent reminded me of mama's honey buns. She would always make them special for one of our birthdays or Christmas morning. She worked so hard on those buns — making the dough from scratch and when they were just the right shade of golden brown, she would drizzle honey and roasted pecans all over the tops of them. They were so gooey and sticky you had to eat them with a tall glass of milk; otherwise, they stuck to the roof of your mouth. I couldn't decide if it was the smell or the memory of mama and the honey buns that finally caused me to stretch and open my eyes. Princess was still at my side curled in a small ball. I stared at the ceiling trying not to clutter my thoughts of the past 24 hours. Willing myself to move, I finally sat up and swung my legs over the edge of the bed. Grabbing worn out sweatpants that displayed my high school's mascot on the leg and pulling my hair into a messy knot I shuffled my way towards the smell. When I neared the kitchen, I could hear multiple voices talking in hushed conversation.

"There she is," Austin said looking up from the conversation as I walked in. I grunted in response, waving my hand and grabbing the fridge door.

"Milk's already on the counter," Austin added. Pausing for a moment to allow his comment to sink in, I again grunted in response, closing the fridge and shuffling further to the counter. The honey buns looked exactly as I remember them. Suddenly ravenous, I dug my fingers into the bun closest to where I stood and shoveled it into my mouth. To my surprise, it tasted exactly like mama's honey buns and tears formed in the corner of my eyes.

"Good Lord, I have never seen anyone cry over a pastry," a voice said causing me to glance up, only to realize Gladys was standing in the kitchen with her apron on.

"This tastes just like my mama's...how in the world?" I finally commented once I was able to form fully comprehensible adult words.

"It was Austin — he called your mother for the recipe and then supervised Gladys the entire time," Caroline chimed in.

"In an annoying 'get the heck out of my way,' kinda way," Gladys said with a short smile, clearly not amused.

"I know how much your mama's cooking means to you," he said with a shrug. He looked so vulnerable for a moment and my heart skipped a beat. I looked at him for a long moment before Princess who had finally joined us in the kitchen interrupted with her barking.

CHAPTER 20

The three of them watched me eat in silence. I wasn't really looking at them, but I could feel their eyes on me as I crammed another honey bun in my mouth. Princess was sitting next to my feet occasionally pawing at my leg. The clock said it was almost four in the afternoon, so she probably needed to go out, and soon.

"Logan, I think..." Austin started.

"Don't," I shot back, lifting my eyes to meet his for the first time. It wasn't that we didn't need to talk because we did and I wanted to talk but not to him, or Caroline, or Gladys, at this very moment.

"Aren't you being..." Caroline started.

"Don't you either," I said holding up my index finger. Caroline huffed at me and crossed her arms in front of her chest.

"I need some time," I slowly followed up only mildly appeasing everyone in the room. "I have to walk Princess and I need to shower and make a phone call..."

"You're calling him?" Austin said with clear disgust on his face.

"Who I call is none of your gosh-darn business," I spat back in his direction.

"Children, settle down," Gladys interrupted. "You go walk the dog, that's what you're hired to do. I'm going to cook everyone dinner because that is what I'm hired to do. Caroline, isn't there something you're hired to do?" Caroline blushed and meekly nodded at Gladys. "And you, I know there is something you could be doing."

"No, ma'am, I got nothing to do," Austin said with confusion.

"You do now, grab me a cutting board from that cabinet over there," she instructed, throwing Austin an apron. I snickered and Gladys gave me a look that rendered me quiet.

"Well, go," she said after a moment clapping her hands sending us going in all different directions.

******

I now sat cross legged on the floor in my room looking out of the floor-to-ceiling windows over the vast city. Princess was curled on my lap sleeping. It seemed like hundreds of people milled around the streets below, each one in a hurry to get to their next destination. In that sudden moment, I felt more homesick than I had ever been, which included the time at sleep-away camp where I cried for two hours after Betsy Anne stole my stuffed horse, named Ed, and threw it in the lake. It took staff over an hour to fish it out and figure out how to dry him off. Idly, twirling my hair with my right hand, I held my cell phone in my left hand as I waited for someone to pick up the phone. I felt a nervous energy wash through me when a male voice answered the phone.

"Hello?"

"Papa?"

"Logan?"

"I'm...so...sorry," I blubbered through tears that I suddenly couldn't control.

"Logan...there is no need for tears. Everything is mended bridges," which was his way of saying things were fine.

"But Austin is here and..."

"Is that boy causing trouble? I told him not to go up there, that boy doesn't have the sense God gave a goose."

"It's just that I had this plan and when he showed up..." hiccups interrupted my words.

"Logan, honey, why don't you talk to your mother. She always has a way with words that I don't. Just know I love you and you come back home when you're ready, you are always welcome...we all miss you," he paused and I could hear some muffled voices before mama got on the phone. When I heard her sweet voice the flood gates opened again, and I babbled my way through what was going on from the moment Austin showed up to this morning with the honey buns. She interrupted me only to clarify a couple points, but she let me get it all out until I felt empty of emotions and tears.

"Logan it looks like you got some figuring out on what to do. Sounds like you are finally confronting some of those ghosts you ran away from."

"I don't know what to do," I whined.

"Yes, you do. You have always known what you wanted and how to get it from the day you were born. Your papa and I named you after your great-grandpa Logan. It caused quit a ruckus, us naming you after him and not one of the boys. But we just knew after meeting you that you had that same toughness and quite strength that he had, and you have not proved us wrong. Big decisions in life usually scare normal people but they have never scared you. You have always embraced a challenge. Logan, do you know why I wasn't worried about your going off to New York City all by yourself?"

"No," but it came out as a hiccup instead.

"Because of all my children, you could handle it. I didn't have to worry about your trusting the wrong people, squandering your savings, going all wild, and compromising your values. I knew you would have the adventure you were meant to have in only the way you were meant to have it. I only hope that the people you meet can keep up with your stubborn, brave, and expressive self."

"Mama, maybe you're wrong, maybe I'm meant to come home."

"Logan, I'm sorry but I've already given your bed away. You're going to have to stay in New York a little bit longer," she said with a sigh.

"You're just saying that mama."

"No really, after you left, I let Becky move into your room."

"You what?! Are you plumb crazy?"

"Logan Hunter you watch your words with me," she said in a stern voice. I could see her eyes narrowing even through the phone.

"Sorry ma'am."

"Logan, you weren't using the room and Emily and Becky had shared a room for too long, it was time they split up."

"Yes, ma'am."

"We have to go, we are late for Mrs. Martin's birthday."

"Love you, mama."

"Stay strong Logan...and Logan..."

"Yes?"

"You can come home whenever you need too...but just not yet."

"Clear as mud, mama."

"I know," she said with a smile in her voice and we disconnected. I ran my fingers through my hair, pulling at the knots and straightening my damp hair as I thought about what my mama said to me.

"Logan?" I heard my name as Austin gently knocked on the bedroom door.

"Come in," I said turning to look at the door and leaned back against the large glass window.

"You could fall," Austin commented his eyes widening.

"Austin, the windows don't open. I'm not going to fall out of them. I know you're scared of heights ... would it make you happier if I moved?" He nodded in the affirmative and I moved Princess from my lap and laid out on my stomach looking at him. He paused a moment before sitting down on the floor leaning against the door frame. Neither of us spoke for several long minutes.

"I really messed up," Austin finally commented looking down at his hands.

"You weren't dancing alone," I said back rolling onto my side so I could see him clearer.

"What happened to us?"

"In general, or within the last day?"

"You know what I mean. We had these big dreams, fell in love young, we both loved the ranch. We had this perfect little bubble that was just us."

"It wasn't meant to last, we can't just stay the same … never changing, never growing. There are so many good memories, but I wasn't lying last night when I said it didn't feel the same to me anymore."

"Aww...I know Logan...but things went all cattywampus so quickly. Caroline was being sweet on me and then that guy..."

"Luca?"

"Yeah, he shows up and I just never felt so part of your past as I did in that moment."

"I didn't mean for that to happen, Austin."

"I know," Austin said as we both took a long pause.

"Austin, I never told you, but I appreciate the effort you made by coming to New York."

"Didn't do me any good."

"You let us write our own crazy ending instead of always wondering."

"I'm leaving to go home."

"I know."

"You do?"

"Wait, what do you mean?"

"I'm leaving now to go home."

"So soon?"

"Can't be soon enough," he said with a chuckle and I laughed after a moment.

"Can I help?"

"No, if it wouldn't trouble you, I was hoping that Ms. Caroline would drop me off at the airport."

"Oh, no, that's fine. Whatever you want," I felt as if I should have been upset or felt some type of feelings about the request, but I didn't feel anything. I could tell Austin was searching my face for how I was really feeling about the situation.

"No really, I'm okay with that." I stood up and motioned him to as well.

"I'll always remember you with your cowboy hat, squinting up at me whenever I rode in from working with the horses. It was the moment I looked forward to the most in my day," I said as I wrapped him in a big hug.

"From the first day I met you, I always thought you were the prettiest girl in the room, and I felt so lucky to have called you mine — even for a short amount of time." I could feel a tear slide down my cheek.

"Time to go," Austin said. He hated good-byes and preferred things to be short and sweet.

"Sure is," I said pulling away. Princess in the meantime had wandered over to us and was now sniffing Austin's leg but made no effort to bark or growl at him.

"Sure, now she likes me," he commented as he turned to head into the hallway.

"She knows you're leaving," I said in a mocking tone as I followed him down the hallway and down the stairs and through the apartment.

"Caroline," I said as we approached the front door.

"Logan," she said meekly.

"Caroline," Austin chimed in.

"Safe travels," I said to Austin leaning in for one more hug.

"When are you coming home?" Austin asked as he picked up his bag.

"I don't know. Mama said I don't have a room anymore."

"Yeah, Becky moved into your room almost the day you left."

"You knew?"

"You didn't know?" With that any tension we had was gone. The playful banter we had felt natural and I knew that Austin and I would never rekindle what we had. We would be civil and we might even be friends one day. I waved as Caroline and Austin got into the elevator and stood there for a couple more moments after the elevator door closed. Mama was right, this was hard but I felt like I had finally risen to the occasion and done what I should have done before running away and that was closure. Not everyone gets the answers they want or the finality of a relationship and for that I was grateful.

CHAPTER 21

Life kept going after Austin left, almost as if he hadn't been there at all. For the next several days, I walked Princess and continued to work on odd jobs. I was radio silent to any friends I had made since arriving in New York, needing to ground myself a little back to reality. The only exception was Luca. We had texted a couple times since the incident but in general his response to me was distant. It was the end of a random Tuesday and I was sitting on the sofa, snuggling Princess watching one of those 'feel good' romance movies about a girl who finds herself in a love triangle that makes the audience root for her and look forward to the sappy happy ending that was inevitable. I was lost in thought when I felt Princess jump up first, letting out a low growl. She jumped down from the sofa and slowly crept to the door as the hair on her back stood on end. Not knowing what was going on, I ran into the kitchen and grabbed the rolling pin that Gladys left on the counter this afternoon after making homemade apple and cherry pies. I could now hear low muffled sounds in the hallway as I crept closer to the door trying to push Princess to the side but she refused to move as she continued to alternate between growling and barking in the direction of the door. There was scraping against the door followed by a jingling noise as the front door popped open.

"Stay back," I yelled jumping in front of the door brandishing my rolling pin as Princess scurried under my legs barking. I heard a familiar voice scream and another curse before I opened my eyes not realizing I had closed them.

"Caroline? Mac?" I said in confusion as they stood frozen in place.

"Surprise?" Caroline said sheepishly.

"Hells bells, y'all scared the living daylights out of me."

"What are you doing with a rolling pin?" Mac questioned setting a bag down by the door.

"It was the first thing I grabbed," I said setting it down on the entry hallway table. "Did y'all think of calling first?"

"We have...four times," Caroline commented holding up four fingers in case I didn't hear her.

"I called more times than I care to admit or deem respectable," Mac said wiping his brow with a handkerchief.

"I ain't been in a mood to talk," I commented pulling out my phone only to see more than a dozen calls and text messages but nothing from Luca.

"Ain't been ...what is happening to you?" Mac said crossing the room to stand in front of me.

"Aww, Mac, I don't know if I found my rope or lost my cow," I mumbled. He didn't hesitate a moment longer and embraced me in a big ol' bear hug.

"Are you guys done? We have actual work to address," Caroline fidgeted next to us.

"Work?" I questioned as I took a moment to straighten myself back out after Mac released me.

"Work can wait for five more minutes. First, I brought this," Mac said leaning over to grab the bag he had and giving it to me with a ceremonious flare. "Those things you said about me were not untrue and for that I sincerely apologize for my behavior. I got too caught up in my love for the dramatic that I didn't consider what I was doing. You have been a good friend to me, and I didn't return the favor."

"Thank you," I tried to say but a cough got stuck in my throat.

"Well open it already," Caroline said impatient with our dialog. I took the bag from Mac and inside was a tiny teal box with the Tiffany's insignia on it.

"Ain't that the berries!" I exclaimed dropping the bag and holding the box. "I can't accept this."

"You don't even know what it is yet," Caroline said clearly annoyed. I carefully lifted the lid and there was a small silver necklace with a diamond horseshoe pendant.

"It's beautiful," I gasped with my hands slightly shaking.

"Oh, it's lovely," Caroline said looking over my shoulder, her annoyance dialed back for a moment.

"It's a sincere gesture," Mac said motioning for me to hand him the box. I did so thinking he was going to take it back but instead he lifted the necklace out of the box and motioned for me to turn around. I did so almost immediately and he clasped the closure around my neck.

"Consider it Texas with a New York flare," he said kissing the top of my head.

"Thank you."

"Are you two done?" Caroline said looking at us and tapping her foot on the floor.

"She's in a horn-tossing mood tonight," I commented after several minutes looking at Mac.

"Don't pay her too much attention. She is stressed out over this plan May has concocted."

"It's ludicrous," Caroline said throwing her hands up.

"The rapper?" I said confused.

"Of all the things you don't know, you know who that is?" Caroline snapped.

"I think it could totally work, she's got May's bone structure," Mac said ignoring her.

"But she has the grace of a cowboy," Caroline said combing her hands through her hair only for it to fall perfectly back in place.

"Hey, I'm standing right here and I am a cowboy," I snapped back getting annoyed.

"So Tex, how do you feel about making some extra money?" Mac asked and Caroline raised her eyebrows in his direction.

"What is the catch?"

"You don't have to do much actually."

"Really, that's what you're going to say?" Caroline said clearly not pleased.

"Can someone just start from the beginning and shoot straight with me?"

"Fine, I'll do it," Caroline said. "May insisted on having some surgery," she paused for a moment and Mac pointed to his nose. "May insisted on having some surgery on her nose."

"She had a nose job?" I asked and Mac nodded.

"Fine, yes, she had a nose job and it didn't go well. She is flying to Canada to see a specialist in the morning. However, she is due back in New York for a couple of days for some press and appearances. She feels that missing these obligations will raise too many red flags causing people to look for her or ask questions."

"Why does she care?" I asked not really understanding the big deal.

"May always cares...about everything," Caroline continued. "May wants Mac here to find her a body double to attend the events dressed as her."

"That's crazy as a bullbat."

"Actually, May wanted Caroline to do it but we have determined that won't work and Caroline got her feelings hurt," Mac said dropping to a whisper.

"I heard that and my feelings aren't hurt."

"Tex, I think you would be perfect!" Mac said with as much enthusiasm as he could muster.

"I hear you clucking but you MUST have lost your nest," I said before busting out laughing.

"I'm serious."

"He's serious," Caroline echoed.

"Y'all can't be," I said settling down allowing the reality of the situation to sink in. "Y'all want me to...what? Dress like May?"

"Yes," Mac said and Caroline nodded.

"Go out in public looking like her?"

"Yes."

"Mingle with other famous people like her?"

"Yes."

"Talk to these people?"

"NO!" They both cried at the same time.

"No talking," Caroline reiterated.

"The bottom line is that you are the same height, build and overall body type like her. We can dress you up and put on some makeup, a wig, and as long as you don't talk this will totally work," Mac explained.

"Do I really have a say in this?" I said looking at both of them.

"I want you to think you do," Mac commented back with a sheepish smile.

"Mac already told her you would do it," Caroline said and Mac frowned at her.

"We said a united front," he shot back at her and she stuck out her tongue.

"What exactly does this list of things entail?" I asked wandering over to the sofa and sitting down. The credits of my movie now rolling in the background.

"Nothing big ... a charity fashion show, final curtain call for Luca Gaines, some dog-sponsored event with Princess," hearing her name Princess barked in response.

"Will I be alone at these events?" I asked horrified.

"No, Mac or I will be with you at all times. We can fill you in on who May knows and doesn't know so you can nod or smile appropriately. Maybe we tell them she has lost her voice, so they don't try talking to her?" Caroline directed the second part to Mac.

"No, that won't work because she is still filming. A rumor like that can set her back in production," Mac responded and Caroline nodded.

"Are you sure there is no one else? What about all your fancy friends, Mac?"

"That is the problem ... they are my 'fancy' friends. Most of them have the same friends as May and the other half don't want to dress up as May; they want to be friends with her, rub elbows with her, be seen with her. Anyway, none of them can keep a secret."

"PLUS, you are the only one who can really handle Princess," Caroline again commented.

"What about Grey?" I was desperate. I knew she was way too short but it was worth a shot.

"Crazy that you mention her because she will be here in a little bit to fit you for a wig and do some makeup," Mac said with a sheepish grin.

"What?"

"Also I'm going to need you to sign a NDA," Caroline said riffling through her bag and pulling out several sheets of paper.

"An NRA?"

"No," Caroline said aghast. "N-D-A, non-disclosure-agreement. Meaning you can't tell anyone or talk to anyone about this or May has the right to sue you for breach of contract."

"Who would believe me?" I said rubbing my temples.

"I know you don't think so but crazier things have happened my dear," Mac said patting me on the shoulder.

"I need to take Princess for a walk, do I have time for that?" I said suddenly standing, needing to clear my head.

"Sure, Grey will be here in about fifteen to twenty minutes. I nodded, my head spinning with questions and information as I headed out with Princess on our walk.

******

As promised, Grey was waiting for me when I got back from my walk with Princess. Caroline was pulling stacks of clothes out from May's vast closet and Mac was on the phone pacing by the windows.

"We are really going to do this?" I questioned as Grey motioned me to sit down.

"Yes, but I need you to sign the contract first," Caroline insisted, pushing the document in front of me.

"Well, I need to read it first," I said taking it from her. As I read through the four-page document, Grey and Mac each signed an agreement without so much as reading a single word.

"Don't you want to know what your signing?" I asked.

"Nope, as long as I get paid this dollar amount, I'm good," Mac said pointing to a big figure in the center of the first page.

"That's what she is paying you?" I said with more shrill than I intended.

"No, that is what she is paying YOU. I make this much," he said pointing to a smaller figure right below.

"Has anyone considered that May needs to see a doctor, maybe have her head examined? Is she medicated?" I was grasping at reasons on why someone would go through all this trouble just to be 'seen' and then pay a ridiculous amount of money to do it.

"Oh, she has a doctor for everything and a pill to match," Caroline said waving my comment off as absurd.

"Ladies, focus," Mac said steering us back to the task at hand. With that the conversation died down and Grey started in first with shaping my eyebrows to match May's. She then made several attempts to put fake eyelashes on but I kept squinting and fluttering my lashes;

by the fourth attempt they were actually secure. With a full face of makeup, she starting messing with a long brunette wig.

"Does anyone have a current picture of May? Is she still a brunette? Long hair? I pulled several pictures I could find but nothing current," she said showing Caroline and Mac some photos.

"I got this photo from her two days ago," Caroline said flipping through photos on her phone.

"Okay, the color looks good...any idea on length?"

"Well, when she left for the movie it was long but she said she was going to have to cut it at some point during the movie shoot but I don't think that is for several more weeks. I think we are good with long hair, if not people will think it's extensions or something," Caroline commented again moving clothes from one pile to the next on May's bed.

"Caroline, what are you doing?" Mac said agitated with her fidgeting.

"I'm pulling things out that May would wear to these kinds of events and then I'm putting them into piles of what Logan would actually wear from that pile."

"Not that it matters, when are the comps arriving?" Mac asked.

"Comps?" I questioned as Grey tucked and tugged my hair.

"Comp dresses. One of the events is during this charity fashion week so people will want May to wear something they designed so it gets photographed."

"I hope it's something edgy," Grey commented from behind me

"May doesn't do edgy," Caroline said crinkling her nose.

"Oh wait, we need the trademark beauty mark," Grey muttered to herself as she stood in front of me, hand on hip, examining her work. She reached into her bag for something and quickly smudged something onto my upper lip.

"Okay Logan, last thing you need to do is put these in," Grey instructed holding something up to me.

"Put what in?"

"Colored contacts, your eyes aren't the same color as May's and people are going to notice."

"I'm not sticking those in my eyes," I retorted quickly.

"Tex, just put the contacts in," Mac grumbled from behind me.

"I already had to wrestle with these lashes now you want me to wear these?"

"Yes, it's not a big deal, I'll show you how," Grey calmly said leaning over and demonstrating how to grab the contact and then slip it onto my eye.

"Most unnatural thing I have ever seen," I commented.

"You look like you just ate a lemon, now get to it," Mac instructed. I carefully pinched the flimsy lens and tugged at the bottom of my eyelid and tried to drop it in just like Grey showed me. My eye had other plans and squinted shut causing the contact to slide around my finger.

"I can't do this," I whined.

"Yes you can, let's try again," Grey patiently responded. Ten minutes later and after beads of sweat broke out on my brow, which Grey gently patted away, the contacts were in.

"These are the most unnatural thing I have ever worn," I commented, as I continued to blink.

"Stop with all the blinking or you will make them fall out," Caroline commented.

"Logan, you are fine, it takes some getting used to but you won't even notice them after a couple minutes," Grey responded.

"Doubtful," I muttered.

"I'm done," Grey said abruptly causing all eyes in the room to look at me.

"Amazing...go put this on," Caroline said holding up what looked to be a black romper as she peered around Grey's shoulder.

"Pair it with those studded black leather blocked-heel sandals, I saw in the there," Mac called after Caroline and me as we walked into May's closet. As I got dressed, Caroline kept muttering to herself, I could hear an 'OMG' and 'this is unbelievable', as she handed me jewelry to complete the look.

"Here she comes," Caroline called from behind me as I walked out of the closet to astonished looks on Grey and Mac's faces.

"You're the perfect spitting image of her," Grey said with her hands clasped together.

"I told you this would work," Mac said to Caroline.

"Y'all, I just feel like this whole thing is a little...," I trailed off as I saw my reflection in the mirror. Or rather it wasn't me, but May McKenzie was staring back at me.

"You look like her, but you sure don't sound like her," Caroline said from behind me.

"Shhhh, your ruining the moment," Grey commented.

"May wanted a picture of May," Mac said holding his phone up for several pictures.

"We should see how she does in public," Caroline said, her head cocked to one side.

"I'm not a Ford you take out on a test run," I hissed back.

"Definitely not May, but I don't see how it would hurt," Mac mused. "Tex, what are you currently in the mood for?"

"Ice cream," I responded.

"May is allergic to dairy...actually she isn't, she loves it, but the public persona of May is gluten free, dairy free, and will only eat organic and grass fed food," Caroline responded.

"What about a hamburger?" I asked trying to see if it met all the criteria.

"I can work with that, there is a place in the Flatiron district called ABC Kitchen that would work. Let me call ahead and let them know we are coming. Then I will call George."

"Who is George?"

"He is May's driver," Mac said as Caroline was already on the phone. From the sound of it, she just made the night much more interesting for whomever answered the phone.

"Okay, they will seat us upon arrival, are we ready to go?"

"I don't know...am I ready to go?"

"As ready as you will need to be," Mac said motioning for Grey and Caroline to grab their things.

"Let me go put Princess in her crate," I said resigning myself to the idea of going out as May.

CHAPTER 22

We arrived at the ABC Kitchen in no time. It was a brick building that had been painted a flat black but had shiny black and ivory accents surrounding the entrance. During the car ride, Mac had instructed me to put on a pair of big black sunglasses which Caroline had grabbed from May's closet. Initially I protested because it was dark out, but his look told me not argue with him. Grey fussed with some last-minute touch-ups to my lipstick and blush before we exited the town car.

"Remember, don't say anything," Caroline repeated to me as I exited the car, I simply nodded as it prevented me from smarting off to her. At first everything was fine; I even waited patiently for George to hold the car door open for me which I normally did not appreciate. As instructed, I got out and stood on the curb for Mac, Caroline, and Grey to exit the car but then I walked in front of them into the restaurant.

"I'm sorry, but we are full for the evening," the young lady said as I approached. I was trying to see her name tag but the sunglasses that Mac had me wearing were smudged, so I pulled the sunglasses down the bridge of my nose and looked at her name tag. At least that is what I thought I was doing. Mac would later tell me, what I was doing was very 'May' and the 'look' I gave the young woman was all attitude. Caroline was sternly talking about our call-ahead, before a gentleman showed up and whisked us away to our table much to the young woman's confusion.

"She didn't know who I was," I whispered to Mac.

"She must be living under a rock," he whispered back. We were seated in the back of the restaurant out of the way of most people. Once seated, Mac told me I could remove my sunglasses and that I could speak but I was to keep my voice down and not speak to the staff. Caroline placed my order for me, and Mac placed my drink order. When the food arrived, my hamburger was slightly undercooked to my liking, but I was fine to eat it. Caroline insisted that is not what May would do and sent it back on my behalf using a tone that I hadn't heard from her yet.

"Doesn't that get tiring?" I asked after the waiter scurried away with my plate.

"Does what get tiring?"

"You always doing someone else's bidding?"

"Most days I love what I do but, yes, it can get tiring. It's worse when I am on set. Then I'm running around trying to pull strings and arrange things in a strange city. At least here in New York I know the shops she likes to shop in, the restaurants she likes to eat in, and the people to call to make last minute things happen."

"Why aren't you on set?" Mac asked somewhat aggressively causing me to kick him under the table.

"Not that we don't love having you around," I amended with a small smile.

"No, it's fine. Sometimes I think I spend so much time with May, her worst and best personality traits start to rub off on me. I was supposed to fly out soon to join her before the fiasco," she whispered pointing to her nose. "She took Rachel with her this time and it's for the better. I'm more useful to her here."

"Who's Rachel?"

"Rachel is me in training. She has been around for about six months but hasn't ever been on remote with May. The studio has worked with May before so they have her set up much to her liking, so it was a good way for Rachel to ease in. This new development probably has her going crazy over there but that's how we all learn. I remember my first remote location trip with May. It was to Chile and then Hawaii for the movie, *Death of Alice Walker*. This was before she flew privately, so the airline lost her luggage, she got the flu on the third week of filming, and lost her voice. She was also attending the big awards that year — Golden Globes, Screen Actors Guild, and the Oscars. We were having dresses flown in and trying to do fittings, it was a nightmare. I almost quit...like...seven times during that two-month shoot."

"Quit slouching, May does not slouch," Mac said pointing his finger at me, causing me to sit up straighter.

"Why this work?" Grey asked as she sipped on her martini, ignoring Mac's comment completely.

"I kind of fell into this work. I went to Parsons School of Design here in the city. One of my faculty advisers knew Vivian Banks," just the mention of her name made me shudder but Caroline continued. "They heard that an up-and-coming actress needed an assistant for all things related to fashion. I was reluctant to interview but my adviser said that there would be an opportunity to tailor clothes and even introduce my own designs. That was four years ago and here I am."

"Have you continued to design your own clothes?" I asked completely intrigued by this new side of Caroline. If I focused on the conversation, I almost forgot how uncomfortable I felt dressed in someone else clothes, wearing the wig that tugged at my scalp, the contacts that burned my eyes, and my stiff posture that ached my back.

"I have continued to design my own clothes but May never wore anything I designed so I stopped asking."

"I'll wear it...I mean May will wear it...I mean I will wear it dressed as May so it's like May wearing it," I rushed, excited to push the envelope a little.

"She would never go for that," Caroline commented twisting her napkin in her lap.

"It's better to ask for forgiveness than permission, my older brothers always said." Caroline seemed to mull this over as the rest of our food finally arrived. We continued to chat over dinner and I forgot I was May, it seemed like a normal meal. There was no extravagant food being served, endless drinks, or crazy adventures. It felt like friends going out to eat and enjoying each other's company. At the end of the meal, Caroline squared the bill and called for George to come pick us up. Mac reminded me to put my sunglasses on as we got up from our table and started to exit the restaurant; it was only then that I noticed the hum of activity. Outside the doors of the restaurant were crowds of people and when they noticed our group, they started yelling and screaming.

"What the Sam Hill?" I asked in confusion.

"They all want to see May," Mac said beside me.

"They all want to see me?"

"Well yes, but not you per se, they want to see you dressed as May," Mac tried to explain.

"Remember don't say anything and keep moving," Caroline said getting to the front of our group, pushing the door open. The sheer volume of the crowd became deafening. There were people of all ages, gender, and background calling for May's attention. People had their phones out and were snapping pictures or video recording my every movement.

'May, over here!'

'Picture, May?'

'Autograph for my son/daughter, May?'

'You're so beautiful, May.'

'Loved your work in your last film.'

Caroline tried to push us forward through the crowd so that we could get to George, but it wasn't working. The large crowd started to push back and enclose on our group. Without thinking, I put my thumb and index finger together and let out a loud whistle. Everyone, I mean everyone, froze to look at me. Caroline had a horrified look on her face while Mac looked mostly disappointed. Grey jumped into action and with the momentary pause pushed us through to the waiting car and we jumped in. People banged on the car and windows trying to get 'May' to open up or let them in. After what seemed like eternity but was more like minutes, George was able to pull away from the crowd and whisk us away into the night.

"What in the world was that?" Caroline and I asked each other at the same time.

"We told you not to speak," Caroline finally blurted out.

"I didn't speak," I said defensively.

"That was intense," Grey said to no one in particular.

"It usually doesn't get that bad. I can usually anticipate it better and we can sneak out the back. I'm sorry, Logan, I didn't really think this was going to work and I didn't think through a plan that involved people actually thinking you were May."

"It's okay I didn't think it was going to work either."

"But it did!" Mac exclaimed much to his own delight. After arriving back at the apartment with no further problems, Grey helped me remove the wig, contacts, eyelashes, and makeup. Afterwards, Caroline, Mac, and Grey had a small meeting to discuss logistics of this new plan. I took Princess on an unscheduled walk just to clear my head. During the walk in an unguarded moment, I called Luca and he didn't answer. I called my mama next and she didn't answer. I was just about to call Austin, but I talked myself out of it. It wasn't right to call him and involve him in a life that I clearly told him he wasn't a part of. Twenty minutes later, I returned to the apartment feeling just as conflicted as I did when I left.

"Oh good, you're back," Caroline said to me as I entered the apartment.

"Is something wrong?"

"No, I just need to take your measurements and send them out to a couple of the fashion houses."

"We are still on this crazy idea?"

"It's not just a crazy idea anymore," Mac said. "May called us while you were out and said she saw the pictures from our restaurant outing and was absolutely pleased."

"She said that?"

"No...she actually said, 'you'll do'."

"Well, glad everyone is on board, what could go wrong?"

"Logan, I don't know why you're so upset about this. Most people would love to be in the good grace of 'THE' May MacKenzie."

"Well then, you could go find one of these people and ask them. I didn't come to the city to be someone else, I came to the city to figure out who I was."

"You can still do that while you're doing this," Mac said with a cheesy grin. I just waved my hands in the air towards him and wandered back towards the kitchen. Looking in the fridge I saw we were out of beer but an open bottle of some red wine sat on the table. I poured myself a glass and wandered over to the panoramic view of the city. I wanted an adventure and I was sure going to embark on my biggest one yet.

"Fine, I'm all in," I said turning around to the group. If I was going to do this I might as well try and be a good sport about it.

CHAPTER 23

Princess and I had attended the grand opening for a boutique pet store named Wags in the West Village two days later. Apparently, the owner was Vivian Bank's niece and May had promised to make an appearance with Princess over a year ago. Grey got me ready and Caroline picked out this super short dress and tall wedge platforms. Princess even made an extra special trip to the groomers in preparation for the occasion and was now sporting a bandanna that complimented my outfit. It was an event that I was sure I wasn't going to worry about speaking at because I was concentrating so hard not to fall in those ridiculously tall wedges. As we pulled up to the boutique it looked low key, people milling around with their own dogs, casually talking, and browsing the items on the sidewalk pulled out on display. The boutique was a pale-yellow whitewash and had sky blue shutters and an awning. I had never seen one in person, but it looked more like a surf shop that belonged in California than New York City.

"It's so kitschy," Caroline said under her breath as George pulled up curbside. It seemed low key, that is until people realized 'May' had arrived. Suddenly, there were flashes of light and May's name being called every which-way. I held Princess snugly in the nook of my arm as we exited the car, pulling on my large over-sized sunglasses.

"I'm so glad you were able to make it," a tall woman with olive skin and mini dreads said approaching Caroline and me. She outstretched her arm as Princess gave a warning growl from my arm and the woman put her arm down.

"Gia," the woman said indicating her name, and I nodded slightly.

"Gia what is the agenda here?" Caroline asked brusquely. She had been in a sour mood all morning but didn't want to talk about it, even after I asked five times.

"We are just waiting on my Aunt to arrive and then we are going to do a ribbon cutting. After which there will be a couple of photo ops and interviews and then the food truck is arriving," Gia said with a large warm smile.

"Food truck?" Caroline repeated slowly. I inched my foot over closer to her as they talked. I was about to stomp on her toes when a limo pulled up honking.

"Over the top," Caroline huffed to herself pulling out her phone and quickly typing something to someone.

"Caroline," I hissed getting her attention.

"Yes, May," she said so sweetly looking up at me.

"Will we have a problem with Vivian Banks?" I asked feeling myself start to sweat out of all the pores in my body.

"May, you..." Caroline trailed off for a moment in a daze before blinking several times.

"Holy...Logan...I forgot for a second that you weren't May," she said leaning into me and hissing into my ear which only caused Princess to start barking.

"My darling, it pleases me to see you here," Vivian appeared cooing in my direction. "I heard a vicious rumor you were otherwise indisposed..." she said letting the sentence and insinuation hang in the air.

"Vivian how are you doing?" Caroline interrupted.

"Caroline," Vivian said curtly before trying to lean in and give me one of those fake side hugs. However, Princess ended up being my best line of defense because she wiggled in my arms and started on a tirade of barking in Vivian's direction.

"I see Princess is behaving as always," she commented walking away but not before sliding her eyes towards her own assistant who cringed and then fell in step behind her.

"Don't say a word," Caroline said to me as if she could read my mind. I casually slid my sunglasses down my nose, raising my eyebrows and looked at her. She sighed and I nodded and pushed them back up. I had long learned from my mother that you didn't need actual words to convey exactly what you were thinking and how you were feeling. I gently patted Princess who settled back down as Caroline led us further into the crowd.

"Good girl," I whispered to Princess scratching her ear when Caroline was otherwise occupied with an older woman waving a notepad asking for an exposé. Somehow Caroline persuaded the women to focus on the event at hand and that focusing on May would be an absolute disservice to entrepreneurs or aspiring business owners on the entire planet. About ten minutes later, Gia called everyone's attention and a ribbon-cutting ceremony took place. Someone handed Gia an absurdly large pair of scissors as another pair stretched out a thin velvety red ribbon. Vivian looked on proudly as Gia cut the ribbon and then smashed a bottle of champagne against the side of the building much to the delight of everyone. The few news outlets present walked around and took pictures. Several stopped to get 'sound bites' from May but Caroline intercepted them all and gave a stock quote. It was bizarre. I was standing right there and from outward appearances it was as if I couldn't be bothered to talk with anyone, feeling as if I were above them in some way and everyone just accepted it. No one thought it was bizarre or even argued with Caroline about it. Gia did come over and talk quietly with Caroline for another ten minutes before disappearing.

"I'm calling George," Caroline said turning to me.

"Time to go?"

"Close, you have to take no less than fifty photos and then we are gone." Caroline didn't lie. We took fifty-eight photos to be exact because I counted. Princess and I took photos by ourselves in front of the shop, with Gia, with Vivian, with Gia and Vivian, with several investors, and finally a select grouping of fans that Caroline hand selected. But by the time George pulled up twenty minutes later we were ready to go. I smiled and waved at the crowd and then gave short curt waves towards Gia and Vivian who each nodded in my direction as I climbed into the car.

"That was exhausting, and I didn't say a thing," I exhaled once we were safely in the car.

"Logan it's eerie, you being May. I don't know why I ever doubted it. I thought that everyone would see through this but there were times today I was sure you were May, and this was all just some mind game."

"That went as fine as cream gravy but do not worry I'm still me," I said with a smile.

"When you talk like that, I believe you."

That evening, Caroline informed me that the photos from the opening came out 'great' according to the real May, who was closely monitoring everything from the private care facility in Canada.

The next event that Caroline and Mac were prepping me for was for a charity fashion show that was supposed to be like an actual fashion week but not, as described to me by Mac. Grey came early and worked on my makeup and hair this time styling my hair a little differently because of all the press was that was going to be present. Caroline laid out several outfits, but I didn't really feel comfortable in any of them.

"The goal is not comfort," Caroline sighed at me in exasperation.

"Oh, well, if that's the case, they all work," I hissed back.

"What about that outfit?" I asked spying what I thought was a romper that that had long billowy pants in a bold red color.

"That's nothing."

"No, what is it?" I said making my way closer to the outfit.

"It's not finished," Caroline said trying to hide it under a pillow.

"Is this something you made?" I asked pulling it out from under the pillow realizing it was separate pieces.

"Yes, I was working on it this morning, but I can't get the hem right for the pants."

"No wonder you carry such a big bag...well then sew me into it."

"What?" Caroline asked giving me a weird look.

"I've seen that on shows before, right? It's an actual thing...you can just sew someone into an outfit. It will be a Caroline original."

"I don't think May would approve."

"I am May and I approve, now sew me into the dang outfit," I said pointing my finger towards her sewing kit that had scattered over the bed when I pulled the pants out.

"I can get fired over this."

"You can just say I made you do it. Come on Caroline, it's beautiful from what I can see and what better time than now."

"I guess." Secretly, I was thrilled the outfit was more comfortable than any other choices I had that day. She ushered me into the closet where I stepped into the pants and then ever so carefully she sewed the high waisted pants closed. Her stitching was delicate and so precise. For the top she had made a sheer crop top that had lace elements in the same bold red color as the pants. The entire outfit fit to perfection and was made with such attention to detail.

"Caroline, in all seriousness this outfit is amazing," I said looking in the mirror again.

"Really?...thank you," she finally said admiring her work.

"Now slide these on," she pushed a pair of black heels covered in mini spikes towards me.

"These seem dangerous," I commented picking them up. "Oh wait, Caroline, the bottoms are red, what a great match!"

"It's not a match it's Louboutin."

"Lou-Bow-Ton?"

"They are expensive fancy shoes, don't ruin them," she said in exasperation. The limo service buzzed up announcing their arrival and Caroline walked me down to the limo where Mac was waiting.

"Who are you wearing?" Mac inquired admiring my outfit.

"It's an original piece," I said, and Mac took it as an original piece from one of the fashion houses and seemed pleased. I winked at Caroline and she nervously waved back at me.

"This is my first time in a limo," I commented to no one in particular.

"Of course, it is," Mac said getting in beside me.

****

"I am surprised how many people are actually here. They are all here to watch other people walk around in clothes?" I tried to whisper but it came out more like a hiss.

"Good Lord, let's hope Anna Wintour didn't hear you," Mac hissed back.

"What about winter?"

"Win-tour"

"Winter"

"Never mind. Stop fussing with the sunglasses and walk straight."

"Look, there's Luca!" I started to wave my arm to get his attention before I realized I was nervous to see him. We had sent several more texts and had each left several phone messages but had not connected since that night.

"Would you put your arm down. You look spastic and remember who you are supposed to be," annoyance crept into his voice as he grabbed my arm lowering it down.

"Oh, Luca, darling," I said again, this time quickly escaping Mac's grip and doing my best casual walk in stilettos over to where Luca was standing.

"Nope not even a good impression," I heard Mac say behind me as he followed in my direction.

"Luca." He was talking in a small group and when I spoke several people raised their eyebrows in my direction.

"May." He seemed to visibly retract from me but gave me a halfhearted smile.

"Mac?" he said slightly confused by his sudden appearance at my side.

"Do not go running off on me like that again, do you understand?" Mac reprimanded me.

"Mac, a dead bee can still sting," I said frustrated by the current situation.

"Umm...will you excuse me," Luca said suddenly to his group and pulled at my arm, spinning me around so that now Luca, Mac, and myself formed a very small circle.

"Logan?" Luca questioned.

"Yes," I said pulling my over-sized sunglasses down a bit. Honestly, I didn't understand why anyone would ever want to wear sunglasses inside, you can't see anything.

"What the hell are you doing?"

"Why is everyone so horn tossing mad with me today? First Caroline and now you...I'm just doing as instructed. Put the wig on, fake a mole, wear the sunglasses, sit front row, and don't talk to anyone."

"You're failing on the don't talk to anyone part," Mac interjected.

"It's just Luca," I commented.

"Luca is someone who actually dated May and had a very public and horrendous break up with her to the point she won't even say his name out loud," he said pointing to Luca. "He is the he who must not be named in her inner circle, so this is a problem," Mac said wiggling his finger back and forth between me and Luca.

"What is your connection to May MacKenzie?" Luca now asked in a hushed tone with his arms crossed.

"She actually can't explain herself because she signed a NDA," Mac said giving me a look.

"It's just Luca," I repeated myself.

"Who you haven't really spoken to in almost two weeks," Mac pointed out.

"I've been busy," Luca defended himself.

"If we keep up this little pow-wow, people will start to talk," Mac again commented.

"What people?" I asked.

"Industry people, tabloid people, casual people...all people," Mac said.

"I actually agree," Luca commented with a frown.

"Move now," Mac said shoving me to the left.

"What in the world?" I asked back.

"Vivian Banks," Mac said and Luca quickly went right, and Mac dragged me further left.

"May darling," Vivian called.

"You have to stop and acknowledge her," Mac said finally after several steps. I stopped and turned to Vivian giving her a half smile and a nod in recognition.

"Darling, are you feeling okay? You have been awfully quite the last couple of times we have seen each other," she inquired looking at me.

"Hi, Vivian. I'm Mac Houston, May's go-to guy," Mac said jumping in and introducing himself.

"I've heard about you from several different people. Always making arrangements, very reliable, and hush hush. Pleasure to finally meet you," she said reaching out her hand in a way that only her fingers connected with Mac's extended hand.

"You're a pleasant change from that Caroline," Vivian commented. I felt an immediate allegiance to Caroline and was about to speak my mind on the subject when Mac squeezed my arm and mouthed the word 'no' when Vivian wasn't looking. He knew me too well.

"May, I asked you a question?" she said turning her attention back to me. "Well, are you going to answer me?" She asked again after several moments. I started to sweat and without thinking, I started to respond.

"I'm fine, just busy," but with a little bit of luck the announcer came on over the loud speaker calling people to their seats as the show was about to start which drowned out my response.

"That's good darling," Vivian said reaching in for a half hug as her assistant ushered her to her seat.

"That was close," Mac said wiping his brow with a handkerchief.

"You're telling me, I was nervous as a fly near a glue pot."

"Ms. MacKenzie, please follow me," a young women said flagging me down in an attempt to get me seated. I had already spoken more than intended so I just nodded and followed her. May's seats were of course front row; Vivian was seated a row back and several sections down from where we were seated. Mac whispered that Vivian's status was slipping, and she only clung to May in order to make herself more important or relevant. It made me feel sad for her, but I was glad we didn't need to sit with her. I looked around for Luca and saw that he was sitting almost directly across from us on the other side of the catwalk. He was starring rather intently at me. He finally picked up his phone and made a gesture that I should do the same.

What is going on? It's uncanny how much you look like her, the text read.

Not right now, I responded trying to be discreet so Mac wouldn't see me.

When?

So are we talking now? I shot back with annoyance. Mac was right; it had been almost two weeks and Luca had made no real effort to try and connect.

I know. I haven't been around much. He replied and when I glanced up, he shrugged and mouthed the word 'sorry'.

"Put that thing away," Mac said elbowing me in the side.

Can we talk later? He sent as a quick follow up.

Yes.

"Just smile...actually never mind, just continue this pout face your making it's perfect, very May MacKenzie," Mac said as the lights dimmed and the show started.

******

"Just walk as straight as possible, pose for a couple photos, and don't say anything. You only have to make it twenty yards and then get in the limo and I'll be waiting. It will be easy," Mac said.

It wasn't easy.

About ten yards into the longest walk of my life, I had already stopped twice to pose for photos and only had a minor stumble that I was hoping no one saw when I heard a slight cough behind me and I turned to find Luca standing next to me.

"What are you doing?" I said in a fierce whisper.

"May, funny running into you here," he said with an amused smile plastered on his face. I was about to say something, instead I frowned and I tried to turn and walk away.

"Luca, a picture with yourself and May?" a random photographer asked.

"Sure," he said, sliding his arm around my waist and twisting me slightly toward the camera.

"Smile," he whispered into my ear and I further pouted in his direction.

"Thank you," he replied back to the photographer. There were other calls for pictures, but Luca waived them off.

"Escort you to your limo, May?" he asked, and I simply nodded. I could feel steam rising from my head due to how angry I felt inside and yet powerless in this moment to say anything.

"Ms. MacKenzie your limo is ready," a valet said as we reached the end of my twenty-yard walk. I nodded and waited as he held the door open. I carefully shimmied in.

"See that wasn't so bad..." Mac started as Luca suddenly slid in behind me.

"I thought I might catch a ride with y'all," he said tipping an invisible hat in my direction.

"What in the world is he doing here?" Mac finished.

"He is as welcome as a wet shoe," I finished with my arms crossed over my chest staring at Luca and Mac. Both looked at me for a long pause and burst into chuckles.

"It sounds like you're really mad but the words that are coming out of your mouth don't make any sense to me," Luca finally said.

"Explain yourself," I finally said showing a faint smile.

"You first, May MacKenzie," he said reaching over and pulling off my sunglasses. "Still not better, what happened to your eyes?"

"Oh right," I leaned forward and quickly popped the contacts out and dumped them unceremoniously into my purse. It was always easier getting them out than in and Grey had what seemed to be hundreds more back at the apartment.

"Better, you look like you," he commented finally leaning back in his seat.

"This was all her idea," I said tugging at the wig only for it to get stuck on a bobby pin.

"Let me help," Mac said sliding over and pulling off the wig. My braids fell free and I worked my fingers deftly through my hair quickly undoing them, letting the wavy mess of hair fall freely around my face.

"Just one more thing," Luca said reaching over and rubbing the beauty mark off from above my lip.

"How do you know May?" Luca asked again.

"I'm her dog sitter."

"More like her dog whisperer," Mac commented and I smiled.

"Princess isn't that bad y'all."

"Princess is May's dog?" he commented almost as if puzzle pieces were suddenly fitting into place.

"So, I am to assume that Mac here got you that job?" I nodded in agreement. "All you do is watch her dog?"

"Well, I currently live in her apartment while she is shooting a movie. My main job is to take Princess on walks, feed her, run her around to different appointments. Generally, spoil her," I said thinking about how much that little dog had changed my life.

"Have you ever met her?" Luca asked appearing curious about this.

"Once for less than fifteen minutes. Mac here made the introduction and Princess took to me right away. I moved in several days later."

"When we met the first time, had you already met May?"

"No? I don't think so. When we met, I was still staying at a hotel...I am pretty sure...why?" I asked suspicious of his questioning.

"Just trying to get some clarity on the situation. I am not a fan of May nor is she a fan of mine, which is no secret. I'm trying to understand this complicated connection we suddenly have," he said lost in thought for a moment before asking another question. "How do you go from dog sitter to impersonator?"

"Well...she had a ...complication but needed to be 'seen' at several events. A couple of those events included Princess. Since Logan can pass for her physically, she came up with this scheme," Mac finished not being able to stay out of the conversation.

"The resemblance between you with this get up is striking...scary actually," Luca said making a face at me.

"I wasn't going to do it, I don't know how to act in these situations... obviously," I said thinking to the disaster that just happened. "But Caroline and Mac convinced me otherwise," I said almost crestfallen.

"And if this plan fails?" he asked his eyebrows furrowed into a straight line.

"She will probably fire me and then I'll be homeless," I said with a shrug.

"We are supposed to make sure she looks the part, knows the people who she knows, and stay out of trouble," Mac said pulling out his handkerchief and wiping his brow. "A feat too great, apparently."

"No one can keep Logan in line...you did the best you can," Luca said and they both nodded in commiseration together.

"Well now the plan is busted."

"What did you have left?"

"Ummm...I had one more of these fashion shows tomorrow. What is the deal with this anyway? Why are all these people sitting around watching these perfect human beings walk around in clothes that no normal human being could ever wear anyway? I mean did you see how sheer that last lace dress was? My mama would think I was in my knickers and not let me leave the house...What?" I said eying them both.

"I'm touched you got the material right...you have been paying attention," Mac commented with his hands over his heart in dramatic fashion.

"I don't think I will ever get tired of seeing the world through your perspective," Luca said leaning over for what I thought was a kiss but instead he just brushed a stray hair from my face.

"Besides the fashion show, anything else?" he asked.

"Final curtain call for one Luca Gaines at *Franklin* on Saturday night," Mac said reading from the list he had saved on his phone.

"That May sure is a piece of work," he said shaking his head. It was quiet for a couple moments before Luca spoke again, "Since I just inserted myself into this narrative, mind if I tag along?"

"Inserted yourself?" I asked.

"That photo we took will be viral within the hour if it isn't already," he commented pulling out his phone and scrolling through.

"See," he said showing me the picture we took not fifteen minutes ago. It showed a pouty May MacKenzie with Luca leaning over and whispering something into her ear as he smiled with the caption, *'Rekindled Romance?'*

"It....I...really look like her," I said in amazement. I was there in that moment and looking at the picture I still question myself if it wasn't her. Just then Mac's phone rang, he held up the screen so we could all see that it was May calling.

"This is going to be bad," Luca said.

"May," Mac said smoothly answering the phone. He didn't get any further as the voice on the other side was shrill and loud.

"You saw the picture...no, of course he doesn't know...I see...anything could be arranged...money isn't a problem...yes, of course...he won't see it coming...yes, of course...anything for you May."

"Sounds like you were arranging a hit...my hit," Luca commented when Mac was through.

"Well, May is just delighted by this change in events."

"She is WHAT?! Is she horn tossing mad?"

"See, I've heard that one before, and now I get it," Luca said distracted from the conversation at hand.

"As I was saying...as long as Luca is completely convinced that Logan is her, she is delighted. She wants Logan aka herself to invite Luca along for as many things as he can attend, make it very public, lots of photos, and then she wants Logan to dump him and break his heart."

"I don't want to do that?"

"But it's not you, it's you acting as May, and May would very much do that," Luca commented clearly amused.

"You're okay with all this?"

"I am up for anything as long as you're upfront with me. Last time things got really intense and I believe some of it could have been avoided if you had just told me about Austin," he said, and I nodded in resignation.

"Now the predicament we are currently in, I can certainly rise to the occasion."

"Being a celebrity is complicated and it's all just a show," I commented.

"Not for everyone but for some yes, they live on the drama. Fame does weird things to people. May used to be a pretty normal person but a lot has changed, she has changed. None of this is surprising to me. I was just upset she might have turned you over to the dark side of fame. But I can clearly see that is not the case."

"Mac, anything else?"

"Oh yes, she said that May MacKenzie doesn't slouch so walk straighter next time."

"She did not," I said throwing my wig in Mac's direction.

CHAPTER 24

The following day I was sitting in a chair in the bathroom with Princess in my lap as Grey fussed with my hair when Caroline came bursting in; she was uncharacteristically red cheeked and out of breath.

"Whoa there," I said as she practically skidded to a stop.

"Logan," she rasped as she tried to catch her breath.

"Caroline?"

"The outfit you wore, my outfit is all over the tabloids!"

"Of course," I said with a slight shudder. The picture of 'May' and Luca was across every magazine on every newspaper stand this morning when I walked Princess. It was obnoxious how much people cared about one person.

"I just got off the phone with a stylist at Vogue asking who May was wearing and where they can buy it!" Is what I believe she said but it came out so rushed it was hard to understand.

"What did you tell them?"

"That I would have to get back to them. I mean what do I tell them?"

"That it was yours?"

"No, I can't do that? Can I? Logan, this was VOGUE," she said emphasizing the last word as if I were a child.

"I know what Vogue is," I said with mild defiance.

"Caroline, that is huge," Grey encouraged as she continued to tug on my hair.

"Tell them it was yours," I again repeated as Grey motioned for me to close my eyes.

"I'm not ready to tell them it was me."

"Then don't tell them it was you," I said trying to keep still for Grey.

"I can't do that can I?"

"Caroline, I'm really excited for you but you are not helping," Grey finally said from somewhere behind me.

"Oh right, sorry," she commented. I could hear her shuffle around the bathroom. The next time she spoke she was much closer to where I was sitting on the floor.

"Logan...do you think you can wear another outfit today?" she whispered.

"Me? You're the stylist Caroline. Do you think I can wear another outfit today? Do you have an outfit for today?" I said cracking an eye.

"Logan keep those eyes closed," Grey commented touching my shoulder.

"The theme of today's show is 'white out,' I think I have something that will work. Let me go get it ready," she said but it was as if she were talking to herself more than Grey and I.

"She is wound tightly some days," I murmured to myself as she walked out of the bathroom.

"Don't you know it," Grey commented.

****

An hour later I was dressed in a white jumpsuit with a wide fit off-the-shoulder neckline, large side pockets, and long puff sleeves. Again, Caroline sewed me into the garment saying she didn't have time to add the zipper. Since the pant legs were so long, she paired them with a very tall pair of white lace Louboutin heels. Grey decided to make a last-minute adjustment to my styled hair and just like that I was May again.

"This is amazing," I said looking in the mirror but talking to Caroline.

"We aren't done yet," she said emerging from the closet with several Grey and blue boxes. "These arrived earlier today while you were walking Princess."

"What are they?"

"Harry Winston."

"I said what not who."

"No, the jeweler is Harry Winston, these are on loan," she said in exasperation. "Diamond drop earrings set in platinum, step-cut octagonal emerald cut diamond ring and your statement necklace," she said opening a large box that held what looked like braids of roped diamonds.

"That is a lot of bling," Grey said letting out a low whistle.

"Are those real?" I said tentatively reaching out to touch the necklace.

"Are they real? That is like asking if Louboutin shoes are red bottomed. Of course, they are real. It's close to two million dollars in jewelry," she said casually as she started to fuss with the clasp on the necklace.

"Can you repeat that?" I asked as I suddenly heard a faint whistle and my face got flushed.

"Are you okay?" Grey asked suddenly.

"For a second, I thought Caroline lost her rocker saying I was wearing two million dollars in jewelry tonight."

"I did say that," Caroline said looking up.

"Your must have lost your mind. I'm not wearing those."

"Why not? May does it all the time. This one time she wore a five-million-dollar ring from Harry while doing yoga in Central Park, it was for a photo shoot, but she misplaced it. That whole crew looked for two hours and someone finally found it rolled up into one of the yoga mats on set. It was totally fine; anyway May has insurance for these kinds of things," she said moving toward me with the necklace.

"I don't know if I can do this. That's a lot of money. What if I lose it or someone tries to rob me and I beat them up? You know I wouldn't be able to sit still and do nothing..." I started to ramble.

"I love that your first inclination is to fight the hypothetical robber," Grey said with a chuckle.

"Logan it's fine. You will have Mac with you, nothing will happen." I looked at her with complete disbelief as she fastened the necklace.

"There are times I just don't understand this life," I mumbled to myself as the doorbell rang.

"That must be Mac, I'll go get it," said Caroline.

"Grey I don't know if I can do this."

"You're overthinking. Every little girl has dreamed of playing dress up, dripping in diamonds. You get to live the ultimate little girl fantasy," she said admiring the ring.

"I guess," I sighed, looking at my reflection and all the sparkle in the mirror.

"Don't you look beautiful," Luca said to my surprise moments later.

"I couldn't stop him," Caroline commented coming around him and checking my appearance one last time. Princess started barking with the sudden appearance of a stranger in the apartment.

"I thought you weren't attending the show tonight?" I said feeling my cheeks flush.

"Plans change," he said with a casual shrug.

"Where is Mac? You are going to be late," Caroline fussed.

"Oh, he's not coming, I told him to stand down," Luca said again surprising everyone.

"What are you doing?" Caroline said getting agitated. "This is not a game, you're playing with fire and I'm afraid we are all going to get burned."

"You sound like Logan," Grey commented packing up her makeup kit. Caroline made a face at Grey and threw up her arms and stormed out of the bedroom.

"My plans changed. The actor who is taking over my part needed another run through so the director thought it would be best that he goes live tonight to try and work out any kinks before I end my run."

"Is that normal?" I asked.

"Not entirely but the director is known for being very unconventional."

"Are you two ready?" Caroline said coming back into the room.

"Ready as I'm going to be," I sighed still unsure of the responsibility of what I was wearing. Luca gave me a questionable look but I just shook my head.

"Logan you are going to be fine. Just remember when you come home tonight the jewels must go back into these boxes. The currier is going to pick them up first thing tomorrow." I nodded in understanding and with that Luca and I went and met the limo that had arrived.

"Are you sure this is a good idea?" I asked him once we were alone. Caroline's comments had frayed my already unraveling nerves. The truth was that ever since that night on the bus when I learned about how May felt about Luca and that Caroline knew about my relationship with Luca and my feelings about Vivian, I was always on edge. Caroline had not said a word about that night to me since nor had she given any indication she was going to tell May but I felt as if this web of secrets was just too good to continue.

"I'm not sure any of this is a good idea but I'm also not going to let May call all the shots in this game she is playing...no offense to you," he commented.

"Sounds like things were pretty bad between you," I said trying to ignore the fact that Luca might in fact use me as a pawn in this game May was playing.

"Things were never good. May didn't break my heart because I wasn't ever in love with her but the lengths she went to after were unimaginable. Did you hear that she set my clothes on fire?" I nodded in the affirmative. "She set up a camp chair and toasted s'mores while everything burned. The fire marshall cited her for violating city burning ordinances."

"I told y'all she was crazy as a bullbat but no one ever listens," I added for commentary. Luca gave me a lop-sided grin and reached for my hand giving it a short squeeze.

"It's going to be okay."

****

The second day of the charity fashion show was mostly uneventful. Once we arrived at the venue, Luca had the limo drop him off about a block earlier. Stating he wasn't going to play by May's rules, but he didn't want to be ostentatious either. He was still seated across from me in the room. Every now and then I would catch his eye and he would make some goofy face in my direction causing me to grin. Thankfully, Vivian was not at this event so no actual speaking on my part was required. At the end of the show, which I found much more interesting today, mostly due to the fact that the designer had the models dressed as if they had just rolled in the mud and crawled through tumbleweeds, Luca approached me to remind me that we needed to be photographed, otherwise May wouldn't know what was going on. Capturing the moment was easy, I walked down the white carpet and approached Luca engaging him in conversation. From outward appearances, the conversation looked serious. In reality, I was asking Luca what his favorite ice cream flavor was and when his birthday was…strawberry and June 21, respectively. Photographers flocked to take pictures while we stood there in conversation. Luca turned first to acknowledge them, and we took one more photo and then I left in the limo. We picked Luca up right where we dropped him off, about a block away.

"Wasn't that fun," Luca said once in the limo.

"I will be glad when this is all over. I don't like not being me."

"I don't like your not being you either."

"Come to dinner with me," Luca blurted out after a moment.

"As me or May?" I asked suddenly confused.

"Oh, I don't care about May, come out as yourself."

******

It was a little after eight as I walked back out on the New York City street. As I was leaving the apartment a small group of people were gathered in front of the building. Walking by I could hear them talking about May and Luca.

"Do you think he's up there right now?" a woman asked a man who shrugged.

"This is completely out of hand," I thought to myself. As I walked the seven or so blocks to the restaurant Luca had sent me directions to, I wondered what mama would think about this. I was sure that she would not approve but would know just what to say to help me through this crazy mess I had gotten myself into. When I arrived at the address, I saw nothing but a black building and black door with the simple address 540 in silver letters on the front. Cautiously, I turned the nob and entered a dark lobby area. I stood for a moment as I waited for my eyes to adjust to my surroundings.

"May I help you?" A younger man said while approaching a small desk.

"Yes sir. I'm meeting a friend. I think I'm in the right place or at least this is the address he gave me."

"What is tonight's drink special?" he asked me casually.

"Isn't that your job?" I replied as my phone dinged.

The drink special tonight is a Black Manhattan, Luca's text read.

"Wait...tonight's drink special is a Black Manhattan?" I read out loud to the young man.

"Yes ma'am. Right this way," he said picking up a menu. Somewhere in the confusion of the conversation, I noticed a door behind the desk and the young man led me into another room. The room was larger than the lobby and the sound of conversation could suddenly be heard. As we rounded a corner the room opened up and tables and booths were filled with patrons. The room was brighter than the lobby but still somewhat dimly lit. A haze hung in the air, but it wasn't tobacco smoke...it reminded me more of incense.

"I believe the gentleman you're waiting for is in the back booth," the waiter pointed towards the back corner and I could see a vague figure sitting alone in the booth. As I wove my way through the crowd, the red and orange accents set against dark wood furniture reminded me of one of the saloons papa would frequent back home.

"Logan is that you?" Luca said as I approached the booth.

"Luca what in the Sam Hill is this place," I said rather exasperated but curious all at the same time.

"It's a speakeasy."

"Speakeasy?"

"During the day of Prohibition, they were all over the place hiding patrons who still wanted to indulge in not so legal activities. Over the last couple of years some of them have opened back up. This was an original speakeasy that was recently restored. I enjoy the extreme privacy a place like this affords me," he commented as I slid into the curved booth but sat mostly across from him.

"Drink order?" a young woman asked.

"I'll have the drink special tonight," Luca commented. The woman looked at me next.

"Ummm...Moscow Mule," I blurted out. It was a drink I had seen Mac order several times. I remember thinking it looked interesting and now seemed like the best time to try something new.

"How did you find this place?" I asked trying to restart the conversation.

"Several of the actors working with me heard about it and passed it along. It's been open a little over a year so they got bored with it and have moved on to the next 'it' place but I really enjoy it here, so I come at least once a week."

"How are you feeling about ending your show?" I asked trying to choose my words so that they made some sense.

"I'm ready for this run to be over. I have another project starting in four or five weeks that will be shot in Budapest and London so I'm looking forward to moving around a bit."

"Wow...those places sound amazing. What is a place you couldn't forget?"

"Interesting question...a place I can't forget is New York City. It's not exotic but in a time in my life where everyone is moving to L.A. and pushing me to do so I feel the pull of New York City, it's in my blood. I think I will always live in New York. How about you, you travel much?" I heard the question and I knew he was being genuine, but I couldn't help but belly laugh in response.

"Me? No. Other than the great state of Texas, I have been to Oklahoma once for a wedding and to New Mexico once to a friend's cabin. New York is my greatest adventure."

"Has this adventure been everything you wanted it to be?"

"Yes and no. I'm not entirely sure I knew what I wanted when I left so I don't know how to say it was a success."

"You left because of Austin?" he asked and I nodded. "You were engaged?" I again nodded. "That's serious business," he finally commented.

"Perhaps, part of it felt like child's play having known each other so long but then part of it felt serious and heavy, hence the reason I left. The reality is we have become two different people. We have known each other our whole lives. He works for my papa and wants to be a rancher. I love working with the horses, but ranching isn't really my thing. My mama had told us stories of New York growing up and I wanted to get out and have my own adventure so when he asked me to marry him, I felt I had to leave; otherwise, I was going to be stuck in a life I didn't want. The first person I met when I arrived was Mac. He got me set up at the Plaza and took me out showed me the sights, and introduced me to his friends," I rushed through the story.

"But Austin showed up here," Luca prompted.

"Yes, I sent a package home and he bribed my sister for the address and that rascal got on a plane and flew here to bring me home!" I said with exasperation.

"Didn't you fly here?"

"No, I took multiple trains…never been on a plane."

"Okay, go on," he said with an amused grin on his face.

"He just showed up here and wouldn't leave. I was so busy with Princess and working other odd jobs for Mac I didn't have time to address anything. The night of the party bus we finally got a moment alone and were able to talk. We were in a good place until you showed up," I said blowing a stray piece of hair out of my face.

"My first fight, yes I remember."

"Again, sorry about that," I said with a shrug.

"So, tell me about these odd jobs of yours."

"It started out just organizing people's closets but soon everyone wanted me to organize something for them. It's unimaginable all the stuff some people have and just how much they can squeeze into the smallest of places. Who knew my ranch work would translate to 5th Avenue. Mac is helping me manage the appointments. My time at the hotel was running out and I was looking for a place to stay then Mac got me a live-in dog watching job for...Princess."

"May's dog?"

"Yes."

"Logan when I first met you on that rooftop you were the singular fresh breath of air I was looking for in a somewhat crowded city. When I saw you on the street walking Princess the second time, it was more than fate. I knew that you were different, and I needed to get to know you. I was cavalier in my approach...I knew my fame was not impressive to you so I tried to be the big-time city boy showing the new girl the sites. On that party bus I saw another side to you and it grounded me back to reality. Your story and struggles are just as important as my own and I lost track of that. It's why I took a step back, I've been a little distant these past couple weeks and for that I wanted to apologize. I just needed some time to ground myself back to reality to be fair to you and give this, us, a fair chance." I just nodded when he was done speaking. It seemed as if Luca had been giving me as much thought as I had been giving him.

"I'm sorry about not being honest about Austin. I never imagined y'all would ever meet but it should not have happened like that," I added, and he nodded. We were silent for a moment as the waitress came over with our drinks.

"I'm curious as to what else is planned for your adventure?" he asked after taking a slow sip of his drink.

"I feel stuck now having to be with Princess so much of everyday. I feel as if my adventure has been paused. I still really want to see the ocean."

"You've never seen the ocean?!"

"No sir. Mama and papa took us to Galveston a couple times, but I want to see the actual Atlantic and someday the Pacific too," I added for good measure.

"I think we will have to remedy that," he said with a twinkle in his eye. With that he launched into a battery of questions, quizzing me on Texas and other things I have done and haven't done. It was well after midnight when we left 540. Luca offered to walk me several blocks back towards the apartment. As we walked, he pointed out several landmarks that had special meaning to him. After rounding one block in particular we encountered a large group, and someone must have recognized him because they shouted out his name. He initially just waived but tried to keep walking. Unsuccessful, we stopped, and Luca took several pictures with the group before we moved on. As we did he grabbed my hand as we strolled towards the apartment. About two blocks away he paused squeezing my hand.

"This is where I leave you," he stated leaning over and kissing me on the forehead. "Logan, I'm glad we were able to get everything out in the open tonight. In my business it's hard to find an authentic person that you can trust."

"Luca, what you're looking for isn't impossible to find. Back home what you're describing is everyone you encounter…the neighbors, the grocer, the general store manager, or the person who sits next to you in church. People are naturally good."

"That hasn't always been my experience, but I trust you and most importantly, I believe in you." I glanced as his features and for that moment it was as if time stood still. No matter where my life took me, I would remember that moment with Luca. It was the magical moment I had dreamed about since I was a little girl. The moment a spark happens between two people. A stranger passed by his — phone ringing that broke the spell.

"I should go," Luca said hailing a cab.

"Have a good night," I said stepping back from the curb.

"Sweet dreams Logan," he said getting into the cab. I stood and watched as the cab drove off. It was a moment made for the movies and I wasn't sure if I was still living in my daydreams or if this was reality, but I practically floated back the apartment unable to hide my smile.

CHAPTER 25

On Friday, I woke up to a still house. For the first time since living at May's apartment I had no plans, and no one was looking for me. Gladys had the weekend off and was going to visit her grandchildren in Long Island. Caroline who had become a close friend in the oddest of circumstances had some errands to run in the morning and was then treating herself to a massage this afternoon. Mac was with Sabrina shopping for wedding dresses and Luca had an early call this morning as this was his final performance weekend for *Franklin*. No additional jobs were scheduled and I sat in the living room cross legged with Princess in my lap casually sipping on coffee just watching the world.

"Are you ready to go on your walk?" I asked Princess rubbing her behind the ear. She let out a half bark as she jumped down off my lap and headed for the door.

"I guess that's a yes," I mumbled back with a smile. I slipped on a pair of shoes and got her leash on and we headed out into the city. Yet again this morning I could see a crowd outside the lobby from the elevator.

"I can't wait for Ms. MacKenzie to move out," I heard someone comment to Joe who worked in the lobby.

"We appreciate all our tenants until they leave us," he replied very diplomatically.

"Ahh, it's not her they want to see anyway. They are trying to catch a glimpse of the dreamy Luca Gaines," an older woman with silver hair replied causing Joe to chuckle. It was all I needed to hear as I crossed the lobby and exited out the door. Princess and I took our usual walk but as we neared the apartment, I couldn't stand the thought of going inside. The weather in New York had finally gotten a little cooler in the mornings and evenings. You could feel fall ready to settle in any day now as Labor Day quickly approached. I was excited about the idea of seeing a real fall with leaves changing color and temperatures adjusting accordingly. In Texas, all we had was yellow grass and green grass seasons, meaning it was either hot or cold; there was never a fall or spring. Instead, Princess and I changed directions and we headed to Central Park. Once there I found a lush piece of grass and laid down looking up at the clear blue sky. Princess, excited about all the grass, pranced around until she too, settled down curled up next to me. Soft snores could be heard from Princess as the phone in my pocket vibrated. Seeing it was Mac, my curiosity got the best of me and I answered.

"What are you doing?" he yelled with no greeting.

"Hello to you to sir," I replied turning over onto my side, much to Princess's dismay.

"You can't play both the role of May MacKenzie current love interest to Luca Gaines and the mistress," he blasted at me.

"What are you talking about?" I said feeling defensive.

"It's you in that picture, isn't it?" he accused.

"What picture?"

"The picture on the front of all the magazines. Sabrina and I are at Monique Lhuillier and I get this text from May just ranting about how deceitful Luca is being and how dare he 'cheat on her'...even though technically it's not even her. I tell May I don't know what she is talking about and she sends me a picture of Luca and you out and about in the city. Now I know it's you but May doesn't know it's you. You're two-timing the system Tex," he said exasperated.

"I didn't know anyone took a picture or cared," I said rather meekly.

"Tex, what are you doing?" He asked in a much softer tone.

"It was just me and Luca going out to dinner…it was just dinner."

"There is no such thing with Luca Gaines."

"What happens now?"

"I don't know but BE CAREFUL…May is not someone who deals with jealousy or deceit very well."

"I'm sorry I wasn't thinking," I said suddenly thinking about how this was going to affect Luca as well.

"Tex, I have to go but keep your head down and try to stay out of trouble."

"Yes sir."

"And Tex?"

"Yes?"

"Don't call me sir," he said, and I laughed knowing he was no longer angry with me.

"Well Princess, as usual I have made a mess out of things," I said scratching behind her ear when Mac and I disconnected. It was only a matter of moments later that my phone again vibrated. I reached down glancing at the number and saw that it was May's apartment building that was calling.

"This is Logan," I replied.

"Ms. Hunter, I do apologize for calling you, but Ms. Ester is not available," Joe responded referring to Gladys.

"She is out of town; how can I help?"

"There is a package here that needs to be signed for and instructions specify it has to be someone from the actual residence."

"Of course, I'll be there shortly."

When I entered the lobby there was no one there. I waited for a couple minutes at the desk even dinging the bell that sat on the counter. I finally gave up and went over to the elevator swiping my card for access to May's floor. When the doors to the elevator finally opened Joe stepped out.

"Sorry Joe, I came as fast as I could."

"It's no problem, Ms. Hunter. I was able to put the package in the suite."

"Oh okay." Joe stepped out and Princess and I stepped in. It was odd that he would have accepted a package on May's behalf but maybe the carrier was in a hurry. We got off the elevator and entered the apartment building.

"Hello?" A voice greeted me from inside the apartment startling me and causing Princess to erupt into a tirade of barking. After I had processed the voice, tears sprung from my eyes and streamed down my face.

"Mama?"

"Logan," she said coming through the kitchen and was now standing in front of me. Curiously, Princess quieted down and stood there wagging her tail.

"Mama." We embraced and stood there for at least five minutes.

"Logan it's okay," she said pulling away and taking in my full appearance.

"What are you doing here?" I questioned gathering myself together a little bit, trying to wipe away the tears.

"I saw some interesting pictures in this magazine the other day and I just figured it was time for me to come out here."

"What pictures?" I said warily but a hiccup escaped my lips causing it to come out 'wHHHAAtttictur'.

"There is time for that, why don't you show me around. This place is amazing." She changed the subject in a way only mothers can.

"Well let me do introductions first, this is Princess." I said scooping her up and coming closer to mama.

"Aww, isn't she adorable. Not nearly as menacing as Austin described her." To my surprise Princess did not bark and willingly let my mother pet her.

"Ain't that the berries," I exclaimed. "She usually doesn't like many people."

"I also heard that."

"What in fact did you hear from Austin and who is he blabbing to?" I narrowed my eyes now curious over what she already knew.

"Austin was just concerned about you, sweetie. But he just talked to me, didn't involve your sisters or anything." A small feeling of relief washed over me. I put Princess down and walked mama around the apartment. She would 'oohhh' and 'ahhh' at the appropriate parts until she saw May's bathroom.

"I love the ranch, don't get me wrong, but there are times I just miss a big old tub."

"Well you can certainly take a soak this evening." I commented surprised by this. I had never known mama to take a bath but the tub at home was older and small; she could never stretch out in it. We found our way back down to the living room where mama settled down on the sofa and Princess jumped up and snuggled with her.

"Anything to drink mama? Tea?"

"Wine?" she asked completely surprising me.

"White or red?"

"How about a big glass of red wine?"

"Red it is," I said pouring two glasses. I handed her a glass and we sat for several moments, enjoying the silence.

"The city has changed so much, and it hasn't at the same time," Mama finally commented.

"Did you fly?"

"Yes."

"Does papa know you're here?"

"Of course."

"Who will supervise everyone on the ranch?"

"You give me too much credit. The ranch will run itself just fine without me." I was skeptical but I nodded in agreement.

"Did Austin tell you where to find me?"

"Not so much Austin, but his friend Caroline."

"Caroline? She knew and she didn't tell me!" A flare of anger passed through my gut.

Big City Dreams

"It was a surprise visit Logan. Caroline is a good secret keeper." I said nothing just sat and waited. I knew Mama had something on her mind but from learned experience it was best to just let it come. Mama would share when she was ready.

"Logan honey, you look so different. So, grown up...your hair," she said reaching over and gently moving wayward pieces from my face.

"You mean it's not a fuzzy mess?"

"Or in a messy bun at all times."

"I have a friend, Grey. I hope you get to meet her. She is wonderful but has really shown me how to deal with all that stuff."

"I'm glad you finally listened to somebody." My phone buzzed in my pocket indicating a text message and out of reflex I glanced at the caller ID. It was Luca asking about late dinner plans.

"Is that the dreamy Luca Gaines?" Mama asked and I nodded without thinking.

"Wait...did Austin?" I commented, my eyes growing wide.

"Well Austin did mention a 'pretty looking dumb actor boy,' his words not mine," she said with a smile and I rolled my eyes.

"He's got a ten-gallon mouth."

"Logan, he was concerned. The Logan he came to see in New York City was not the same Logan who left Texas. He was not prepared for that. It's been a lot for him to process but I think Caroline is helping a little bit." I narrowed my eyes. I had suspected that they continued to talk but mama just confirmed it. I knew Austin was not my business anymore, but it still stung a little bit.

"What did Luca want?" mama asking, bringing us back around.

"He wanted to do dinner tonight after the show."

"I think that would be nice."

"I don't know... I have kind of messed things up."

"In what way."

"Well, I was hired to do this job and seeing him kind of complicates things."

"Logan that is the most tactful thing you have ever said," she said with pride in her voice.

"You think?" She nodded and got up from the sofa and reached into her bag.

"It wouldn't have anything to do with this?" she said, setting down two magazines in front of me. One was with me as May and the other was from last night with Lucan and me on the street.

"What about May?" I said automatically.

"Logan, I'm your mother and I know my daughter when I see her."

"Mama, I can't...people can't..."

"I asked your sister if she thought it looked like you and she rolled her eyes and said, 'in Logan's dreams' and dismissed the idea so I think your secret is safe."

"You asked Becky?" I cried, guessing at which sibling she was talking about.

"Just observationally."

"Mama!"

"Logan, start at the beginning." It was a statement not a request and I knew it. I sat there for several seconds contemplating what to say and mulling it over in my stubborn head. I knew mama would win, she always does. There was no secret keeping and not talking to mama was not an option. It was only a matter of time and she would wait. She always did. So, I did what she asked and I told her the whole story. She of course knew parts of it already from the times we had talked on the phone...but without interruptions or time limitations, I told her the whole story. When I was done, I got up and refilled our wine glasses.

"Well I think we should go to dinner with Luca tonight," she finally said.

"I just told you all that and you think that is a good idea?"

"Logan, I don't think any of this has been a great idea but we have to eat."

"And to clarify you want to meet Luca Gaines?"

"Well, I want to meet the man at the center of this but mostly because he's important to you. I can tell the way you talk about him that he means a great deal to you." I just nodded my head mostly out of nerves and took my phone out. It did not go unnoticed that the only option mama gave was dinner as a threesome. Going to dinner alone with Luca tonight was out of the question.

"Hey Luca," I said, a bit surprised when he answered.

"Logan, I don't have a lot of time, but I was wondering if you were free for dinner tonight."

"Luca, I had a surprise guest this afternoon."

"Another ex-boyfriend?"

"Well, aren't you funny. No, my mama came for a surprise visit."

"Your mother?"

"Yes."

"You should spend time with her then."

"Actually, would you be up for dinner with us both?"

"I don't want to intrude. I know you haven't seen her in a while."

"Her words, 'we have to eat'."

"If you're sure. I know just the place but it will be late."

"Luca nothing fancy, just a normal dinner."

"I got it, don't worry. I have to go."

"Bye."

"Don't worry Logan, this will be great. See you later." I wasn't sure but I disconnected.

"We are all set for dinner tonight. Do you want to take a nap or rest up?"

"Logan, I may be older but this is a city that doesn't sleep. Let's get dressed and go exploring. See what I remember around here."

"Yes ma'am." With that I went upstairs to get ready for a totally unexpected adventure.

CHAPTER 26

We had not made it very far into our adventure as we were waiting in line at Starbucks, per mama's request. She declared that while the coffee at home was good, she missed the variety that a coffee shop had to offer. I was seeing my mama in a whole new light every twist and turn of this trip. She was in the middle of telling me a story about when she and her cousin Loraine were on a field trip to the city in the eighth grade and got separated from their group. If I had to guess, it sounded like more on purpose than by accident, but it was just a guess. Instead of panicking, they asked the next available stranger directions to Macy's and spent the afternoon wandering around the department store. She said they eventually met back up with the group when my phone vibrated in my pocket. I ignored the call and focused on the rest of the story that mama was telling. The phone vibrated a second time and mama stopped and looked at me.

"Sorry, I can turn it off."

"You are the worst at answering calls, just answer the call."

"It's just my friend Mac."

"Will I get to meet him?"

"Get to meet who?" Mac's booming voice came from behind me.

"Mac?" I said surprised and delighted by his appearance.

"I was passing through the neighborhood, seeing what you were up to and needed some caffeine. I thought it was you but couldn't be sure because I didn't recognize this beautiful woman standing with you," he said turning to mama.

"Catherine Hunter." It was odd to hear her use her full name. Papa and people who were not her children always called her Cat on the ranch.

"Logan's sister?" Mac replied and I couldn't help but roll my eyes. It was too much, too over the top.

"My mama," I replied as the barista asked for our order.

"Aren't you sweet," I heard mama say as I ordered a venti iced vanilla latte, mama ordered a grande iced cafe americano with an extra shot of espresso, and Mac ordered a grande lightly sweet chi latte with almond milk.

"What are you dolls up to now?" Mac inquired.

"Mama wanted to reacquaint herself with New York City. How was dress shopping with Sabrina?"

"Over the top — and I loved every minute of it. I think she said 'yes' to a dress, but we will see. Sometimes she changes her mind at the last minute."

"What kind of dress?" Mama asked.

"Wedding," I said.

"Monique Lhuillier" Mac said at the same time.

"Well, those are two different things," Mama said with a smile. I suddenly had a feeling that mama's New York experiences were much more educational in fashion and such than she led on.

"You are a fan of Lhuillier?" Mac questioned. I could see the wheels turning in his head, assuming he was making the same connections as I was.

"Who isn't?" she replied.

"Am I the only one? I'm still not sure if I know exactly what Lhuillier is," I sighed in defeat as Mac and mama laughed. I thought with mama being there I might have some strength in numbers, seems I was wrong.

"Mama what next?"

"Is John's Pizza still a thing?" she asked.

"On Bleecker street?" Mac replied.

"Yes, that is it! I have missed real New York style pizza, you just can't get the real thing in Texas," she exclaimed with delight.

"I guess that is where we are headed next." Mac lead the way and chatted with mama the entire way as I hung behind. I didn't mind, I was still trying to wrap my head around the new side of 'Catherine Hunter.' It was moments like these that I missed home and commiserating with my sisters.

By some miracle when we arrived, we were seated within thirty minutes and Mac ordered a round of beers and a large margarita pizza.

"Mac, are you in cahoots with Logan on her current adventure?" Mama casually asked as she sipped her beer. I knew this game, it was a trap and I had no way to warn Mac.

"Which adventure do you want to know more about?" He replied not fully taking the bait. '*Well played*,' I thought to myself taking a sip of my beer. My eyes darting back to mama.

"The one that landed her on the front page of *People*." I avoided eye contact and continued to sip my beer.

"Catherine, Logan is the greatest partner in crime," Mac replied instead, unphased by the Spanish Inquisition from mama.

"Hmmm, very true. When she was in high school, she would sneak out of her room and climb down this ridiculous oak tree right outside the house. She was clever enough to remember to bring dog treats to bribe the dogs. Now I know most nights she was going to the hay barn. But on one particular night she headed to the road and got into a parked car with no lights on." Mac was hooked…he was leaning in, in anticipation. My mind was reeling over the revelation that mama knew about my night time adventures, she had never said a word.

"At first I thought it was Austin she was creeping off with probably to go necking or something…"

"MAMA," I said in sheer embarrassment.

"What?"

"Necking is not a thing and totally gross."

"Anyway…when I looked closer it was the car of the daughter of the Minister," she said her voice almost dropping to a whisper.

"Uh-oh," I commented, and mama flashed me a mega smile.

"Why uh-oh?" Mac commented lost.

"Uh-oh because the next morning all the floors in high school were covered in a fine layer of cooking grease and on top of the grease was a single layer, packed wall to wall of hundreds if not thousands of water balloons. It took the administration days to clean it up. With the grease they couldn't get a good hold on any of those slippery suckers nor could they get any type of standing. To this day no one knows who did it, the prank is infamous. I on the other hand have my suspicions." I could feel their eyes on me.

"Why do you think of me?" I replied sheepishly.

"In a class of maybe one hundred people, there was only a handful smart enough to come up with the idea and execute it. There was the sneaking out at night the night before, our paint sprayer went missing, and I think what did it for me is you never once gossiped about it or brought it up. I mean this was the talk of the town for weeks, still comes up now years later, and you didn't have an opinion? No not my Logan." She had me, they were fair points.

"Tex, was it you?" Mac said.

"I did not work alone," I finally said and burst into laughter. "Mama you never said a word!"

"You could have been suspended."

"Don't I know it," I said with almost relief in my voice.

"How did you do it?" Mac asked.

"Warmed the grease and put it in the paint sprayer. If you did it quick enough it came out evenly. Once the coat was down, we just kept dumping water balloons until the place was full. We almost got busted, it took all night. We were leaving out the back when Principle Skidmore was coming in the front."

"Who was with you?"

"Not my place to tell."

"After all this time."

"Yes, after all this time," I replied. The reality was I had almost forgotten about the prank. I had a good dose of fear about being caught and suspended prior to graduation but the adventure was worth the risk.

"Mac, the point of this story is that if Logan could do this and never tell a soul. I know she must be up against a wall if she came clean about your current fiasco."

"You told her?"

"She's my mama plus she had both covers," I sulked.

"Catherine, if I'm being honest it carries a bit of risk but more for the actress than us. Plus, the money was too good to pass up."

"I like an honest man."

"Logan was a willing participate," he added.

"You and I remember that conversation completely differently," I commented back, and he gave me a stupid grin just as the pizza arrived.

"I'm not saying I'm against it..." mama started.

"You're not?" All this time I was waiting for the lecture, the moral high ground, values story and it wasn't coming.

"Nope. Logan you are a grown woman. You make your own decisions. This one is a bit crazy, even for you. What I needed to know is if this group of people you have assembled and befriended have your back."

"That's a good mama," Mac said and I couldn't help think if it made him think of his own family.

"The best," I finally said leaning into her and she kissed the top of my head.

"Catherine, you know how to raise'em," Mac finally said raising his mostly finished beer in our direction.

"Thank you, sir," she commented and I smiled. I knew what Mac would have to say about that.

******

After pizza, Mac wandered around with us for a little bit before he bid us adieu. He announced he had a date and was going out on the town, so he needed to go 'make himself presentable.' Mama and I left him at the subway station and headed back to May's apartment.

"Mama, did you really come here just to meet my friends?"

"Mostly. Austin painted a rather unreliable picture of what was going on in the city."

"Austin did not enjoy his New York experience."

"He doesn't understand this life."

"Do you miss this life?" I asked her in response.

"Sometimes, but it's a fleeting thought here and there. I am, however, glad for the visit under the guise of helping you out."

"I bet Becky loved that."

"Oh, the girls begged to come with me. That would not have been helpful and those girls couldn't hang," Mama said causing me to bust out laughing.

"You think I can?"

"You are my daughter and I have heard your stories. I know you can."

"Fair enough," I said locking my arm with mama and leaning my head on her shoulder as we strolled back to the apartment.

******

It was now close to eleven in the evening and mama and I were waiting by the stage door of the Walter Playhouse where the production of *Franklin* was playing. After leaving Mac and going back to the apartment, mama and I took Princess on an extended walk. After that mama made a couple phone calls back home to make sure everything was in order while I flipped through the numerous movie channels, deciding on nothing. After mama finished up her calls, she declared she needed to shower and clean up. I started thinking about what I was going to wear and was moving clothes from one stack to another and I was no further along when mama appeared in my doorway.

"Still at it?" she commented coming over to look at my stacks.

"What are you wearing, mama?"

"I thought I might come and see what you had to offer," she said now peering over my shoulder.

"How about this?" I held up a light creme sweater with a very subtle navy detail. Mama mulled this over finally nodding in approval.

"I have a pair of dark wash jeans," she said over her shoulder as she exited the room just as quickly as she entered. I finally settled on a pair of moss green billowy pants with a belted waist and a black blouse with lace sleeves.

"You look very nice, Logan," mama said as we stood at the door.

"You don't look like my mama," I commented back. She looked so youthful, carefree. New York City was good for her.

"But I still am," she said with a gentle smile.

"I found this after you left. It will look good as a layer," I said holding a white jean jacket up for her.

"A layer? New York has really changed you," she commented to herself taking the jacket.

"I was just thinking about the effect the city has on people."

"I always liked to think it was a city that gave you room to grow."

"Profound as always," I commented as we walked out the door and headed for the elevator.

We stood by the back door waiting on Luca. He had sent me a text earlier stating that the show was over around ten, but he had a donor thing and would be out by the door as soon as he could. Now we waited. It wasn't long before the door opened, and a group of seven people emerged all laughing and talking amongst themselves. At the back of the group was Luca. He was seriously studying his phone, he had a crease over the bridge of his nose that made him look a little angry. When he glanced up and saw us, his expression changed and he flashed us a big smile.

"Logan," he said giving me a big hug and a small kiss on the forehead.

"Luca, this is my mama, Mrs. Catherine Hunter."

"Mrs. Hunter," he said as she extended her hand. He looked at her for a moment and went in for a hug instead.

"Catherine works," mama said with a chuckle as Luca hugged her.

"Where to?" I asked.

"Uncle Richard's Tavern," he said stepping up to the curb and hailing a cab. In no time, a yellow cab pulled up and Luca held the door open for us.

"How was the show?" I asked after a moment of silence in the cab.

"It was good, it's strange to believe that tomorrow will be my last night."

"What is next for you?" Mama asked.

"I have a movie coming up that will require some travel. Maybe a small vacation? I always think the possibilities are endless, but the projects quickly seem to add up."

"How was the donor thing?" I inquired.

"It was good. It was a big hot shot law firm. They are huge donors so the group there was eclectic. I met some fascinating people. There was this young girl who was this snowboarding prodigy there with her uncle. She seems to be traveling more than I am. She was off to Europe next week for another competition. I was more interested in her story than telling my own. Then there was a group of friends that seemed to be having their own party within a party. They were cool, turns out they have known each other since grade school. One of the women just had her novel on the New York Time's Bestseller list and her husband is a rock star."

"Doesn't sound that boring," Mama commented.

"Tonight was great. I don't know if I was just being nostalgic over the ending of my run in the show or just appreciating the moment more than normal. But enough about me, Catherine what brings you to the city?"

"I always meet all of Logan's boyfriends," she deadpanned.

"Long list?" Luca commented without missing a beat.

"MAMA have you lost your..." I was so embarrassed I couldn't even finish my statement.

"I'm kidding y'all," she said in a fit of giggles.

"I'm so glad you're tickled."

"Logan, it's fine," Luca said reaching over and giving my hand a little squeeze.

"I just came for a visit. It's been a long time since I've been here. Plus, Logan has been telling me about all her adventures and I wanted to come see for myself."

"Austin told her that I was involved with a group of misfits," I added as commentary.

"Logan, be nice."

"I was."

"How is Austin?" Luca asked rubbing his cheek and now it was my turn to burst into a fit of giggles. I was saved only by the fact that we had arrived at our destination. Uncle Richard's Tavern was not a large establishment — it was long and narrow. There was a total of ten tables lined up, five on the left and five on the right. It seemed they were expecting us because as soon as we entered Luca gave his name we were whisked off to the furthest table.

"You eat here often?"

"Often enough," he said cryptically.

"Luca! It's been too long," the waiter said leaning over and giving Luca and awkward side hug.

"Joey, I didn't know you worked here now?"

"They roped me in, you can only stay away from the family business for so long."

"Let me introduce you to Logan and Catherine," Luca said by way of introductions.

"This is Joey Balaste, his father is Richard."

"And y'all are related?" I asked for clarification.

"Uncle Richard is literally my uncle," Luca replied. "Well he is an uncle to a dozen or so of us — I'm not special or anything," he clarified.

"Ain't nothing special about you Luca," Joey teased in an accent that was thicker than any Texas accent I had ever heard. "But I'm being rude, what can I get everyone to drink?" Joey took our drink orders and gave us the specials of the evening before departing the table.

"You know everyone," I commented

"Not everyone, but I know a good handful of people."

"Catherine, what is your favorite part of the city?" Luca asked.

"There are so many great things but I'm a traditionalist. I love Macy's which includes the parades and the Brooklyn Bridge and Central Park."

"All solid options."

"Logan do you have a favorite spot yet?" Mama asked.

"I don't know if I have a favorite spot yet...The Plaza was pretty fantastic," I mused thinking back to my first couple of nights in the city.

"The Plaza is a staple," Luca commented as Joey came back with our drinks.

"Ready to order?"

"I think we are," Mama said before launching into her order. Our conversation continued to flow through dinner and desert until it was nearly two in the morning, long past closing but a benefit of being related to the restaurant owner.

"Thank you for letting me tag along," Mama said as we now stood outside of the restaurant. Luca had hailed us a cab for the ride home.

"The pleasure was mine," he said and reached out for a hug with mama. After the embrace mama climbed into the cab leaving us on the curb.

"Tonight was special and probably the most normal I have felt in a long time," I admitted to us both.

"Will I see you tomorrow?"

"Me, no, but you will see May one final time," I commented which only caused me to think about tomorrow's agenda.

"I'll be glad when this whole thing is over."

"Me, too, but regardless I am excited to see your show."

"I'll be interested to know what you think."

"Good night, Logan," Luca said and leaned down and kissed me.

"Good night Luca." With that I got in the cab and waived at Luca as we pulled away. I leaned over resting my head on mama's shoulder with a loud sigh.

"I know, sweetie, I know." Mama said stroking my hair.

"Know what?" I mumbled.

"I know the sigh of love when I hear it."

"Love?"

"You may not see it yourself but it's there." I was too tired to argue with her. I just sat in the back quietly as our cab whisked down the dark city streets headed back to the apartment.

CHAPTER 27

The end was finally in sight, the last day I was going to be May. I had not realized how much I wanted this to end until the day arrived. I had been mulling over mama's question about my favorite spot in the city all morning, making the realization that my personal adventure was on hold. Originally, I thought dressing up like May and doing all the events as her was its own adventure. What I had learned was that the time and energy spent turning me into May, babysitting me as May, and then wrapping up the event, was mentally taxing and draining.

"Tell me how this all works?" Mama questioned me as we sat on the sofa waiting for everyone to arrive. It was just a little past three in the afternoon.

"I put on a wig, go out, wave, stay quiet, and come home."

"You stay quiet?"

"Most of the time."

"You do this alone?"

"Oh no, Grey does the makeup, Caroline does the clothes, and Mac does the babysitting."

"Wow, it takes a whole team?"

"To be fair, I think she has this team and then some when she's here in person."

"As your grandmama says 'sounds like she has a bulb or two burned out on that string'."

"Exactly."

"I hate to say it Logan, but you might too, to go along with it."

"Mama, but the money..."

"What does your papa say about money?"

"Health is better than wealth."

"Mmmm."

"It's the last time," I said, and I could hear the slight whine in my voice. We were both staring at each other when the doorbell rang. Princess got up from her pillow and followed me to the door, barking the entire way.

"Grey!"

"Logan, Princess, as always good to see you," she teased coming in without giving Princess any attention. I scooped Princess and cooed with her. From the kitchen, I could hear mama introducing herself to Grey. Before I shut the door completely, I heard another voice.

"Hold the door." I peeked around the door to see Caroline coming down the hallway, arms full of bags.

"What is all that?" I asked trying to take a bag from her.

"I couldn't decide on a final outfit but also the dry cleaning."

"Grey and my mama are here."

"Your mama?!"

"Oh, don't act all sweet. I know that you knew."

"I was asked to keep it quiet," she said meekly going past me into the apartment.

"You could have given me a clue."

The apartment had a steady hum as Caroline sorted clothes from the bags she brought, occasionally going into May's closet and coming out with another piece of this or that. Mama chatted with Grey as she took all her makeup out and set it up in May's bedroom.

"I'm going to take Princess on a walk," I said entering the bedroom.

"I'll go with you, sweetie," mama said looking up from her conversation.

"Are you sure?"

"I want to soak up as much time as I can in the city."

"Sounds like a great plan." I waved to Caroline and Grey as I got Princess's leash and we were out the door. I let mama lead the way on the walk, only stopping once to get coffee and pastries.

"Mama, why haven't you traveled back to the city with papa? I can tell you miss it."

"I tried once."

"Papa has been to the city?!" I was flooded with hundreds of images of the city, but I could not place papa in any of them.

"Well..." Just as she started my phone vibrated. Looking quickly I saw it was Caroline and I hit ignore.

"You were small - maybe 4 or 5?" My phone rang. I hit ignore.

"Did you fly?" I asked as the phone vibrated again and I switched it to silent after mama gave me a look.

"Answer it."

"No, I want to hear your story first."

"Yes, we flew, it was a couple weeks before Christmas. Your papa did fine with flying. I think he was nervous, but he never let on even during the slight turbulence we had right before landing. We landed, got our luggage, and checked into a hotel. Things were going well. We got dressed for dinner and ventured out just as it started snowing. It felt magical — to me. His complaining started around the time the ground had a light dusting on it. It was too cold, too crowded, people were driving too fast, the food was too expensive, the portions were too small, the people were stand-offish. You pick something — he found something wrong with it. By the next morning there was almost a foot of snow on the ground. I convinced him to leave the hotel and walk around and see the sights anyway. There was more complaining. His feet were wet, his fingers were frozen, the subway smelled, the cabs were dirty, the coffee was too fancy. By the second morning, I was ready to inflict serious bodily harm to him. There had not been a moment he wasn't complaining. I could never pinpoint a specific moment or event that happened to make him so unhappy other than it wasn't Texas. We cut the vacation short and flew home a day early. We didn't speak for the entire trip home nor the drive home. It was two days later when I was calm enough to ask him more about the trip. He simply said, "it wasn't for me." After that I never asked him to go with me again. I figured if I came back to the city it would be by myself or with one of you girls. I never imagined one of my girls would take off for the city without me."

"I never heard that story before."

"It's not that interesting," she commented as we entered the lobby.

"Are you ready for this?" she asked as we entered the elevator.

"I know this sounds crazy but I'm actually excited to see Luca's performance tonight. It doesn't matter how I'm dressed, it's still me living the experience."

"That it is," she said as I unlocked the apartment and instantly heard shouting. Princess started pulling on the leash, barking frantically. I barely had a chance to unleash her and she took off on a barking tirade into the apartment.

"Hello?" I called out. The only thing that responded was more shouting and barking. I quickly followed the noise.

"Why the hell won't she stop barking?" I heard again, unable to place the voice.

"Princess," I called coming up the stairs. Moments later Princess came toward me wagging her tail.

"Who are you?" I heard directed at me as I scooped up Princess. When I stood up, I came face to face with May MacKenzie.

"Logan, ma'am."

"Logan who? Why is my dog barking at me?"

"Logan is the dog sitter," Caroline now came up behind May. Her whole demeanor was different. When we made eye contact, she mouthed 'sorry' and motioned to her phone, indicating she tried to call me.

"Princess, come to mama," May cooed at Princess who let out a slight growl.

"You have brainwashed my dog," she shrilled.

"You must be plumb crazy," I said unable to help myself. I took several steps toward May.

"Catherine Hunter, it's a pleasure to meet you," Mama said suddenly appearing from behind me with her hand outstretched.

"Who the hell are you?" May responded yet again. Ignoring mama's hand.

"I'm Logan's mother, just in for a visit," she said sweet as sugar.

"Guests in my house — that is not allowed."

"Actually, May, per the contract she is allowed to have one guest stay at the residence as long as you are not present," Caroline chimed in, in a monotone voice.

"I'm present now, aren't I?" she snapped back.

"But you're not supposed to be. Hence without proper notice she is not in violation."

"Whose side are you on? AND why can't I hold my dog?"

"No one said anything about your not being able to hold Princess," Mama said very calmly, nudging me slightly.

"Here you go," I said holding Princess out ever so slightly. Princess wiggled in my arms but May reached out and took her. Princess grunted but did not bark or growl.

"Good girl," both May and I said at the same time toward Princess.

"You are dismissed," May said toward me turning around. I stood there awkwardly unsure of what was going on. Caroline looked at me and the retreating figure.

"May, what are your plans this evening?"

"I'm going to the show tonight with Luca."

"You're what?" I asked unable to stay quiet.

"Why are you talking?"

"I think what Logan meant to say was that I know you had made previous arrangements, which we are perfectly happy to carry out."

"Where is that girl that plays me?"

"It's Logan."

"Who's Logan."

"The woman who has been covering for you is Logan."

"The dog walker?" She now turned around and looked at me for the first time, taking in my full appearance.

"You?"

"Me."

"Well, your services are no longer needed. When I break up with someone, I do it in person," she said once again turning and leaving.

"Caroline..." she snapped her fingers. She said something that was mumbled but I was able to make out the end of her statement, "she doesn't even look like me." My blood boiled as she walked away from me. I had every intention to follow her when mama stepped in.

"Logan, sweetie. Let's go."

"But mama she is meaner than a wasp."

"Not now Logan," she said in her 'don't mess with me' voice.

"Yes ma'am," I replied automatically. She led me by the elbow out of May's bedroom and down the stairs to her own room, closing the door. I instantly started pacing.

"Who does she think she is? What is she doing here? She makes a wasp look cuddly." I stopped to look at mama who was now sitting on the bed.

"Maybe you should make a couple phone calls."

"Luca!" I cried, thinking of the horror that awaited him this evening. I pulled my phone out to see no less than a dozen missed calls from Caroline and one text that read, 911. I dialed his number and got his voice mail, leaving a message. I then sent a couple texts with my own warning.

"There."

"And..."

"And what?"

"Maybe you should call Mac?"

"How are you thinking straight? She was off her rocker."

"One of us needs to be calm." She replied as I hit send on his number.

"Mac!"

"Tex, what is going on? I got a series of crypt texts from Caroline."

"The May MacKenzie showed up in the apartment just now."

"Shut your mouth."

"I'm not joking. She is planning on attending the show tonight because in her words 'when I break up with someone, I do it in person'."

"This is not good."

"Did you talk with her?" He followed up quickly.

"Talk with her? I barely got a word in and when I did, she didn't like what I had to say. I was about to pop her in that new nose of hers when mama stepped in."

"Tex, did she say anything else?"

"She said and I quote, 'she doesn't even look like me' about my looks."

"Is that all?"

"Isn't that enough."

"Perhaps, but with May you never know."

"Let me figure out what is going on."

"Mac, I need to get into that show tonight. I cannot let her humiliate Luca."

"Tex the show is beyond sold out…it has been for months."

"Mac, please?"

"I'll see what I can do," he said and disconnected. I continued to pace back and forth when there was a knock on the door.

"Come in," mama called back. Grey poked her head into the room.

"You guys want any company?"

"Did she kick you out too?"

"She called my products second rate and told Caroline to call Javier immediately for her 'usual'," she said using air quotes for the last part.

"Come in." Grey rolled her cosmetics suitcase into the room and sat down next to mama.

"Mama, she is…"

"I know Logan, you have made your opinion on this very clear."

"I second that opinion for what it's worth," Grey commented.

"Your hair is beautiful," Grey said distracted by mamas' hair.

"That is kind of you."

"Can I style it?"

"I don't think that is necessary anymore."

"Mac told me to make sure you were both presentable."

"Presentable for what?"

"For the final curtain call for one Luca Gaines."

"Shut the front door, no way."

"That man is incredible," mama remarked.

"That he is." With that Grey started helping mama with her hair and makeup. They chatted like life-long friends who were not in the middle of a storm named May MacKenzie.

"My clothes are upstairs but I ain't going near that witch."

"See if Caroline will bring you anything," Grey commented.

"Poor Caroline," I said thinking of her following May around.

"No one was more disappointed when May came bursting through that door than Caroline. She went white as a ghost and it was only seconds later that May was yelling at her to do this and do that. She glanced at the clothes Caroline had been laying out and pushed them all to the floor so she could lie on the bed. She laid down with her arm over her face telling Caroline how she had fired her other assistant and just had to come home. I thought Caroline was going to start crying." I sent a text to Caroline unsure if she would respond.

My phone pinged, it was a text from Mac, 'You and your Mom are a go for *Franklin*. Look presentable. Pick up the tickets from Gabe at the ticket counter. Tickets under Dr. Jackson.'

'You're amazing,' I texted back.

'I owe a friend a HUGE favor. I hate being indebted to anyone.'

'I REALLY appreciate it.' I knew Mac would not let me live this down. He was used to people owing him, not the reverse.

'We will see if it makes a difference,' he texted back. There was soft scratching at the door. I opened it to find Princess standing on the other side wagging her tail.

"You are going to get us into trouble," I commented picking her up and scratching behind her ear.

"I think you might get to keep her," Caroline commented coming down the hallway with a bag in her hands.

"Why?"

"She bit May's finger causing her to chip a nail."

"The horror."

"Logan, watch yourself," Mama warned from under a set of large curlers.

"I brought several options I was going to have you choose from for tonight," Caroline continued as if mama had not spoken.

"Won't May wear them?" I asked.

"Not a chance in hell. These were mostly my creations anyway. Completely off brand."

"Caroline, are you doing okay?" Grey asked.

"It's fine, this is my job."

"Your job sucks," I said unable to hold back. Caroline darted her eyes at me, and I could see them get glassy.

"Oh no, I didn't mean..."

"Yes, you did...and my job does suck. It was different before. I hate to say it Logan, but you have grown on me. It was just different working with you and Mac around and not being around May almost 24 hours a day, seven days a week. Having the break and her just showing up didn't give me any time to mentally prepare. But what would I do if I don't do this?" She suddenly wailed causing everyone to stop what they were doing.

"Literally, anything," I commented back.

"Caroline, honey, I think what Logan is trying to say is that you're very talented and could explore other options. You would be slightly confused by what she just said because she didn't use her best words." Mama was always lecturing me about this. I wasn't sure if I should give Caroline a hug — I took a couple steps closer to her.

"What are you doing?" she suddenly said.

"I was going to give you a hug."

"No that will make it worse. Plus, we have to get you ready. I don't know what is going to go down tonight but May seems fired up about it." I just nodded, not knowing what to say. Grey finished with mama's hair and started in on my hair while Caroline dressed mama. When she was done with Mama, she focused her energy back on me.

"Let's go ahead and slide you into this." She held up a pretty navy dress. It wasn't until it was mostly on that I saw it was actually a very fine lace pattern.

"Caroline, this doesn't fit." I said tugging at the front that was now exposing most of my bra.

"You will need to take your bra off."

"You must be off your rocker."

"No really, Logan. We will use double sided tape to make sure the dress won't go anywhere."

"You're going to duct tape me into this dress?"

"It's not duct tape, this stuff costs twice as much. It's fashion tape."

"Because that makes a difference."

"Logan have you been this difficult the entire time you have been here?" Mama asked.

"Yes," replied Caroline very quickly.

"I just don't understand. If you must tape me into it, aren't you showing too much?"

"No," everyone in the room replied. I threw my arms up in the air in defeat. Caroline started cutting squares of tape and I removed my bra.

"The key is not to have too many moments," Caroline was explaining to mama who had asked her a question that I didn't hear.

"You can't have a high slit, low back, high collar, dramatic cape, and then be risqué at the same time. You have to keep it classy."

"Caroline, this is so elegant."

"Logan, come here," Grey called me into the bathroom. Caroline followed still taping me in places I did not want to be taped.

"This material gives the illusion of being transparent, but you will be mostly covered."

"Sounds good."

"Well it won't get the same attention it was going to get if you were May but at least you will appreciate it," she said rather harshly when she stepped back.

"Thanks?" I replied.

"Sorry, I'm in a mood."

"Sure thing."

"Oh Logan, you look stunning," mama commented when I emerged from the bathroom. Caroline helped me fasten a pair of very tall black strappy heals on while Grey fussed with final details.

"Thank you, mama."

"Let's take a picture."

"Mama is that necessary?"

"This makes your prom dress look like a Wednesday evening chapel service." I didn't argue with her. I was relieved that when I finally looked in the mirror, I still looked like myself. I will admit it was a more glamorous version of myself, but it was still me.

"Are you going to be able to walk in those?" Mama suddenly asked, eyeing my shoes with skepticism.

"Mama, believe it or not, these are not the tallest shoes Caroline has dressed me in."

"Not by a long shot," Caroline commented.

"Now what?" I asked.

"You and your mother go and enjoy the show. May will be leaving later as she wants to make a grand entrance but not too early; she has to wait around and talk to everyone before the show starts."

"Aren't you going?"

"I am going to be there but not in the show. I will walk whatever carpet or entrance they have to make sure she looks okay but once she is seated, I will probably come back to the apartment and wait for May to come back unless she wants me to stay in which case I usually wait in the car."

"Why not go home?"

"There is an after party. We will do an outfit change."

"Am I going to the after party?"

"Heck if I know. The original plan did not have you going to the after party as May."

"Logan, you wanted an adventure."

"Let's go and see what this night holds for us." Princess barked and wagged her tail, coming over to sniff my dress.

"That material is not puppy proof," Caroline said kneeling down and grabbing Princess.

"Caroline!"

"What?"

"You just picked up Princess."

"OH MY, I did…I wasn't thinking. Well I was thinking about not ruining the dress. She has never let me hold her before." Caroline was now beside herself. Scratching her ear and rubbing her face into Princess's neck. Princess let out a grunt as she snuggled into the nook of Caroline's arm.

"What a day today has been," mama commented.

"You need to go," Grey said as she gathered her things from around the room.

"Thank you both so much." Grey and Caroline nodded and then shooed us out of the apartment.

CHAPTER 28

Mama hailed us a cab and we slowly made our way over to the theater. It would have been faster to walk but Mama said that we had to think about our feet. The area was crowded and the front entrance was blocked for all the VIP arrivals so the cab driver had to drop us off at the corner and we walked the last block anyway. As we got closer to the entrance so many people were moving around and people were taking photos; names were being called out left and right. We stood there for a couple of moments with mama mumbling nice things about so many of the people around us.

"Excuse me miss," a man with a camera approached us.

"Yes sir?"

"Are you here with anyone?"

"We are here to see Luca," I stammered. With the mention of Luca's name, the man's eyebrows rose in what appeared to be interest.

"What she means to say is that we are excited to see Luca Gaines in his last performance. Aren't you honey?" Mama said sweet as honey butter. The man was completely caught off guard with mamas' statement and just nodded in amusement.

"Well how about a photo to capture the evening?" he followed up. I was so used to having my picture taken as May that this request did not seem odd or out of place to me. Mama on the other hand declined the invitation and sent the man on his merry way.

"These people are strangers — can't just be taking your picture," she finally said when he was gone. I just shrugged my shoulders and continued my way to the box office weaving through the crowded lobby. The call window where Mac said the tickets would be had the longest line. As we stood in line, I could tell there was a buzz of excitement in the air; people milled around chatting with each other, laughing and having a good time. I on the other hand was a nervous wreck. I kept scanning the room hoping by some miracle Luca would be walking around. I had tried to call him two more times in the cab ride over. Mama told me to stop fussing but I couldn't help it. I felt personally responsible for Luca being in this situation. The line slowly crept forward and mama tugged at my arm.

"Stop fidgeting and act like you belong here." It was something she said to each and every one of my brothers and sisters almost all the time. When she said it, she meant that we needed to stop what we were doing and remember that we were in a public space where people can see us, and we needed to act a certain way. One time when we were younger, she even fussed at papa with her phrase. I could never really remember what had occurred to make her say it, but I sure remembered everything after that moment. Papa got really red in the face and mama just sat there with her hand flat on the table in front of her and starred at him. He eventually set his beer down, got up and walked quickly and quietly out of the restaurant. We children sat there still as still could be for about 10-MISSISSIPPIs before we launched into a series of questions for mama. She did not answer a single question and gave us all a certain look she had, where she would raise just one eyebrow slightly and then stare directly into your eyes without blinking. It was an intense look and one that you never wanted to be on the receiving end. After we all settled down, we ate the rest of the meal in silence. When dinner was done, she got up calmly, paid and we followed. Papa was waiting in the truck for us. On the ride home the only sound was that of the radio playing an old country western song.

"Mama, back when we were little, you once fussed at papa, why?"

"What brings that up now?"

"The memory just popped into my head, thought I would ask."

"Your father had had a little too much to drink and said something inappropriate to the waitress. We had a long discussion about it when I was ready."

"How long did that take?"

"Five days."

"Y'all didn't speak for five days?"

"It wasn't something that should be taken lightly."

"I never knew."

"You don't need to know everything Logan. Sometimes things are best left for two people to figure out on their own." With that we were finally at the box office. The woman behind the counter was very nice but looked exhausted from the dark bags she had under her eyes.

"Long day?" I asked without expecting an actual answer.

"The longest day you could imagine. Been here since nine this morning and my six-month-old at home didn't sleep last night — up all night with a fever and cough. Going on fumes."

"Is Gabe here?" I questioned reading from Mac's text.

"He's on break," she commented back.

"Can you help me with tickets then? Under Dr. Jackson." She nodded and started flipping through several stacks of small envelopes.

"Cold with your baby?" Mama inquired of the lady. The lady looked startled for a moment and lowered her voice to explain the symptoms to mama. Mama was mulling them over as I tugged on her sleeve. She shushed me with a quick glance. It was long enough for me to pull out my phone again and text and call Luca, again, still no answer.

"Mama," I whined a little bit in her direction. She finally said something and came over to where I was.

"Logan, you catch more bees with honey than vinegar."

"What does that mean?"

"If you really listen to people sometimes, they tell you what you want to hear. For example, Beth at the window had a sick infant and just wanted someone to validate her feelings and her tiredness. After that she did share that you will not see Luca before the show as he is doing major press before the performance tonight. Also, VIP guests, including May, are sitting stage right but we are sitting stage left."

"She told you all that?"

"Sometimes you just need to listen."

I heard what mama said about Luca, but it didn't stop me from scanning the crowds as we navigated our way to our seats. I had

Big City Dreams

a moment where I considered running up to the stage and quickly darting behind the curtain before anyone caught me. After I had the thought, I quickly realized how crazy it sounded. I might be on an adventure but visiting the New York City Jail was not anywhere on the list. The lights flickered indicating that the show was about to start. Feeling disappointed in not being able to reach Luca, I stirred in my seat until mama put her hand on my knee indicating that I needed to stop. I had not seen May arrive either. Secretly, I was hoping she would change her mind and skip out on the performance all together.

******

As it turned out our seats were in the first row of the mezzanine section. The woman next to me quickly introduced herself and inquired if we were Mr. Houston's friends. I indicated that we were, she said she was glad that the seats didn't go to waste. They had originally been her parent's seats but her father had to leave for Chicago for some experimental surgical team he was on. Turns out she was a doctor as well and was at the show with her soon-to-be stepdaughter. To be fair, mama got all this information. I was acutely tuned to the stage and the audience. I turned to mama to whisper something and suddenly the lights went out and the music started. Mama shushed me and I turned back to the stage. The first person on stage was a little boy pulling a kite, he was not but ten steps on stage when he broke out into song. He was soon joined by an equally young group of boys and girls, all of which could sing and dance to my amazement. I was transfixed which is why I almost missed May's arrival. Almost. There was a whisper that floated through the audience and then a louder murmur. I glanced down to see almost a dozen people standing as May moved around in her section. I could see Caroline standing stonily off to the side. I couldn't tell what was going on, but it looked as if people were moving seats as two ushers were quickly trying to accommodate everyone. I glanced back at the stage and the young cast finished up a second song and seemed to be slowly exiting the stage. Next a very tall, very tan, and very fit man strolled on stage. He spoke three words before he broke into song with one of the most haunting voices I had ever heard. It was about twenty seconds into his song when I heard someone shout from May's section. There was a pause and then a louder shout. I dragged my eyes away from the man on stage and saw that May was now the only one standing and she had her arms in the air and was waving at something. I couldn't see if Caroline was still around. I saw an usher moving quickly back toward May. I looked back on the stage and the man was moving diagonally across the stage. He was telling us a story and I didn't want it to end. As crazy as it sounds, I forgot about Luca until he appeared on stage five or six minutes later. His entrance was sudden, and his voice was a striking contrast to the man who had been singing. There was something equally as haunting in Luca's voice but in a completely different way. I had heard him sing before on the street and bus, but this was different. This was as if I had been transported to another time and place. Once Luca began to sing, I couldn't take my eyes off of him or the stage. For the next hour I sat completely still and transfixed. When the final bar of the first half was sung and the curtain closed indicating intermission, I exhaled as if I had been holding my breath the entire time.

"Wow," mama said next to me.

"I know, right?" I responded still unable to fully bring myself back to the present. The woman we were sitting with asked if anyone needed anything and got up to stretch her legs. I should have done the same, but I could not; instead, I wiped a tear from my cheek as it slide down.

"There is no need to cry," mama said gently.

"I've never been so..." I didn't have the words to explain the emotion, but mama knew. She just reached over and grabbed my hand and gave it a tight squeeze.

CHAPTER 29

My emotions were no better during the second half of the performance. I had been to other shows before as Becky was involved in theater during high school. This was just so different; I had never seen something of this caliber or talent. Watching my younger sister play Sandy in the *Grease Revival* show during her senior year of high school had ill prepared me for this moment. When the show ended, I was first on my feet clapping and cheering. Luca and the cast came back for an encore and again the audience stood. Luca gave a final bow and waved as thunderous applause echoed through the room for no less than fifteen minutes. It did not go unnoticed to me, that he waved in May's general direction. I couldn't tell from where I was seated if this gesture registered with May or not. Once everyone had cleared the stage, we began the ever frustrating process of trying to leave. We were trying to wait as our row cleared when my phone vibrated. Hoping it was Luca I was slightly disappointed that it was a text from Caroline.

'May is going backstage to see Luca.'

"Mama, we have to get backstage!" I fiercely whispered.

"Logan honey, I don't know how you think we are going to do that."

"But we have too." I heard the whine in my voice and paused a minute. I had been in New York and I had been doing okay thus far

—I needed to get creative with the new skills. Leaning over Mama to the woman next to her, I had a plan that was starting to develop.

"Excuse me, ma'am. What was your name again?"

"Danielle but everyone calls me Dani and this is Chelsey," she said beaming as she introduced her soon-to-be stepdaughter. Chelsey just waved in my direction and then shyly tucked herself into Dani's side.

"Dani you wouldn't by any chance know how we would get a chance to meet Luca Gaines would you? My mama and I are big fans," I said as sweetly as I could. Dani chuckled a moment.

"Ummm, no sorry I don't." Chelsey pulled at Dani's sweater and whispered something into her ear causing Dani to smile. I sent a text to Mac and Caroline, trying to pull any strings I had left to get myself back stage.

"Logan, I think you need to try something else." Mama was not really being patient with me now.

"Mama this will work out," I said out loud hoping it to be true. Mac responded that he was working on it but people were not responding. Caroline reported that May was being stopped at the stage door and was suddenly being sweet to get herself backstage.

"Miss Logan?" I heard from behind me causing mama and me to turn around.

"Thomas?" I was so surprised that it took my breath away. I had told mama all about my friends I had made when I first arrived in the city, but we had not yet been over to see them. It took me a moment, but I regained myself before I leaned in for a hug. No matter what was going on, seeing him brought me pure joy and lifted my spirits.

"Mama, this is Thomas. He was very kind to me when I first got into the city."

"Thomas, I have heard so much about you," Mama said extending her hand to Thomas.

"Miss Logan is unlike any guest we have ever had," he said winking at me causing me to chuckle.

"Ummm, sorry to interrupt. We just need to squeeze by," Dani said. Chelsey again said something, and Dani smiled.

"Well tell her," Dani whispered back.

"You look exactly like May MacKenzie only prettier," Chelsey said after a moment.

"That is sweeter than honey, Miss Chelsey. Can I give you a hug?" I said feeling myself turning red in the cheeks. Chelsey came out from Dani's side and I swept her up into a big hug.

"You are very pretty yourself and don't you forget that," I whispered into her ear.

"Thank you both," I said setting her down. Dani nodded and she and Chelsey left our row making their way out of the theatre.

"Miss Hunter's Mama, you raised this one right," Thomas said again when it was quiet.

"Thank you," Mama said beaming a little.

"Thomas you need to excuse us — we are trying to get back stage," I said suddenly remembering our current dilemma.

"Why didn't you say so. I've been working backstage for a couple weeks now. Mac set me up with this as the hotel was cutting some hours." It was now I saw the green badge that said 'crew' on it.

"Come on, follow me," Thomas said with a wave of his hand and led us down the stairs and to the stage right through a small door.

"They are pretty tight about guests backstage but James owes me a favor. I let his niece backstage last week to meet Ariel, the female lead...Did you both hear the ruckus that a guest caused during the first act?" he said all in one breath without breathing.

"You mean May MacKenzie?" I confirmed and he nodded.

"She tried to bring her dog into the theater and then when that was denied she felt her seats were not good enough and we had to accommodate her request to change seats."

"But why Thomas? Why not just ask her to leave?"

"The usher told me that people like her always have the potential to be donors, so we do our best to accommodate their requests."

"It ain't right," I pouted. As we wove our way through the hallways, we saw more and more people, some still in costume some in plain clothes. "Mr. Gaines is going to be back down that hallway," Thomas pointed. I gave him a quick squeeze and then headed down the hallway.

I turned left and saw the door that said 'Luca Gaines' on it slightly ajar. I peeked inside and the room was full of people but from a glance Luca was not there. I frantically scanned the hallways and saw a flash of what looked to be May going down another hallway.

"This way mama," I said pulling her down the hallway with me. I was too late to stop anything from happening but just in time to see it all go down. Caroline was standing behind May making a face as if she had just eaten a lemon. Luca saw May from across the room and a broad smile came across his face as he approached May — arms outstretched, almost as if he was going in for a kiss. I slide into the back of the room with Mama beside me so that I was now behind May but trying to get into Luca's direct line of sight. As Luca reached in, May pulled back her arm and slapped him across the face. His initial reaction was confusion as he took a couple steps back. When he looked back up, I took a step forward and waved trying to get his attention. I saw his eyes flicker in my direction and then back to May. His eyes immediately hardened as he straightened himself up.

"May, always a pleasure to see you," he commented stepping around her and walking over to me. He didn't make it far before May spoke.

"Where the hell do you think you're going? We aren't done."

"May I'm very done with you," he replied pausing for a moment to look at her.

"What are you doing here?" she practically spat in my direction now seeing me behind Luca. Caroline in the background looked frantic as she suddenly started to clear the room and ask those with cameras to put them away. She worked quickly in the background and soon very few people were in the room. May on the other hand had started towards me with her finger in the air and her head shaking back and forth.

"You're the dog walker, you have no right to be here," she shrilled.

"Do you even know her name," Luca said from his place between us. I didn't have words, but my immediate impulse was to step towards May.

"Logan honey, deep breaths," Mama warned from beside me.

"It doesn't matter what her name is. She's fired," May continued to yell. "I want all your things out of my place now, now leave so Luca and I can finish our conversation." She said essentially dismissing me.

"May, you can't speak to her like that," Luca started to say. I didn't give him a chance to finish.

"Who in the world do you think you are?" I mouthed off stepping around Luca and now facing May directly on.

"I underestimated you," May smirked closing the distance to me.

"Logan," Luca warned from behind me.

"How do you know her name?" May said suddenly distracted by Luca.

"How do you not?" Luca countered.

"Did you break the contract? I'm going to sue you and your whole country backwoods family for breach of contract," she was now screaming.

"You are crazier than…," I commented as May screamed and turned in circles looking for someone or some thing.

"Caroline…CAROLINE," she screamed but Caroline was no longer in the room. Caroline had disappeared.

"You're the one from the photos." She now turned to me again and put her finger right in my face.

"Put your finger down or I'll do it for you," I stated calmly as I stared her down in the eyes.

"I'm May MacKenzie who the fuck are you?" she said moving her finger from my face and jabbing it into my chest instead.

"Logan, don't, it's not worth it," Luca said coming up next to me and putting his hands on either side of my shoulders.

"Look at you, so weak. Always falling for some no class no-one. Together we could have been huge, we could have been unstoppable, Luca. But you go and sleep around and with a backwoods Barbie with no status or no job. She was probably raised by some hillbillies, barefoot and uneducated…," she didn't make it any further.

"Don't you dare talk about my daughter or family that way," mama said coming up from behind me and slapping May right across her face. She never saw it coming. The expression on her face and mine and Luca's probably matched.

"Who are you? You broke my nose, I'm going to sue for everything you have," May said now hunched over and holding her nose. I could see a little blood escaping her fingers as it dripped onto the floor.

"I'm the uneducated barefoot hillbilly you just spoke about. Now, you're going to get up and get yourself to a doctor and none of us are ever going to speak about this again."

"I'm going to sue…"

"No you're not and here's why. Because if you dare come after my daughter or my family, or even Mr. Gaines over here, we are going to share your whole story. The whole stupid crazy story."

"You can't do that."

"Maybe I can and maybe I can't, but I don't think your reputation can survive another scandal."

"What other scandal?" May questioned righting herself.

"Logan dear, can I see your phone?" Too stunned to say anything else. I handed mama my phone. It took her a minute as she pulled up an article, "May MacKenzie to be replaced by Gina Matthews on big blockbuster film."

"What that isn't true," May said horrified. "They can't replace me on my film. I'm the star." Just then her phone rang.

"What?" she answered.

"I just saw that, that can't be true."

"I've been busy. I can't answer all my calls."

"What do you mean? They can't fire me, I'm May MacKenzie."

"But I wasn't in New York when I should have been on set, I was…no, you're right —there are photos of me in New York."

"Yes, Vivian…I'm leaving the theater now, send a car for me up front." She hung up and stood there for a moment. She took a deep breath and turned to face us still holding her nose.

"I don't have time to deal with you all. If I never see you again, that would be fine by me." With that she walked herself right out the door. There was a ten-second pause, before I could move.

"Mama, I have no words…thank you," I said leaning over and giving her a big hug.

"I know I'm always telling you that fighting is not the solution but that woman was just out of control. You don't speak about people and their families that way."

"Amen," Luca commented coming up from behind me.

"I now know where Logan gets her quick temper," he teased.

"Oh no, she gets it from her papa," she said with a mischievous grin on her face.

"How about I take you lovely ladies out to dinner?" Luca offered after a moment.

"Don't you have an after-party?" I asked confused.

"There is nowhere I would rather be than with you tonight," he said finally releasing my shoulders and spinning me around and leaning in to kiss me.

"Your whole family is a bunch of fighters. I think if I continue to hang out with you I'm going to have to take some lessons or something," he joked as he pulled away.

"Nonsense," Mama fussed causing us all to laugh.

CHAPTER 30

"Keep your eyes closed," Luca whispered into my ear. His breath tickled my neck and sent goosebumps down my back. I could hear water splashing somewhere close by and I could smell salt in the air.

"Okay, now what?"

"Wait just a minute," he said his voice now off in front of me.

"Okay now open them," he instructed, and my eyes popped open. Directly in front of me was the vast expanse of a body of water.

"It's darker than I imagined," I commented as a smile spread across my face.

"Would you like to come aboard?" Luca said to my left, patiently extending his hand to me. It was only once he spoke that I finally saw him standing next to a large boat.

"That's for us?" I commented now trying to take the boat in. It wasn't the biggest boat on the dock we were standing on, but it wasn't the smallest either. On the back of the boat it read, 'Seas the Day.'

"It's not mine but we are borrowing it for a couple days. Thought you might want to get out of the city for a bit and see some other sights along the coast."

"You bet I do!" I exclaimed walking over to him and embracing him.

"I remember you once saying you had never seen the ocean. I thought this might be the best way to start checking off some of those bucket list items. Of course, I can't compare to the adventures you and Mac have had, but I thought we might try and have our own adventure."

"This is amazing, just like you."

Once aboard, I realized there was a two-man crew. Luca made quick introductions and we were soon off and headed north towards Martha's Vineyard. It wasn't long before I was staring out over the deep blue vastness of the ocean. I always felt that the rolling hills of Texas had the ability to make one feel small but this was different. There was nothing around us for what seemed like miles. A cool breeze whisked by causing me to shiver and zip my jacket up further.

"Are you ready for dinner?" Luca called from the interior cabin, distracting me from my thoughts.

"Just a moment," I wanted to drink it all in. So much had happened in the last week that again sent my adventure in a different direction. After the confrontation with May at the theatre, I was, of course, without a job and a place to live. Caroline had quit as May's assistant that day. She wasn't without a job for long, she signed on with a fashion house doing design work two days later. She told us that after May's epic meltdown she was done but I think she was done long before that. However, before she officially quit she was kind enough to arrange that all my things be moved out of May's apartment quickly and quietly so that May would not set them on fire and burn down her building or half of New York. She had them shipped over to Mac's place with his blessing of course. Literally, on her way out the door she took Princess with her as she tells the story. She said May had been talking about Princess not acting right and that teacup pigs were more in and that maybe she should change up pets as she started over. Caroline who had developed a soft spot for Princess didn't want to see anything happen and scooped her up and just took her with her as she walked out of May's apartment. Mama stayed for a day or two longer, we finally got to see the sights properly and Luca joined us for several occasions as his scheduled allowed. His people weren't please he skipped out after his last show, so he had some interviews and press to catch up on. He now had a couple weeks off before he was due on set of his new film.

Rooming with Mac so far hasn't been bad. Turns out we are rarely home at the same time and when we are we enjoy some good pizza, beer, and watching bad reality TV. May was in fact replaced on the set of her movie. The producers of the film thought she was on medical leave and when the photos of 'her' around New York began to surface they got upset. Apparently, she wasn't taking their calls either but the final straw had been actually in the theatre. One of the families that was displaced by May's antics that night was one of the producer's beloved grandmother and grandfather. According to Mac, who was still in her good graces, her team was now doing some major PR on her image. Mac has said that when mama slapped May she might have knocked some sense into her. As far as her nose, 'the slap' actually realigned her nose and no surgery was needed. I last saw a picture that she had dyed her hair jet black and got a pixie cut as part of the restyling.

"Logan are you coming?" Luca now said poking his head out from the interior of the cabin.

"Yes," I said turning and heading in. On the table was a spread of cheese, crackers, little meats, olives, two glasses, and a bottle of red wine.

"What were you thinking about?" Luca asked as he poured two glasses at the table.

"I was just processing the last couple of weeks. It's been a bigger adventure than I could have ever imagined."

"Logan, when we first met you told me you were on this adventure to find out who you were, correct?" I nodded as he handed me a glass. I put my nose in the glass as I kept observing everyone else doing it but every time all I could smell was alcohol. Never the berries, dried wood, or vanilla that others promised.

"Did you find what you were looking for?" He asked coming close to me and staring intently at me.

"Yes and no. I learned that I didn't need to be anyone else. There was enough room for me in this world."

"Barely," he teased and I scrunched up my nose.

"I learned that I don't have to talk like everyone else or act a certain way. People that were meant to be in my life love me for me,"

"We do and I do," Luca commented putting his wine glass down and putting his hands on my hips pulling me forward.

"I also learned to be open to trying new things and saying yes when an opportunity presents itself but I also learned that there are things I'm just not going to like."

"Like what?" Luca mumbled burrowing his nose into my neck.

"Red wine," I commented, and I could feel his body shake with laughter against mine.

"Logan, why didn't you say something earlier?"

"I felt that in order to fit into this life I needed to like certain things...but I have tried, Lord knows I have tried...but I can't do it, it just doesn't taste good to me."

"Logan, you always need to be true to yourself, it's one of your best qualities. Plus, I don't mind drinking the whole bottle myself," he commented pulling away from me. He took my glass and set it on the table and headed to the mini-fridge.

"I always come prepared," he said reaching in and pulling a beer out causing me to grin.

"But I felt so lost and confused when I left Texas I really felt like I had to find myself," I said ignoring his comment.

"Logan, you don't need finding because I don't think you were ever lost," he commented handing me the beer. "Maybe you were anxious and even a little scared but never lost. You have such grit, determination, and maybe your inner values are a little different for this neck of the woods, but it's what I love most about you."

"So, you think I'm where I'm supposed to be?" I asked walking towards him and sliding my hands around his waist this time.

"Squarely."

"Luca?"

"Hmmm?"

"I love you, too," I said laying my head on his shoulder as he wrapped his arms around my shoulders. I felt him sigh and relax as we stood there for several moments.

"Now let's eat," he said carefully spinning me around to face the table.

"You know how to speak directly to my heart, city boy."

Dear Reader,

Thank you so much for reading! I hope you enjoyed, *Big City Dreams* as much as I loved writing it. Conceptually this novel started as a short story, some of you may have even read, *Big City Dreams: Finding Logan Hunter* (a novella). After finishing that story, I knew there was much more adventure and mayhem left for Logan and her friends. Logan was an entertaining and easy character to write. I enjoyed researching and using all the southern colloquialisms and as much fun as that was it was important for Logan to grow throughout the story.

Characters Mac, Grey, Caroline, Princess, and Luca were the best supporting ensemble that a main character could ask for. Each unique with a distinct voice (or bark). A quick note about the character of Caroline. The character was named after a fan who entered a T.S. Krupa contest in the summer of 2016. Big shout out to Caroline for playing, winning and trusting me with the character.

Big City Dreams, took almost four years to complete. Which for me has seemed like a lifetime. But I have been busy! During that time, my husband and I had a little girl, moved (twice!) and navigated career changes. It has been one of the most gratifying accomplishment to finish this story and, finally, be able to share it with you.

If you have enjoyed the story, hated the characters or even related to what they are going through, I would love to hear from you. You can always email me at ts.krupa@yahoo.com, visit my website at www.tskrupa.com or leave me a review.

Thank you from the bottom of my heart for your interest, time and feedback.

Best,

T.S. Krupa

Acknowledgements

There are so many people I want to thank who have supported me along the way. As always, my husband who continues to read draft after draft after working a full day and completing his graduate coursework. My parents who always encouraged me to write and who I continuously pushed back on. To my sister who reads whatever I put in front of her and gives open and honest feedback. To my friends who read my drafts without hesitation no matter how busy their lives are. I am a better writer and most importantly person because you are all in my life.

About the Author

T.S. Krupa was born in New Haven, Connecticut. Raised in a Polish household with a blended American culture, she is fluent in Polish. She graduated with her bachelor's degree from Franklin Pierce University, where she played division II field hockey. She earned her Master's from Texas Tech University and graduated with her Doctorate degree from North Caroline State University. She lives in North Carolina with her husband, daughter and two dogs – Chase and Penny. *Big City Dreams* is her fourth full length novel. To learn more about her other novels, *The Ten Year Reunion, On the Edge, Safe & Sound* and other writing project *Chasing Perfection*, visit her at www.tskrupa.com.